THE WISDOM OF FATHER BROWN

G. K. CHESTERTON was born in 1874. He attended the Slade School of Art, where he appears to have suffered a nervous breakdown, before turning his hand to journalism. A prolific writer throughout his life, his best-known books include *The Napoleon of Notting Hill* (1904), *The Man Who Knew Too Much* (1922), *The Man Who Was Thursday* (1908) and the Father Brown stories. Chesterton converted to Roman Catholicism in 1922 and died in 1936.

D1146755

G. K. Chesterton
The Wisdom of
Father Brown

PENGUIN CLASSICS

PENGUIN CLASSICS

Published by the Penguin Group
Penguin Books Ltd, 80 Strand, London WC2R ORL, England
Penguin Group (USA) Inc., 375 Hudson Street, New York, New York 10014, USA
Penguin Group (Canada), 90 Eglinton Avenue East, Suite 700, Toronto, Ontario,
Canada M4P 2Y3 (a division of Pearson Penguin Canada Inc.)
Penguin Ireland, 25 St Stephen's Green, Dublin 2, Ireland (a division of Penguin Books Ltd)
Penguin Group (Australia), 707 Collins Street, Melbourne, Victoria 3008, Australia
(a division of Pearson Australia Group Pty Ltd)
Penguin Books India Pvt Ltd, 11 Community Centre, Panchsheel Park,
New Delhi – 110 017, India
Penguin Group (NZ), 67 Apollo Drive, Rosedale, Auckland 0632, New Zealand
(a division of Pearson New Zealand Ltd)
Penguin Books (South Africa) (Pty) Ltd, Block D, Rosebank Office Park,
181 Jan Smuts Avenue, Parktown North, Gauteng 2193, South Africa

Penguin Books Ltd, Registered Offices: 80 Strand, London WC2R ORL, England

www.penguin.com

First published in 1914
Published in Penguin Classics as part of *The Complete Father Brown Stories* 2012
This edition published in Penguin Classics 2013
001

Set in 10.25/12.25pt PostScript Adobe Sabon
Typeset by Jouve (UK), Milton Keynes
Printed in England by Clays Ltd, St Ives plc

ISBN: 978-0-141-39328-5

www.greenpenguin.co.uk

Penguin Books is committed to a sustainable
future for our business, our readers and our planet.
This book is made from Forest Stewardship
Council™ certified paper.

Contents

THE WISDOM OF
FATHER BROWN

I

The Absence of Mr Glass

The consulting-rooms of Dr Orion Hood, the eminent criminologist and specialist in certain moral disorders, lay along the sea-front at Scarborough, in a series of very large and well-lighted french windows, which showed the North Sea like one endless outer wall of blue-green marble. In such a place the sea had something of the monotony of a blue-green dado: for the chambers themselves were ruled throughout by a terrible tidiness not unlike the terrible tidiness of the sea. It must not be supposed that Dr Hood's apartments excluded luxury, or even poetry. These things were there, in their place; but one felt that they were never allowed out of their place. Luxury was there: there stood upon a special table eight or ten boxes of the best cigars; but they were built upon a plan so that the strongest were always nearest the wall and the mildest nearest the window. A tantalus containing three kinds of spirit, all of a liqueur excellence, stood always on this table of luxury; but the fanciful have asserted that the whisky, brandy, and rum seemed always to stand at the same level. Poetry was there: the left-hand corner of the room was lined with as complete a set of English classics as the right hand could show of English and foreign physiologists. But if one took a volume of Chaucer or Shelley from that rank, its absence irritated the mind like a gap in a man's front teeth. One could not say the books were never read; probably they were, but there was a sense of their being chained to their places, like the Bibles in the old churches. Dr Hood treated his private book-shelf as if it were a public library. And if this strict scientific intangibility steeped even the shelves laden with lyrics and ballads and the tables laden with drink and tobacco, it goes without saying that yet more of such heathen holiness protected the other shelves that held the specialist's library, and the other tables that sustained the frail and even fairy-like instruments of chemistry or mechanics.

Dr Orion Hood paced the length of his string of apartments, bounded – as the boys' geographies say – on the east by the North Sea and on the west by the serried ranks of his sociological and criminologist library. He was clad in an artist's velvet, but with none of an artist's negligence; his hair was heavily shot with grey, but growing thick and healthy; his face was lean, but sanguine and expectant. Everything about him and his room indicated something at once rigid and rest-less, like that great northern sea by which (on pure principles of hygiene) he had built his home.

Fate, being in a funny mood, pushed the door open and introduced into those long, strict, sea-flanked apartments one who was perhaps the most startling opposite of them and their master. In answer to a curt but civil summons, the door opened inwards and there shambled into the room a shapeless little figure, which seemed to find its own hat and umbrella as unmanage-able as a mass of luggage. The umbrella was a black and prosaic bundle long past repair; the hat was a broad-curved black hat, clerical but not common in England; the man was the very embodiment of all that is homely and helpless.

The doctor regarded the new-comer with a restrained

astonishment, not unlike that he would have shown if some huge but obviously harmless sea-beast had crawled into his room. The new-comer regarded the doctor with that beaming but breathless geniality which characterizes a corpulent charwoman who has just managed to stuff herself into an omnibus. It is a rich confusion of social self-congratulation and bodily disarray. His hat tumbled to the carpet, his heavy umbrella slipped between his knees with a thud; he reached after the one and ducked after the other, but with an unimpaired smile on his round face spoke simultaneously as follows:

'My name is Brown. Pray excuse me. I've come about that business of the MacNabs. I have heard you often help people out of such troubles. Pray excuse me if I am wrong.'

By this time he had sprawlingly recovered the hat, and made an odd little bobbing bow over it, as if setting everything quite right.

'I hardly understand you,' replied the scientist, with a cold intensity of manner. 'I fear you have mistaken the chambers. I am Dr Hood, and my work is almost entirely literary and educational. It is true that I have sometimes been consulted by the police in cases of peculiar difficulty and importance, but –'

'Oh, this is of the greatest importance,' broke in the little man called Brown. 'Why, her mother won't let them get engaged.' And he leaned back in his chair in radiant rationality.

The brows of Dr Hood were drawn down darkly, but the eyes under them were bright with something that might be anger or might be amusement. 'And still,' he said, 'I do not quite understand.'

'You see, they want to get married,' said the man with the clerical hat. 'Maggie MacNab and young

Todhunter want to get *married*. Now, what can be more important than that?'

The great Orion Hood's scientific triumphs had deprived him of many things – some said of his health, others of his God; but they had not wholly despoiled him of his sense of the absurd. At the last plea of the ingenuous priest a chuckle broke out of him from inside, and he threw himself into an arm-chair in an ironical attitude of the consulting physician.

'Mr Brown,' he said gravely, 'it is quite fourteen and a half years since I was personally asked to test a personal problem: then it was the case of an attempt to poison the French President at a Lord Mayor's Banquet. It is now, I understand, a question of whether some friend of yours called Maggie is a suitable fiancée for some friend of hers called Todhunter. Well, Mr Brown, I am a sportsman. I will take it on. I will give the MacNab family my best advice, as good as I gave the French Republic and the King of England – no, better: fourteen years better. I have nothing else to do this afternoon. Tell me your story.'

The little clergyman called Brown thanked him with unquestionable warmth, but still with a queer kind of simplicity. It was rather as if he were thanking a stranger in a smoking-room for some trouble in passing the matches, than as if he were (as he was) practically thanking the Curator of Kew Gardens for coming with him into a field to find a four-leaved clover. With scarcely a semi-colon after his hearty thanks, the little man began his recital:

'I told you my name was Brown; well, that's the fact, and I'm the priest of the little Catholic Church I dare say you've seen beyond those straggly streets, where the town ends towards the north. In the last and straggliest of those streets which runs along the sea like a sea-wall there is a very honest but rather sharp-tempered member of my flock, a widow called MacNab. She has one daughter, and she lets lodgings, and between her and the daughter, and between her and the lodgers – well, I dare say there is a great deal to be said on both sides. At present she has only one lodger, the young man called Todhunter; but he has given more trouble than all the rest, for he wants to marry the young woman of the house.'

'And the young woman of the house,' asked Dr Hood, with huge and silent amusement, 'what does she want?'

'Why, she wants to marry him,' cried Father Brown, sitting up eagerly. 'That is just the awful complication.'

'It is indeed a hideous enigma,' said Dr Hood.

'This young James Todhunter,' continued the cleric, 'is a very decent man so far as I know; but then nobody knows very much. He is a bright, brownish little fellow, agile like a monkey, clean-shaven like an actor, and obliging like a born courtier. He seems to have quite a pocketful of money, but nobody knows what his trade is. Mrs MacNab, therefore (being of a pessimistic turn), is quite sure it is something dreadful, and probably connected with dynamite. The dynamite must be of a shy and noiseless sort, for the poor fellow only shuts himself up for several hours of the day and studies something behind a locked door. He declares his privacy is temporary and justified, and promises to explain before the wedding. That is all that anyone knows for certain, but Mrs MacNab will tell you a great deal more than even she is certain of. You know how the tales grow like grass on such a patch of ignorance as that. There are tales of two voices heard talking in the room; though, when the door is opened, Todhunter is always found alone. There are tales of a

mysterious tall man in a silk hat, who once came out of
the sea-mists and apparently out of the sea, stepping
softly across the sandy fields and through the small
back garden at twilight, till he was heard talking to the
lodger at his open window. The colloquy seemed to
end in a quarrel. Todhunter dashed down his window
with violence, and the man in the high hat melted into
the sea-fog again. This story is told by the family with
the fiercest mystification; but I really think Mrs Mac-
Nab prefers her own original tale: that the Other Man
(or whatever it is) crawls out every night from the big
box in the corner, which is kept locked all day. You see,
therefore, how this sealed door of Todhunter's is
treated as the gate of all the fancies and monstrosities
of the "Thousand and One Nights." And yet there is
the little fellow in his respectable black jacket, as punctual and innocent as a parlour clock. He pays his rent
to the tick; he is practically a teetotaller; he is tirelessly
kind with the younger children, and can keep them
amused for a day on end; and, last and most urgent of
all, he has made himself equally popular with the eld-
est daughter, who is ready to go to church with him
to-morrow.'

A man warmly concerned with any large theories
has always a relish for applying them to any triviality.
The great specialist having condescended to the priest's
simplicity, condescended expansively. He settled himself with comfort in his arm-chair and began to talk in
the tone of a somewhat absent-minded lecturer:

'Even in a minute instance, it is best to look first to
the main tendencies of Nature. A particular flower
may not be dead in early winter, but the flowers are
dying; a particular pebble may never be wetted with
the tide, but the tide is coming in. To the scientific eye
all human history is a series of collective movements,

destructions or migrations, like the massacre of flies in winter or the return of birds in spring. Now the root fact in all history is Race. Race produces religion; Race produces legal and ethical wars. There is no stronger case than that of the wild, unworldly and perishing stock which we commonly call the Celts, of whom your friends the MacNabs are specimens. Small, swarthy, and of this dreamy and drifting blood, they accept easily the superstitious explanation of any incidents, just as they still accept (you will excuse me for saying) that superstitious explanation of all incidents which you and your Church represent. It is not remarkable that such people, with the sea moaning behind them and the Church (excuse me again) droning in front of them, should put fantastic features into what are probably plain events. You, with your small parochial responsibilities, see only this particular Mrs MacNab, terrified with this particular tale of two voices and a tall man out of the sea. But the man with the scientific imagination sees, as it were, the whole clans of Mac-Nab scattered over the whole world, in its ultimate average as uniform as a tribe of birds. He sees thousands of Mrs MacNabs, in thousands of houses, dropping their little drop of morbidity in the tea-cups of their friends; he sees –'

Before the scientist could conclude his sentence, another and more impatient summons sounded from without; someone with swishing skirts was marshalled hurriedly down the corridor, and the door opened on a young girl, decently dressed but disordered and red-hot with haste. She had sea-blown blonde hair, and would have been entirely beautiful if her cheek-bones had not been, in the Scotch manner, a little high in relief as well as in colour. Her apology was almost as abrupt as a command.

'I'm sorry to interrupt you, sir,' she said, 'but I had to follow Father Brown at once; it's nothing less than life or death.'

Father Brown began to get to his feet in some disorder. 'Why, what has happened, Maggie?' he said.

'James has been murdered, for all I can make out,' answered the girl, still breathing hard from her rush. 'That man Glass has been with him again; I heard them talking through the door quite plain. Two separate voices: for James speaks low, with a burr, and the other voice was high and quavery.'

'That man Glass?' repeated the priest in some perplexity.

'I know his name is Glass,' answered the girl, in great impatience. 'I heard it through the door. They were quarrelling – about money, I think – for I heard James say again and again, "That's right, Mr Glass," or "No, Mr Glass," and then, "Two or three, Mr Glass." But we're talking too much; you must come at once, and there may be time yet.'

'But time for what?' asked Dr Hood, who had been studying the young lady with marked interest. 'What is there about Mr Glass and his money troubles that should impel such urgency?'

'I tried to break down the door and couldn't,' answered the girl shortly. 'Then I ran round to the back-yard, and managed to climb on to the window-sill that looks into the room. It was all dim, and seemed to be empty, but I swear I saw James lying huddled up in a corner, as if he were drugged or strangled.'

'This is very serious,' said Father Brown, gathering his errant hat and umbrella and standing up; 'in point of fact I was just putting your case before this gentleman, and his view –'

'Has been largely altered,' said the scientist gravely.

'I do not think this young lady is so Celtic as I had supposed. As I have nothing else to do, I will put on my hat and stroll down the town with you.'

In a few minutes all three were approaching the dreary tail of the MacNabs' street: the girl with the stern and breathless stride of the mountaineer, the criminologist with a lounging grace (which was not without a certain leopard-like swiftness), and the priest at an energetic trot entirely devoid of distinction. The aspect of this edge of the town was not entirely without justification for the doctor's hints about desolate moods and environments. The scattered houses stood farther and farther apart in a broken string along the seashore; the afternoon was closing with a premature and partly lurid twilight; the sea was of an inky purple and murmuring ominously. In the scrappy back garden of the MacNabs which ran down towards the sand, two black, barren-looking trees stood up like demon hands held up in astonishment, and as Mrs MacNab ran down the street to meet them with lean hands similarly spread, and her fierce face in shadow, she was a little like a demon herself. The doctor and the priest made scant reply to her shrill reiterations of her daughter's story, with more disturbing details of her own, to the divided vows of vengeance against Mr Glass for murdering, and against Mr Todhunter for being murdered, or against the latter for having dared to want to marry her daughter, and for not having lived to do it. They passed through the narrow passage in the front of the house until they came to the lodger's door at the back, and there Dr Hood, with the trick of an old detective, put his shoulder sharply to the panel and burst in the door.

It opened on a scene of silent catastrophe. No one seeing it, even for a flash, could doubt that the room had been the theatre of some thrilling collision between two, or perhaps more, persons. Playing-cards lay littered across the table or fluttered about the floor as if a game had been interrupted. Two wine glasses stood ready for wine on a side-table, but a third lay smashed in a star of crystal upon the carpet. A few feet from it lay what looked like a long knife or short sword, straight, but with an ornamental and pictured handle; its dull blade just caught a grey glint from the dreary window behind, which showed the black trees against the leaden level of the sea. Towards the opposite corner of the room was rolled a gentleman's silk top hat, as if it had just been knocked off his head; so much so, indeed, that one almost looked to see it still rolling. And in the corner behind it, thrown like a sack of potatoes, but corded like a railway trunk, lay Mr James Todhunter, with a scarf across his mouth, and six or seven ropes knotted round his elbows and ankles. His brown eyes were alive and shifted alertly.

Dr Orion Hood paused for one instant on the doormat and drank in the whole scene of voiceless violence. Then he stepped swiftly across the carpet, picked up the tall silk hat, and gravely put it upon the head of the yet pinioned Todhunter. It was so much too large for him that it almost slipped down on to his shoulders.

'Mr Glass's hat,' said the doctor, returning with it and peering into the inside with a pocket lens. 'How to explain the absence of Mr Glass and the presence of Mr Glass's hat? For Mr Glass is not a careless man with his clothes. This hat is of a stylish shape and systematically brushed and burnished, though not very new. An old dandy, I should think.'

'But, good heavens!' called out Miss MacNab, 'aren't you going to untie the man first?'

'I say "old" with intention, though not with certainty,' continued the expositor; 'my reason for it might seem a little far-fetched. The hair of human beings falls out in very varying degrees, but almost always falls out slightly, and with the lens I should see the tiny hairs in a hat recently worn. It has none, which leads me to guess that Mr Glass is bald. Now when this is taken with the high-pitched and querulous voice which Miss MacNab described so vividly (patience, my dear lady, patience), when we take the hairless head together with the tone common in senile anger, I should think we may deduce some advance in years. Nevertheless, he was probably vigorous, and he was almost certainly tall. I might rely in some degree on the story of his previous appearance at the window, as a tall man in a silk hat, but I think I have more exact indication. This wine-glass has been smashed all over the place, but one of its splinters lies on the high bracket beside the mantelpiece. No such fragment could have fallen there if the vessel had been smashed in the hand of a comparatively short man like Mr Todhunter.'

'By the way,' said Father Brown, 'might it not be as well to untie Mr Todhunter?'

'Our lesson from the drinking-vessels does not end here,' proceeded the specialist. 'I may say at once that it is possible that the man Glass was bald or nervous through dissipation rather than age. Mr Todhunter, as has been remarked, is a quiet thrifty gentleman, essentially an abstainer. These cards and wine-cups are no part of his normal habit; they have been produced for a particular companion. But, as it happens, we may go farther. Mr Todhunter may or may not possess this wine-service, but there is no appearance of his possessing any wine. What, then, were these vessels to contain? I would at once suggest some brandy or whisky, perhaps of a luxurious sort, from a flask in the pocket of

Mr Glass. We have thus something like a picture of the man, or at least of the type: tall, elderly, fashionable, but somewhat frayed, certainly fond of play and strong waters, and perhaps rather too fond of them. Mr Glass is a gentleman not unknown on the fringes of society.'

'Look here,' cried the young woman, 'if you don't let me pass to untie him I'll run outside and scream for the police.'

'I should not advise *you*, Miss MacNab,' said Dr Hood gravely, 'to be in any hurry to fetch the police. Father Brown, I seriously ask you to compose your flock, for their sakes not for mine. Well, we have seen something of the figure and quality of Mr Glass; what are the chief facts known of Mr Todhunter? They are substantially three: that he is economical, that he is more or less wealthy, and that he has a secret. Now, surely it is obvious that there are the three chief marks of the kind of man who is blackmailed. And surely it is equally obvious that the faded finery, the profligate habits, and the shrill irritation of Mr Glass are the unmistakable marks of the kind of man who black-mails him. We have the two typical figures of a tragedy of hush money: on the one hand, the respectable man with a mystery; on the other, the West-end vulture with a scent for a mystery. These two men have met here to-day and have quarrelled, using blows and a bare weapon.'

'Are you going to take those ropes off?' asked the girl stubbornly.

Dr Hood replaced the silk hat carefully on the side table, and went across to the captive. He studied him intently, even moving him a little and half-turning him round by the shoulders, but he only answered:

'No; I think these ropes will do very well till your friends the police bring the handcuffs.'

Father Brown, who had been looking dully at the carpet, lifted his round face and said: 'What do you mean?'

The man of science had picked up the peculiar dagger-sword from the carpet and was examining it intently as he answered:

'Because you find Mr Todhunter tied up,' he said, 'you all jump to the conclusion that Mr Glass had tied him up; and then, I suppose, escaped. There are four objections to this: First, why should a gentleman so dressy as our friend Glass leave his hat behind him, if he left of his own free will? Second,' he continued, moving towards the window, 'this is the only exit, and it is locked on the inside. Third, this blade here has a tiny touch of blood at the point, but there is no wound on Mr Todhunter. Mr Glass took that wound away with him, dead or alive. Add to all this primary probability. It is much more likely that the blackmailed person would try to kill his incubus, rather than that the blackmailer would try to kill the goose that lays his golden eggs. There, I think, we have a pretty complete story.'

'But the ropes?' inquired the priest, whose eyes had remained open with a rather vacant admiration.

'Ah, the ropes,' said the expert with a singular intonation. 'Miss MacNab very much wanted to know why I did not set Mr Todhunter free from his ropes. Well, I will tell her. I did not do it because Mr Todhunter can set himself free from them at any minute he chooses.'

'What?' cried the audience on quite different notes of astonishment.

'I have looked at all the knots on Mr Todhunter,' reiterated Hood quietly. 'I happen to know something about knots; they are quite a branch of criminal science. Every one of those knots he has made himself and could loosen himself; not one of them would have been made by an enemy really trying to pinion him. The whole of this affair of the ropes is a clever fake, to make us think him the victim of the struggle instead of the wretched Glass, whose corpse may be hidden in the garden or stuffed up the chimney.'

There was a rather depressed silence; the room was darkening, the sea-blighted boughs of the garden trees looked leaner and blacker than ever, yet they seemed to have come nearer to the window. One could almost fancy they were sea-monsters like crakens or cuttlefish, writhing polypi who had crawled up from the sea to see the end of this tragedy, even as *he*, the villain and victim of it, the terrible man in the tall hat, had once crawled up from the sea. For the whole air was dense with the morbidity of blackmail, which is the most morbid of human things, because it is a crime concealing a crime; a black plaster on a blacker wound.

The face of the little Catholic priest, which was commonly complacent and even comic, had suddenly become knotted with a curious frown. It was not the blank curiosity of his first innocence. It was rather that creative curiosity which comes when a man has the beginnings of an idea. 'Say it again, please,' he said in a simple, bothered manner; 'do you mean that Todhunter can tie himself up all alone and untie himself all alone?'

'That is what I mean,' said the doctor.

'Jerusalem!' ejaculated Brown suddenly; 'I wonder if it could possibly be that!'

He scuttled across the room rather like a rabbit, and peered with quite a new impulsiveness into the partially covered face of the captive. Then he turned his own rather fatuous face to the company. 'Yes, that's it!' he cried in a certain excitement. 'Can't you see it in the man's face? Why, look at his eyes!'

Both the Professor and the girl followed the direction of his glance. And though the broad black scarf completely masked the lower half of Todhunter's visage, they did grow conscious of something struggling and intense about the upper part of it.

'His eyes do look queer,' cried the young woman, strongly moved. 'You brutes; I believe it's hurting him!'

'Not that, I think,' said Dr Hood; 'the eyes have certainly a singular expression. But I should interpret those transverse wrinkles as expressing rather such slight psychological abnormality –'

'Oh, bosh!' cried Father Brown: 'can't you see he's laughing?'

'Laughing!' repeated the doctor, with a start; 'but what on earth can he be laughing at?'

'Well,' replied the Reverend Brown apologetically, 'not to put too fine a point on it, I think he is laughing at you. And indeed, I'm a little inclined to laugh at myself, now I know about it.'

'Now you know about what?' asked Hood, in some exasperation.

'Now I know,' replied the priest, 'the profession of Mr Todhunter.'

He shuffled about the room, looking at one object after another with what seemed to be a vacant stare, and then invariably bursting into an equally vacant laugh, a highly irritating process for those who had to watch it. He laughed very much over the hat, still more uproariously over the broken glass, but the blood on the sword point sent him into mortal convulsions of amusement. Then he turned to the fuming specialist.

'Dr Hood,' he cried enthusiastically, 'you are a great poet! You have called an uncreated being out of the void. How much more godlike that is than if you had only ferreted out the mere facts! Indeed, the mere facts are rather commonplace and comic by comparison.'

'I have no notion what you are talking about,' said Dr Hood rather haughtily; 'my facts are all inevitable, though necessarily incomplete. A place may be permitted to intuition, perhaps (or poetry if you prefer the term), but only because the corresponding details cannot as yet be ascertained. In the absence of Mr Glass –'

'That's it, that's it,' said the little priest, nodding quite eagerly; 'that's the first idea to get fixed; the absence of Mr Glass. He is so extremely absent. I suppose,' he added reflectively, 'that there was never anybody so absent as Mr Glass.'

'Do you mean he is absent from the town?' demanded the doctor.

'I mean he is absent from everywhere,' answered Father Brown; 'he is absent from the Nature of Things, so to speak.'

'Do you seriously mean,' said the specialist with a smile, 'that there is no such person?'

The priest made a sign of assent. 'It does seem a pity,' he said.

Orion Hood broke into a contemptuous laugh. 'Well,' he said, 'before we go on to the hundred and one other evidences, let us take the first proof we found; the first fact we fell over when we fell into this room. If there is no Mr Glass, whose hat is this?'

'It is Mr Todhunter's,' replied Father Brown.

'But it doesn't fit him,' cried Hood impatiently. 'He couldn't possibly wear it!'

Father Brown shook his head with ineffable mildness. 'I never said he could wear it,' he answered. 'I said it was his hat. Or, if you insist on a shade of difference, a hat that is his.'

'And what is the shade of difference?' asked the criminologist with a slight sneer.

'My good sir,' cried the mild little man, with his first movement akin to impatience, 'if you will walk down the street to the nearest hatter's shop, you will see that there is, in common speech, a difference between a man's hat and the hats that are his.'

'But a hatter,' protested Hood, 'can get money out of his stock of new hats. What could Todhunter get out of this one old hat?'

'Rabbits,' replied Father Brown promptly.

'*What?*' cried Dr Hood.

'Rabbits, ribbons, sweetmeats, goldfish, rolls of coloured paper,' said the reverend gentleman with rapidity. 'Didn't you see it all when you found out the faked ropes? It's just the same with the sword. Mr Todhunter hasn't got a scratch on him, as you say; but he's got a scratch in him, if you follow me.'

'Do you mean inside Mr Todhunter's clothes?' inquired Mrs MacNab sternly.

'I do not mean inside Mr Todhunter's clothes,' said Father Brown. 'I mean inside Mr Todhunter.'

'Well, what in the name of Bedlam *do* you mean?'

'Mr Todhunter,' explained Father Brown placidly, 'is learning to be a professional conjurer, as well as juggler, ventriloquist, and expert in the rope trick. The conjuring explains the hat. It is without traces of hair, not because it is worn by the prematurely bald Mr Glass, but because it has never been worn by anybody. The juggling explains the three glasses, which Todhunter was teaching himself to throw up and catch in rotation. But, being only at the stage of practice, he smashed one glass against the ceiling. And the juggling also explains the sword, which it was Mr Todhunter's professional pride and duty to swallow. But, again, being at the stage of practice, he very slightly grazed the inside of his throat with the weapon. Hence he has a wound inside him, which I am sure (from the expression of his face) is not a serious one. He was also practising the trick of a release from ropes, like the Davenport Brothers, and he was just about to free himself when we all burst into the room. The cards, of course, are for card tricks, and they are scattered on the floor because he had just been practising one of those dodges of sending them flying through the air. He merely kept his trade secret, because he had to keep his tricks secret, like any other conjurer. But the mere fact of an idler in a top hat having once looked in at his back window, and been driven away by him with great indignation, was enough to set us all on a wrong track of romance, and make us imagine his whole life overshadowed by the silk-hatted spectre of Mr Glass.'

'But what about the two voices?' asked Maggie, staring.

'Have you never heard a ventriloquist?' asked Father Brown. 'Don't you know they speak first in their natural voice, and then answer themselves in just that shrill, squeaky, unnatural voice that you heard?'

There was a long silence, and Dr Hood regarded the little man who had spoken with a dark and attentive smile. 'You are certainly a very ingenious person,' he said; 'it could not have been done better in a book. But there is just one part of Mr Glass you have not succeeded in explaining away, and that is his name. Miss MacNab distinctly heard him so addressed by Mr Todhunter.'

The Rev. Mr Brown broke into a rather childish giggle. 'Well, that,' he said, 'that's the silliest part of the whole silly story. When our juggling friend here threw up the three glasses in turn, he counted them aloud as he caught them, and also commented aloud when he failed to catch them. What he really said was: "One, two and three – missed a glass; one, two – missed a glass." And so on.'

There was a second of stillness in the room, and then everyone with one accord burst out laughing. As they did so the figure in the corner complacently uncoiled all the ropes and let them fall with a flourish. Then, advancing into the middle of the room with a bow, he produced from his pocket a big bill printed in blue and red, which announced that ZALADIN, the World's Greatest Conjurer, Contortionist, Ventriloquist and Human Kangaroo would be ready with an entirely new series of Tricks at the Empire Pavilion, Scarborough, on Monday next at eight o'clock precisely.

2

The Paradise of Thieves

The great Muscari, most original of the young Tuscan poets, walked swiftly into his favourite restaurant, which overlooked the Mediterranean, was covered by an awning and fenced by little lemon and orange trees. Waiters in white aprons were already laying out on white tables the insignia of an early and elegant lunch; and this seemed to increase a satisfaction that already touched the top of swagger. Muscari had an eagle nose like Dante; his hair and neckerchief were dark and flowing; he carried a black cloak, and might almost have carried a black mask, so much did he bear with him a sort of Venetian melodrama. He acted as if a troubadour had still a definite social office, like a bishop. He went as near as his century permitted to walking the world literally like Don Juan, with rapier and guitar.

For he never travelled without a case of swords, with which he had fought many brilliant duels, or without a corresponding case for his mandolin, with which he had actually serenaded Miss Ethel Harrogate, the highly conventional daughter of a Yorkshire banker on a holiday. Yet he was neither a charlatan nor a child; but a hot, logical Latin who liked a certain thing and was it. His poetry was as straightforward as anyone else's prose. He desired fame or wine or the beauty of women with a torrid directness inconceivable among the cloudy ideals or cloudy compromises of the north; to vaguer races his intensity smelt of danger or even crime. Like fire or the sea, he was too simple to be trusted.

The banker and his beautiful English daughter were staying at the hotel attached to Muscari's restaurant; that was why it was his favourite restaurant. A glance flashed round the room told him at once, however, that the English party had not descended. The restaurant was glittering, but still comparatively empty. Two priests were talking at a table in a corner, but Muscari (an ardent Catholic) took no more notice of them than of a couple of crows. But from a yet farther seat, partly concealed behind a dwarf tree golden with oranges, there rose and advanced towards the poet a person whose costume was the most aggressively opposite to his own.

This figure was clad in tweeds of a piebald check, with a pink tie, a sharp collar and protuberant yellow boots. He contrived, in the true tradition of 'Arry at Margate, to look at once startling and commonplace. But as the Cockney apparition drew nearer, Muscari was astounded to observe that the head was distinctly different from the body. It was an Italian head: fuzzy, swarthy and very vivacious, that rose abruptly out of the standing collar like cardboard and the comic pink tie. In fact it was a head he knew. He recognized it, above all the dire erection of English holiday array, as the face of an old but forgotten friend name Ezza. This youth had been a prodigy at college, and European fame was promised him when he was barely fifteen; but when he appeared in the world he failed, first publicly as a dramatist and a demagogue, and then privately for years on end as an actor, a traveller, a commission agent or a journalist. Muscari had known him last behind the footlights; he was but too well attuned to the excitements of that profession, and it was believed that some moral calamity had swallowed him up.

'Ezza!' cried the poet, rising and shaking hands in a pleasant astonishment. 'Well, I've seen you in many costumes in the green room; but I never expected to see you dressed up as an Englishman.'

'This,' answered Ezza gravely, 'is not the costume of an Englishman, but of the Italian of the future.'

'In that case,' remarked Muscari, 'I confess I prefer the Italian of the past.'

'That is your old mistake, Muscari,' said the man in tweeds, shaking his head; 'and the mistake of Italy. In the sixteenth century we Tuscans made the morning: we had the newest steel, the newest carving, the newest chemistry. Why should we not now have the newest factories, the newest motors, the newest finance – and the newest clothes?'

'Because they are not worth having,' answered Muscari. 'You cannot make Italians really progressive; they are too intelligent. Men who see the short cut to good living will never go by the new elaborate roads.'

'Well, to me Marconi, or D'Annunzio, is the star of Italy,' said the other. 'That is why I have become a Futurist – and a courier.'

'A courier!' cried Muscari, laughing. 'Is that the last of your list of trades? And whom are you conducting?'

'Oh, a man of the name of Harrogate, and his family, I believe.'

'Not the banker in this hotel?' inquired the poet, with some eagerness.

'That's the man,' answered the courier.

'Does it pay well?' asked the troubadour innocently.

'It will pay me,' said Ezza, with a very enigmatic

smile. 'But I am a rather curious sort of courier.' Then, as if changing the subject, he said abruptly: 'He has a daughter – and a son.'

'The daughter is divine,' affirmed Muscari, 'the father and son are, I suppose, human. But granted his harmless qualities, doesn't that banker strike you as a splendid instance of my argument? Harrogate has millions in his safes, and I have – the hole in my pocket. But you daren't say – you can't say – that he's cleverer than I, or bolder than I, or even more energetic. He's not clever; he's got eyes like blue buttons; he's not energetic, he moves from chair to chair like a paralytic. He's a conscientious, kindly old blockhead; but he's got money simply because he collects money, as a boy collects stamps. You're too strong-minded for business, Ezza. You won't get on. To be clever enough to get all that money, one must be stupid enough to want it.'

'I'm stupid enough for that,' said Ezza gloomily. 'But I should suggest a suspension of your critique of the banker, for here he comes.'

Mr Harrogate, the great financier, did indeed enter the room, but nobody looked at him. He was a massive elderly man with a boiled blue eye and faded grey-sandy moustaches; but for his heavy stoop he might have been a colonel. He carried several unopened letters in his hand. His son Frank was a really fine lad, curly-haired, sun-burnt and strenuous; but nobody looked at him either. All eyes, as usual, were riveted, for the moment at least, upon Ethel Harrogate, whose golden Greek head and colour of the dawn seemed set purposely above that sapphire sea, like a goddess's. The poet Muscari drew a deep breath as if he were drinking something, as indeed he was. He was drinking the Classic; which his fathers made. Ezza studied her with a gaze equally intense and far more baffling.

Miss Harrogate was specially radiant and ready for conversation on this occasion; and her family had fallen into the easier Continental habit, allowing the stranger Muscari and even the courier Ezza to share their table and their talk. In Ethel Harrogate conventionality crowned itself with a perfection and splendour of its own. Proud of her father's prosperity, fond of her fashionable pleasures, a fond daughter but an arrant flirt, she was all these things with a sort of golden good-nature that made her very pride pleasing and her worldly respectability a fresh and hearty thing.

They were in an eddy of excitement about some alleged peril in the mountain path they were to attempt that week. The danger was not from rock and avalanche, but from something yet more romantic. Ethel had been earnestly assured that brigands, the true cut-throats of the modern legend, still haunted that ridge and held that pass of the Apennines.

'They say,' she cried, with the awful relish of a schoolgirl, 'that all that country isn't ruled by the King of Italy, but by the King of Thieves. Who is the King of Thieves?'

'A great man,' replied Muscari, 'worthy to rank with your own Robin Hood, signorina. Montano, the King of Thieves, was first heard of in the mountains some ten years ago, when people said brigands were extinct. But his wild authority spread with the swiftness of a silent revolution. Men found his fierce proclamations nailed in every mountain village; his sentinels, gun in hand, in every mountain ravine. Six times the Italian Government tried to dislodge him, and was defeated in six pitched battles as if by Napoleon.'

'Now that sort of thing,' observed the banker weightily, 'would never be allowed in England; perhaps, after all, we had better choose another route. But the courier thought it perfectly safe.'

'It is perfectly safe,' said the courier contemptuously, 'I have been over it twenty times. There may have been some old jail-bird called a King in the time of our grandmothers; but he belongs to history if not to fable. Brigandage is utterly stamped out.'

'It can never be utterly stamped out,' Muscari answered; 'because armed revolt is a reaction natural to southerners. Our peasants are like their mountains, rich in grace and green gaiety, but with the fires beneath. There is a point of human despair where the northern poor take to drink – and our own poor take to daggers.'

'A poet is privileged,' replied Ezza, with a sneer. 'If Signor Muscari were English he would still be looking for highwaymen in Wandsworth. Believe me, there is no more danger of being captured in Italy than of being scalped in Boston.'

'Then you propose to attempt it?' asked Mr Harrogate, frowning.

'Oh, it sounds rather dreadful,' cried the girl, turning her glorious eyes on Muscari. 'Do you really think the pass is dangerous?'

Muscari threw back his black mane. 'I know it is dangerous,' he said. 'I am crossing it to-morrow.'

The young Harrogate was left behind for a moment emptying a glass of white wine and lighting a cigarette, as the beauty retired with the banker, the courier and the poet, distributing peals of silvery satire. At about the same instant the two priests in the corner rose; the taller, a white-haired Italian, taking his leave. The shorter priest turned and walked towards the banker's son, and the latter was astonished to realize that though a Roman priest the man was an Englishman. He vaguely remembered meeting him at the social crushes of some of his Catholic friends. But the man spoke before his memories could collect themselves.

'Mr Frank Harrogate, I think,' he said. 'I have had an introduction, but I do not mean to presume on it. The odd thing I have to say will come far better from a stranger. Mr Harrogate, I say one word and go: take care of your sister in her great sorrow.'

Even for Frank's truly fraternal indifference the radiance and derision of his sister still seemed to sparkle and ring; he could hear her laughter still from the garden of the hotel, and he stared at his sombre adviser in puzzledom.

'Do you mean the brigands?' he asked; and then, remembering a vague fear of his own, 'or can you be thinking of Muscari?'

'One is never thinking of the real sorrow,' said the strange priest. 'One can only be kind when it comes.'

And he passed promptly from the room, leaving the other almost with his mouth open.

A day or two afterwards a coach containing the company was really crawling and staggering up the spurs of the menacing mountain range. Between Ezza's cheery denial of the danger and Muscari's boisterous defiance of it, the financial family were firm in their original purpose; and Muscari made his mountain journey coincide with theirs. A more surprising feature was the appearance at the coast-town station of the little priest of the restaurant; he alleged merely that business led him also to cross the mountains of the midland. But young Harrogate could not but connect his presence with the mystical fears and warnings of yesterday.

The coach was a kind of commodious wagonette, invented by the modernist talent of the courier, who dominated the expedition with his scientific activity and breezy wit. The theory of danger from thieves was banished from thought and speech; though so far conceded in formal act that some slight protection was employed. The courier and the young banker carried loaded revolvers, and Muscari (with much boyish gratification) buckled on a kind of cutlass under his black cloak.

He had planted his person at a flying leap next to the lovely Englishwoman; on the other side of her sat the priest, whose name was Brown and who was fortunately a silent individual; the courier and the father and son were on the *banc* behind. Muscari was in towering spirits, seriously believing in the peril, and his talk to Ethel might well have made her think him a maniac. But there was something in the crazy and gorgeous ascent, amid crags like peaks loaded with woods like orchards, that dragged her spirit up alone with his into purple preposterous heavens with wheeling suns. The white road climbed like a white cat; it spanned sunless chasms like a tight-rope; it was flung round far-off headlands like a lasso.

And yet, however high they went, the desert still blossomed like the rose. The fields were burnished in sun and wind with the colour of kingfisher and parrot and humming-bird; the hues of a hundred flowering flowers. There are no lovelier meadows and woodlands than the English; no nobler crests or chasms than those of Snowdon and Glencoe. But Ethel Harrogate had never before seen the southern parks tilted on the splintered northern peaks; the gorge of Glencoe laden with the fruits of Kent. There was nothing here of that chill and desolation that in Britain one associates with high and wild scenery. It was rather like a mosaic palace, rent with earthquakes; or like a Dutch tulip garden blown to the stars with dynamite.

'It's like Kew Gardens on Beachy Head,' said Ethel.

'It is our secret,' answered he, 'the secret of the volcano; that is also the secret of the revolution – that a thing can be violent and yet fruitful.'

'You are rather violent yourself,' and she smiled at him.

'And yet rather fruitless,' he admitted; 'if I die to-night I die unmarried and a fool.'

'It is not my fault if you have come,' she said after a difficult silence.

'It is never your fault,' answered Muscari; 'it was not your fault that Troy fell.'

As he spoke they came under overwhelming cliffs that spread almost like wings above a corner of peculiar peril. Shocked by the big shadow on the narrow ledge, the horses stirred doubtfully. The driver leapt to the earth to hold their heads, and they became ungovernable. One horse reared up to his full height – the titanic and terrifying height of a horse when he becomes a biped. It was just enough to alter the equilibrium; the whole coach heeled over like a ship and crashed through the fringe of bushes over the cliff. Muscari threw an arm round Ethel, who clung to him, and shouted aloud. It was for such moments that he lived.

At the moment when the gorgeous mountain walls went round the poet's head like a purple windmill a thing happened which was superficially even more startling. The elderly and lethargic banker sprang erect in the coach and leapt over the precipice before the tilted vehicle could take him there. In the first flash it looked as wild as suicide; but in the second it was as sensible as a safe investment. The Yorkshireman had evidently more promptitude, as well as more sagacity, than Muscari had given him credit for; for he landed in a lap of land which might have been specially padded with turf and clover to receive him. As it happened, indeed, the whole company were equally lucky, if less dignified in their form of ejection. Immediately under this abrupt turn of the road was a grassy and flowery hollow like a sunken meadow; a sort of green velvet pocket in the long, green, trailing garments of the hills. Into this they were all tipped or tumbled with little damage, save that their smallest baggage and even the contents of their pockets were scattered in the grass around them. The wrecked coach still hung above, entangled in the tough hedge, and the horses plunged painfully down the slope. The first to sit up was the little priest, who scratched his head with a face of foolish wonder. Frank Harrogate heard him say to himself: 'Now why on earth have we fallen just here?'

He blinked at the litter around him, and recovered his own very clumsy umbrella. Beyond it lay the broad sombrero fallen from the head of Muscari, and beside it a sealed business letter which, after a glance at the address, he returned to the elder Harrogate. On the other side of him the grass partly hid Miss Ethel's sunshade, and just beyond it lay a curious little glass bottle hardly two inches long. The priest picked it up; in a quick, unobtrusive manner he uncorked and sniffed it, and his heavy face turned the colour of clay.

'Heaven deliver us!' he muttered; 'it can't be hers! Has her sorrow come on her already?' He slipped it into his own waistcoat pocket. 'I think I'm justified,' he said, 'till I know a little more.'

He gazed painfully at the girl, at that moment being raised out of the flowers by Muscari, who was saying: 'We have fallen into heaven; it is a sign. Mortals climb up and they fall down; but it is only gods and goddesses who can fall upwards.'

And indeed she rose out of the sea of colours so beautiful and happy a vision that the priest felt his suspicion shaken and shifted. 'After all,' he thought, 'perhaps the poison isn't hers; perhaps it's one of Muscari's melodramatic tricks.'

Muscari set the lady lightly on her feet, made her an absurdly theatrical bow, and then, drawing his cutlass, hacked hard at the taut reins of the horses, so that they scrambled to their feet and stood in the grass trembling. When he had done so, a most remarkable thing occurred. A very quiet man, very poorly dressed and extremely sunburnt, came out of the bushes and took hold of the horses' heads. He had a queer-shaped knife, very broad and crooked, buckled on his belt; there was nothing else remarkable about him, except his sudden and silent appearance. The poet asked him who he was, and he did not answer.

Looking around him at the confused and startled group in the hollow, Muscari then perceived that another tanned and tattered man, with a short gun under his arm, was looking at them from the ledge just below, leaning his elbows on the edge of the turf. Then he looked up at the road from which they had fallen and saw, looking down on them, the muzzles of four other carbines and four other brown faces with bright but quite motionless eyes.

'The brigands!' cried Muscari, with a kind of monstrous gaiety. 'This was a trap. Ezza, if you will oblige me by shooting the coachman first, we can cut our way out yet. There are only six of them.'

'The coachman,' said Ezza, who was standing grimly with his hands in his pockets, 'happens to be a servant of Mr Harrogate's.'

'Then shoot him all the more,' cried the poet impatiently; 'he was bribed to upset his master. Then put the lady in the middle, and we will break the line up there – with a rush.'

And, wading in wild grass and flowers, he advanced fearlessly on the four carbines; but finding that no one followed except young Harrogate, he turned, brandishing his cutlass to wave the others on. He beheld the courier still standing slightly astride in the centre of the grassy ring, his hands in his pockets; and his lean, ironical Italian face seemed to grow longer and longer in the evening light.

'You thought, Muscari, I was the failure among our schoolfellows,' he said, 'and you thought you were the success. But I have succeeded more than you and fill a bigger place in history. I have been acting epics while you have been writing them.'

'Come on, I tell you!' thundered Muscari from above. 'Will you stand there talking nonsense about yourself with a woman to save and three strong men to help you? What do you call yourself?'

'I call myself Montano,' cried the strange courier in a voice equally loud and full. 'I am the King of Thieves, and I welcome you all to my summer palace.'

And even as he spoke five more silent men with weapons ready came out of the bushes, and looked towards him for their orders. One of them held a large paper in his hand.

'This pretty little nest where we are all picnicking,' went on the courier-brigand, with the same easy yet sinister smile, 'is, together with some caves underneath it, known by the name of the Paradise of Thieves. It is my principal stronghold on these hills; for (as you have doubtless noticed) the eyrie is invisible both from the road above and from the valley below. It is something

better than impregnable; it is unnoticeable. Here I
mostly live, and here I shall certainly die, if the gendarmes ever track me here. I am not the kind of criminal
that "reserves his defence," but the better kind that
reserves his last bullet.'

All were staring at him thunderstruck and still,
except Father Brown, who heaved a huge sigh as of
relief and fingered the little phial in his pocket. 'Thank
God!' he muttered; 'that's much more probable. The
poison belongs to this robber-chief, of course. He car-
ries it so that he may never be captured, like Cato.'

The King of Thieves was, however, continuing his
address with the same kind of dangerous politeness. 'It
only remains for me,' he said, 'to explain to my guests
the social conditions upon which I have the pleasure of
entertaining them. I need not expound the quaint old
ritual of ransom, which it is incumbent upon me to
keep up; and even this only applies to a part of the
company. The Reverend Father Brown and the celebrated Signor Muscari I shall release to-morrow at
dawn and escort to my outposts. Poets and priests, if
you will pardon my simplicity of speech, never have
any money. And so (since it is impossible to get anything out of them), let us seize the opportunity to show
our admiration for classic literature and our reverence
for Holy Church.'

He paused with an unpleasing smile; and Father
Brown blinked repeatedly at him, and seemed suddenly to be listening with great attention. The brigand
captain took the large paper from the attendant brig-
and and, glancing it over, continued: 'My other
intentions are clearly set forth in this public document,
which I will hand round in a moment; and which after
that will be posted on a tree by every village in the valley, and every cross-road in the hills. I will not weary

you with the verbalism, since you will be able to check it; the substance of my proclamation is this: I announce first that I have captured the English millionaire, the colossus of finance, Mr Samuel Harrogate. I next announce that I have found on his person notes and bonds for two thousand pounds, which he has given up to me. Now since it would be really immoral to announce such a thing to a credulous public if it had not occurred, I suggest it should occur without further delay. I suggest that Mr Harrogate senior should now give me the two thousand pounds in his pocket.'

The banker looked at him under lowering brows, red-faced and sulky, but seemingly cowed. That leap from the falling carriage seemed to have used up his last virility. He had held back in a hang-dog style when his son and Muscari had made a bold movement to break out of the brigand trap. And now his red and trembling hand went reluctantly to his breast-pocket, and passed a bundle of papers and envelopes to the brigand.

'Excellent!' cried that outlaw gaily; 'so far we are all cosy. I resume the points of my proclamation, so soon to be published to all Italy. The third item is that of ransom. I am asking from the friends of the Harrogate family a ransom of three thousand pounds, which I am sure is almost insulting to that family in its moderate estimate of their importance. Who would not pay triple this sum for another day's association with such a domestic circle? I will not conceal from you that the document ends with certain legal phrases about the unpleasant things that may happen if the money is not paid; but meanwhile, ladies and gentlemen, let me assure you that I am comfortably off here for accommodation, wine and cigars, and bid you for the present a sportsman-like welcome to the luxuries of the Paradise of Thieves.'

All the time that he had been speaking, the dubious-looking men with carbines and dirty slouch hats had been gathering silently in such preponderating numbers that even Muscari was compelled to recognize his sally with the sword as hopeless. He glanced around him; but the girl had already gone over to soothe and comfort her father, for her natural affection for his person was as strong or stronger than her somewhat snobbish pride in his success. Muscari, with the illogicality of a lover, admired this filial devotion, and yet was irritated by it. He slapped his sword back in the scabbard and went and flung himself somewhat sulkily on one of the green banks. The priest sat down within a yard or two, and Muscari turned his aquiline eye and nose on him in an instantaneous irritation.

'Well,' said the poet tartly, 'do people still think me too romantic? Are there, I wonder, any brigands left in the mountains?'

'There may be,' said Father Brown agnostically.

'What do you mean?' asked the other sharply.

'I mean I am puzzled,' replied the priest. 'I am puzzled about Ezza or Montano, or whatever his name is. He seems to me much more inexplicable as a brigand even than he was as a courier.'

'But in what way?' persisted his companion. 'Santa Maria! I should have thought the brigand was plain enough.'

'I find three curious difficulties,' said the priest in a quiet voice. 'I should like to have your opinion on them. First of all I must tell you I was lunching in that restaurant at the seaside. As four of you left the room, you and Miss Harrogate went ahead, talking and laughing; the banker and the courier came behind, speaking sparely and rather low. But I could not help hearing Ezza say these words – "Well, let her have a little fun; you know the blow may smash her any minute." Mr Harrogate answered nothing; so the words must have had some meaning. On the impulse of the moment I warned her brother that she might be in peril; I said nothing of its nature, for I did not know. But if it meant this capture in the hills, the thing is non-sense. Why should the brigand-courier warn his patron, even by a hint, when it was his whole purpose to lure him into the mountain-mousetrap? It could not have meant that. But if not, what is this other disaster, known both to courier and banker, which hangs over Miss Harrogate's head?'

'Disaster to Miss Harrogate!' ejaculated the poet, sitting up with some ferocity. 'Explain yourself; go on.'

'All my riddles, however, revolve round our bandit chief,' resumed the priest reflectively. 'And here is the second of them. Why did he put so prominently in his demand for ransom the fact that he had taken two thousand pounds from his victim on the spot? It had no faintest tendency to evoke the ransom. Quite the other way, in fact. Harrogate's friends would be far likelier to fear for his fate if they thought the thieves were poor and desperate. Yet the spoliation on the spot was emphasized and even put first in the demand. Why should Ezza Montano want so specially to tell all Europe that he had picked the pocket before he levied the blackmail?'

'I cannot imagine,' said Muscari, rubbing up his black hair for once with an unaffected gesture. 'You may think you enlighten me, but you are leading me deeper in the dark. What may be the third objection to the King of the Thieves?'

'The third objection,' said Father Brown, still in meditation, 'is this bank we are sitting on. Why does our brigand-courier call this his chief fortress and the

Paradise of Thieves? It is certainly a soft spot to fall on and a sweet spot to look at. It is also quite true, as he says, that it is invisible from valley and peak, and is therefore a hiding-place. But it is not a fortress. It never could be a fortress. I think it would be the worst fortress in the world. For it is actually commanded from above by the common high-road across the mountains – the very place where the police would most probably pass. Why, five shabby short guns held us helpless here about half an hour ago. The quarter of a company of any kind of soldiers could have blown us over the precipice. Whatever is the meaning of this odd little nook of grass and flowers, it is not an entrenched position. It is something else; it has some other strange sort of importance; some value that I do not understand. It is more like an accidental theatre or a natural green-room; it is like the scene for some romantic comedy; it is like . . .'

As the little priest's words lengthened and lost themselves in a dull and dreamy sincerity, Muscari, whose animal senses were alert and impatient, heard a new noise in the mountains. Even for him the sound was as yet very small and faint; but he could have sworn the evening breeze bore with it something like the pulsation of horses' hoofs and a distant hallooing.

At the same moment, and long before the vibration had touched the less-experienced English ears, Montano the brigand ran up the bank above them and stood in the broken hedge, steadying himself against a tree and peering down the road. He was a strange figure as he stood there, for he had assumed a flapped fantastic hat and swinging baldric and cutlass in his capacity of bandit king, but the bright prosaic tweed of the courier showed through in patches all over him.

The next moment he turned his olive, sneering face

and made a movement with his hand. The brigands scattered at the signal, not in confusion, but in what was evidently a kind of guerilla discipline. Instead of occupying the road along the ridge, they sprinkled themselves along the side of it behind the trees and the hedge, as if watching unseen for an enemy. The noise beyond grew stronger, beginning to shake the mountain road, and a voice could be clearly heard calling out orders. The brigands swayed and huddled, cursing and whispering, and the evening air was full of little metallic noises as they cocked their pistols, or loosened their knives, or trailed their scabbards over the stones. Then the noises from both quarters seemed to meet on the road above; branches broke, horses neighed, men cried out.

'A rescue!' cried Muscari, springing to his feet and waving his hat; 'the gendarmes are on them! Now for freedom and a blow for it! Now to be rebels against robbers! Come, don't let us leave everything to the police; that is so dreadfully modern. Fall on the rear of these ruffians. The gendarmes are rescuing us; come, friends, let us rescue the gendarmes!'

And throwing his hat over the trees, he drew his cutlass once more and began to escalade the slope up to the road. Frank Harrogate jumped up and ran across to help him, revolver in hand, but was astounded to hear himself imperatively recalled by the raucous voice of his father, who seemed to be in great agitation.

'I won't have it,' said the banker in a choking voice; 'I command you not to interfere.'

'But, father,' said Frank very warmly, 'an Italian gentleman has led the way. You wouldn't have it said that the English hung back.'

'It is useless,' said the older man, who was trembling violently, 'it is useless. We must submit to our lot.'

Father Brown looked at the banker; then he put his hand instinctively as if on his heart, but really on the little bottle of poison; and a great light came into his face like the light of the revelation of death.

Muscari meanwhile, without waiting for support, had crested the bank up to the road, and struck the brigand king heavily on the shoulder, causing him to stagger and swing round. Montano also had his cutlass unsheathed, and Muscari, without further speech, sent a slash at his head which he was compelled to catch and parry. But even as the two short blades crossed and clashed the King of Thieves deliberately dropped his point and laughed.

'What's the good, old man?' he said in spirited Italian slang; 'this damned farce will soon be over.'

'What do you mean, you shuffler?' panted the fire-eating poet. 'Is your courage a sham as well as your honesty?'

'Everything about me is a sham,' responded the ex-courier in complete good-humour. 'I am an actor; and if I ever had a private character, I have forgotten it. I am no more a genuine brigand than I am a genuine courier. I am only a bundle of masks, and you can't fight a duel with that.' And he laughed with boyish pleasure and fell into his old straddling attitude, with his back to the skirmish up the road.

Darkness was deepening under the mountain walls, and it was not easy to discern much of the progress of the struggle, save that tall men were pushing their horses' muzzles through a clinging crowd of brigands, who seemed more inclined to harass and hustle the invaders than to kill them. It was more like a town crowd preventing the passage of the police than anything the poet had ever pictured as the last stand of doomèd and outlawed men of blood. Just as he was rolling his eyes in bewilderment he felt a touch on his elbow, and found the odd little priest standing there like a small Noah with a large hat, and requesting the favour of a word or two.

'Signor Muscari,' said the cleric, 'in this queer crisis personalities may be pardoned. I may tell you without offence of a way in which you will do more good than by helping the gendarmes, who are bound to break through in any case. You will permit me the impertinent intimacy; but do you care about that girl? Care enough to marry her and make her a good husband, I mean?'

'Yes,' said the poet quite simply.

'Does she care about you?'

'I think so,' was the equally grave reply.

'Then go over there and offer yourself,' said the priest: 'offer her everything you can; offer her heaven and earth if you've got them. The time is short.'

'Why?' asked the astonished man of letters.

'Because,' said Father Brown, 'her Doom is coming up the road.'

'Nothing is coming up the road,' argued Muscari, 'except the rescue.'

'Well, you go over there,' said his adviser, 'and be ready to rescue her from the rescue.'

Almost as he spoke the hedges were broken all along the ridge by a rush of the escaping brigands. They dived into bushes and thick grass like defeated men pursued; and the great cocked hats of the mounted gendarmerie were seen passing along above the broken hedge. Another order was given; there was a noise of dismounting, and a tall officer with a cocked hat, a grey imperial, and a paper in his hand appeared in the gap that was the gate of the Paradise of Thieves. There was a momentary silence, broken in an extraordinary

way by the banker, who cried out in a hoarse and
strangled voice: 'Robbed! I've been robbed!'

'Why, that was hours ago,' cried his son in astonishment: 'when you were robbed of two thousand
pounds.'

'Not of two thousand pounds,' said the financier,
with an abrupt and terrible composure, 'only of a small
bottle.'

The policeman with the grey imperial was striding
across the green hollow. Encountering the King of the
Thieves in his path, he clapped him on the shoulder
with something between a caress and a buffet and gave
him a push that sent him staggering away. 'You'll get
into trouble, too,' he said, 'if you play these tricks.'

Again to Muscari's artistic eye it seemed scarcely
like the capture of a great outlaw at bay. Passing on,
the policeman halted before the Harrogate group and
said: 'Samuel Harrogate, I arrest you in the name of
the law for embezzlement of the funds of the Hull and
Huddersfield Bank.'

The great banker nodded with an odd air of business assent, seemed to reflect a moment, and before
they could interpose took a half turn and a step that
brought him to the edge of the outer mountain wall.
Then, flinging up his hands, he leapt exactly as he leapt
out of the coach. But this time he did not fall into a
little meadow just beneath; he fell a thousand feet
below, to become a wreck of bones in the valley.

The anger of the Italian policeman, which he
expressed volubly to Father Brown, was largely mixed
with admiration. 'It was like him to escape us at last,'
he said. '*He* was a great brigand if you like. This last
trick of his I believe to be absolutely unprecedented.
He fled with the company's money to Italy, and actually got himself captured by sham brigands in his own

pay, so as to explain both the disappearance of the
money and the disappearance of himself. That demand
for ransom was really taken seriously by most of the
police. But for years he's been doing things as good as
that, quite as good as that. He will be a serious loss to
his family.'

Muscari was leading away the unhappy daughter,
who held hard to him, as she did for many a year after.
But even in that tragic wreck he could not help having
a smile and a hand of half-mocking friendship for the
indefensible Ezza Montano. 'And where are you going
next?' he asked him over his shoulder.

'Birmingham,' answered the actor, puffing a cigarette. 'Didn't I tell you I was a Futurist? I really do
believe in those things if I believe in anything. Change,
bustle and new things every morning. I am going to
Manchester, Liverpool, Leeds, Hull, Huddersfield,
Glasgow, Chicago – in short, to enlightened, energetic,
civilized society!'

'In short,' said Muscari, 'to the real Paradise of
Thieves.'

3

The Duel of Dr Hirsch

M. Maurice Brun and M. Armand Armagnac were crossing the sunlit Champs Elysées with a kind of vivacious respectability. They were both short, brisk and bold. They both had black beards that did not seem to belong to their faces, after the strange French fashion which makes real hair look like artificial. M. Brun had a dark wedge of beard apparently affixed under his lower lip. M. Armagnac, by way of a change, had two beards; one sticking out from each corner of his emphatic chin. They were both young. They were both atheists, with a depressing fixity of outlook but great mobility of exposition. They were both pupils of the great Dr Hirsch, scientist, publicist and moralist.

M. Brun had become prominent by his proposal that the common expression 'Adieu' should be obliterated from all the French classics, and a slight fine imposed for its use in private life. 'Then,' he said, 'the very name of your imagined God will have echoed for the last time in the ear of man.' M. Armagnac specialized rather in a resistance to militarism, and wished the chorus of the Marseillaise altered from 'Aux armes, citoyens' to 'Aux grèves, citoyens.' But his antimilitarism was of a peculiar and Gallic sort. An eminent and very wealthy English Quaker, who had come to see him to arrange for the disarmament of the whole planet, was rather distressed by Armagnac's proposal that (by way of beginning) the soldiers should shoot their officers.

And indeed it was in this regard that the two men differed most from their leader and father in philosophy. Dr Hirsch, though born in France and covered with the most triumphant favours of French education, was temperamentally of another type – mild, dreamy, humane; and, despite his sceptical system, not devoid of transcendentalism. He was, in short, more like a German than a Frenchman; and much as they admired him, something in the subconsciousness of these Gauls was irritated at his pleading for peace in so peaceful a manner. To their party throughout Europe, however, Paul Hirsch was a saint of science. His large and daring cosmic theories advertised his austere life and innocent, if somewhat frigid, morality; he held something of the position of Darwin doubled with the position of Tolstoy. But he was neither an anarchist nor an antipatriot; his views on disarmament were moderate and evolutionary – the Republican Government put considerable confidence in him as to various chemical improvements. He had lately even discovered a noiseless explosive, the secret of which the Government was carefully guarding.

His house stood in a handsome street near the Elysée – a street which in that strong summer seemed almost as full of foliage as the park itself; a row of chestnuts shattered the sunshine, interrupted only in one place where a large café ran out into the street. Almost opposite to this were the white and green blinds of the great scientist's house, an iron balcony, also painted green, running along in front of the first-floor windows. Beneath this was the entrance into a kind of court, gay with shrubs and tiles, into which the two Frenchmen passed in animated talk.

The door was opened to them by the doctor's old servant, Simon, who might very well have passed for a doctor himself, having a strict suit of black, spectacles, grey hair, and a confidential manner. In fact, he was a far more presentable man of science than his master, Dr Hirsch, who was a forked radish of a fellow, with just enough bulb of a head to make his body insignificant. With all the gravity of a great physician handling a prescription, Simon handed a letter to M. Armagnac. That gentleman ripped it up with a racial impatience, and rapidly read the following:

> I cannot come down to speak to you. There is a man in this house whom I refuse to meet. He is a Chauvinist officer, Dubosc. He is sitting on the stairs. He has been kicking the furniture about in all the other rooms; I have locked myself in my study, opposite that café. If you love me, go over to the café and wait at one of the tables outside. I will try to send him over to you. I want you to answer him and deal with him. I cannot meet him myself. I cannot: I will not.
>
> There is going to be another Dreyfus case.
>
> P. HIRSCH.

M. Armagnac looked at M. Brun. M. Brun borrowed the letter, read it, and looked at M. Armagnac. Then both betook themselves briskly to one of the little tables under the chestnuts opposite, where they procured two tall glasses of horrible green absinthe, which they could drink apparently in any weather and at any time. Otherwise the café seemed empty, except for one soldier drinking coffee at one table, and at another a large man drinking a small syrup and a priest drinking nothing.

Maurice Brun cleared his throat and said: 'Of course we must help the master in every way, but –'

There was an abrupt silence, and Armagnac said: 'He may have excellent reasons for not meeting the man himself, but –'

Before either could complete a sentence, it was evident that the invader had been expelled from the house opposite. The shrubs under the archway swayed and burst apart, as that unwelcome guest was shot out of them like a cannon-ball.

He was a sturdy figure in a small and tilted Tyrolean felt hat, a figure that had indeed something generally Tyrolean about it. The man's shoulders were big and broad, but his legs were neat and active in knee-breeches and knitted stockings. His face was brown like a nut; he had very bright and restless brown eyes; his dark hair was brushed back stiffly in front and cropped close behind, outlining a square and powerful skull; and he had a huge black moustache like the horns of a bison. Such a substantial head is generally based on a bull neck; but this was hidden by a big coloured scarf, swathed round up the man's ears and falling in front inside his jacket like a sort of fancy waistcoat. It was a scarf of strong dead colours, dark red and old gold and purple, probably of Oriental fabrication. Altogether the man had something a shade barbaric about him; more like a Hungarian squire than an ordinary French officer. His French, however, was obviously that of a native; and his French patriotism was so impulsive as to be slightly absurd. His first act when he burst out of the archway was to call in a clarion voice down the street: 'Are there any Frenchmen here?' as if he were calling for Christians in Mecca.

Armagnac and Brun instantly stood up; but they were too late. Men were already running from the street corners; there was a small but ever-clustering crowd. With the prompt French instinct for the politics of the street, the man with the black moustache had already run across to a corner of the café, sprung on one of the tables, and seizing a branch of chestnut to steady himself, shouted as Camille Desmoulins once shouted when he scattered the oak-leaves among the populace.

'Frenchmen!' he volleyed; 'I cannot speak! God help me, that is why I am speaking! The fellows in their filthy parliaments who learn to speak also learn to be silent – silent as that spy cowering in the house opposite! Silent as he is when I beat on his bedroom door! Silent as he is now, though he hears my voice across this street and shakes where he sits! Oh, they can be silent eloquently – the politicians! But the time has come when we that cannot speak *must* speak. You are betrayed to the Prussians. Betrayed at this moment. Betrayed by that man. I am Jules Dubosc, Colonel of Artillery, Belfort. We caught a German spy in the Vosges yesterday, and a paper was found on him – a paper I hold in my hand. Oh, they tried to hush it up; but I took it direct to the man who wrote it – the man in that house! It is in his hand. It is signed with his initials. It is a direction for finding the secret of this new Noise-less Powder. Hirsch invented it; Hirsch wrote this note about it. This note is in German, and was found in a German's pocket. "Tell the man the formula for powder is in grey envelope in first drawer to the left of Secretary's desk, War Office, in red ink. He must be careful. P. H."'

He rattled short sentences like a quick-firing gun, but he was plainly the sort of man who is either mad or right. The mass of the crowd was Nationalist, and already in threatening uproar; and a minority of equally angry Intellectuals, led by Armagnac and Brun, only made the majority more militant.

'If this is a military secret,' shouted Brun, 'why do you yell about it in the street?'

'I will tell you why I do!' roared Dubosc above the roaring crowd. 'I went to this man in straight and civil style. If he had any explanation it could have been given in complete confidence. He refuses to explain. He refers me to two strangers in a café as to two flunkeys. He has thrown me out of the house, but I am going back into it, with the people of Paris behind me!'

A shout seemed to shake the very façade of mansions and two stones flew, one breaking a window above the balcony. The indignant Colonel plunged once more under the archway and was heard crying and thundering inside. Every instant the human sea grew wider and wider; it surged up against the rails and steps of the traitor's house; it was already certain that the place would be burst into like the Bastille, when the broken french window opened and Dr Hirsch came out on the balcony. For an instant the fury half turned to laughter; for he was an absurd figure in such a scene. His long bare neck and sloping shoulders were the shape of a champagne bottle, but that was the only festive thing about him. His coat hung on him as on a peg; he wore his carrot-coloured hair long and weedy; his cheeks and chin were fully fringed with one of those irritating beards that begin far from the mouth. He was very pale, and he wore blue spectacles.

Livid as he was, he spoke with a sort of prim decision, so that the mob fell silent in the middle of his third sentence.

'. . . only two things to say to you now. The first is to my foes, the second to my friends. To my foes I say: It is true I will not meet M. Dubosc, though he is

storming outside this very room. It is true I have asked
two other men to confront him for me. And I will tell
you why! Because I will not and must not see him –
because it would be against all rules of dignity and
honour to see him. Before I am triumphantly cleared
before a court, there is another arbitration this gentleman owes me as a gentleman, and in referring him to
my seconds I am strictly –'

Armagnac and Brun were waving their hats
wildly, and even the Doctor's enemies roared applause
at this unexpected defiance. Once more a few sentences
were inaudible, but they could hear him say: 'To my
friends – I myself should always prefer weapons purely
intellectual, and to these an evolved humanity will certainly confine itself. But our own most precious truth is
the fundamental force of matter and heredity. My
books are successful; my theories are unrefuted; but I
suffer in politics from a prejudice almost physical in
the French. I cannot speak like Clemenceau and
Déroulède, for their words are like echoes of their pistols. The French ask for a duellist as the English ask for
a sportsman. Well, I give my proofs: I will pay this barbaric bribe, and then go back to reason for the rest of
my life.'

Two men were instantly found in the crowd itself to
offer their services to Colonel Dubosc, who came out
presently, satisfied. One was the common soldier with
the coffee, who said simply: 'I will act for you, sir. I am
the Duc de Valognes.' The other was the big man,
whom his friend the priest sought at first to dissuade;
and then walked away alone.

In the early evening a light dinner was spread at the
back of the Café Charlemagne. Though unroofed by
any glass or gilt plaster, the guests were nearly all under
a delicate and irregular roof of leaves; for the orna-

mental trees stood so thick around and among the tables as to give something of the dimness and the dazzle of a small orchard. At one of the central tables a very stumpy little priest sat in complete solitude, and applied himself to a pile of whitebait with the gravest sort of enjoyment. His daily living being very plain, he had a peculiar taste for sudden and isolated luxuries; he was an abstemious epicure. He did not lift his eyes from his plate, round which red pepper, lemons, brown bread and butter, etc., were rigidly ranked, until a tall shadow fell across the table, and his friend Flambeau sat down opposite. Flambeau was gloomy.

'I'm afraid I must chuck this business,' said he heavily. 'I'm all on the side of the French soldiers like Dubosc, and I'm all against the French atheists like Hirsch; but it seems to me in this case we've made a mistake. The Duke and I thought it as well to investigate the charge, and I must say I'm glad we did.'

'Is the paper a forgery, then?' asked the priest.

'That's just the odd thing,' replied Flambeau. 'It's exactly like Hirsch's writing, and nobody can point out any mistake in it. But it wasn't written by Hirsch. If he's a French patriot he didn't write it, because it gives information to Germany. And if he's a German spy he didn't write it, well – because it doesn't give information to Germany.'

'You mean the information is wrong?' asked Father Brown.

'Wrong,' replied the other, 'and wrong exactly where Dr Hirsch would have been right – about the hiding-place of his own secret formula in his own official department. By favour of Hirsch and the authorities, the Duke and I have actually been allowed to inspect the secret drawer at the War Office where the Hirsch formula is kept. We are the only people who have ever known it, except the inventor himself and the Minister for War; but the Minister permitted it to save Hirsch from fighting. After that we really can't support Dubosc if his revelation is a mare's nest.'

'And it is?' asked Father Brown.

'It is,' said his friend gloomily. 'It is a clumsy forgery by somebody who knew nothing of the real hiding-place. It says the paper is in the cupboard on the right of the Secretary's desk. As a fact the cupboard with the secret drawer is some way to the left of the desk. It says the grey envelope contains a long document written in red ink. It isn't written in red ink, but in ordinary black ink. It's manifestly absurd to say that Hirsch can have made a mistake about a paper that nobody knew of but himself; or can have tried to help a foreign thief by telling him to fumble in the wrong drawer. I think we must chuck it up and apologize to old Carrots.'

Father Brown seemed to cogitate; he lifted a little whitebait on his fork. 'You are sure the grey envelope was in the left cupboard?' he asked.

'Positive,' replied Flambeau. 'The grey envelope – it was a white envelope really – was –'

Father Brown put down the small silver fish and the fork and stared across at his companion. 'What?' he asked, in an altered voice.

'Well, what?' repeated Flambeau, eating heartily.

'It was *not* grey,' said the priest. 'Flambeau, you frighten me.'

'What the deuce are you frightened of?'

'I'm frightened of a white envelope,' said the other seriously. 'If it had only just been grey! Hang it all, it might as well have been grey. But if it was white, the whole business is black. The Doctor has been dabbling in some of the old brimstone after all.'

'But I tell you he couldn't have written such a note!'

cried Flambeau. 'The note is utterly wrong about the facts. And innocent or guilty, Dr Hirsch knew all about the facts.'

'The man who wrote that note knew all about the facts,' said his clerical companion soberly. 'He could never have got 'em so wrong without knowing about 'em. You have to know an awful lot to be wrong on every subject – like the devil.'

'Do you mean –?'

'I mean a man telling lies on chance would have told some of the truth,' said his friend firmly. 'Suppose someone sent you to find a house with a green door and a blue blind, with a front garden but no back garden, with a dog but no cat, and where they drank coffee but not tea. You would say if you found no such house that it was all made up. But I say no. I say if you found a house where the door was blue and the blind green, where there was a back garden and no front garden, where cats were common and dogs instantly shot, where tea was drunk in quarts and coffee forbidden – then you would know you had found the house. The man must have known that particular house to be so accurately inaccurate.'

'But what could it mean?' demanded the diner opposite.

'I can't conceive,' said Brown; 'I don't understand this Hirsch affair at all. As long as it was only the left drawer instead of the right, and red ink instead of black, I thought it must be the chance blunders of a forger, as you say. But three is a mystical number; it finishes things. It finishes this. That the direction about the drawer, the colour of ink, the colour of envelope, should *none* of them be right by accident, that *can't* be a coincidence. It wasn't.'

'What was it, then? Treason?' asked Flambeau, resuming his dinner.

'I don't know that either,' answered Brown, with a face of blank bewilderment. 'The only thing I can think of . . . Well, I never understood that Dreyfus case. I can always grasp moral evidence easier than the other sorts. I go by a man's eyes and voice, don't you know, and whether his family seems happy, and by what subjects he chooses – and avoids. Well, I was puzzled in the Dreyfus case. Not by the horrible things imputed both ways; I know (though it's not modern to say so) that human nature in the highest places is still capable of being Cenci or Borgia. No; what puzzled me was the *sincerity* of both parties. I don't mean the political parties; the rank and file are always roughly honest, and often duped. I mean the persons of the play. I mean the conspirators, if they were conspirators. I mean the traitor, if he was a traitor. I mean the men who *must* have known the truth. Now Dreyfus went on like a man who *knew* he was a wronged man. And yet the French statesmen and soldiers went on as if they *knew* he wasn't a wronged man but simply a wrong 'un. I don't mean they behaved well; I mean they behaved as if they were sure. I can't describe these things; I know what I mean.'

'I wish I did,' said his friend. 'And what has it to do with old Hirsch?'

'Suppose a person in a position of trust,' went on the priest, 'began to give the enemy information because it was false information. Suppose he even thought he was saving his country by misleading the foreigner. Suppose this brought him into spy circles, and little loans were made to him, and little ties tied on to him. Suppose he kept up his contradictory position in a confused way by never telling the foreign spies the truth, but letting it more and more be guessed. The better part of him (what was left of it) would still say:

"I have not helped the enemy; I said it was the left drawer." The meaner part of him would already be saying: "But they may have the sense to see that means the right." I think it is psychologically possible – in an enlightened age, you know.'

'It may be psychologically possible,' answered Flambeau, 'and it certainly would explain Dreyfus being certain he was wronged and his judges being sure he was guilty. But it won't wash historically, because Dreyfus's document (if it was his document) was literally correct.'

'I wasn't thinking of Dreyfus,' said Father Brown.

Silence had sunk around them with the emptying of the tables; it was already late, though the sunlight still clung to everything, as if accidentally entangled in the trees. In the stillness Flambeau shifted his seat sharply – making an isolated and echoing noise – and threw his elbow over the angle of it. 'Well,' he said, rather harshly, 'if Hirsch is not better than a timid treason-monger . . .'

'You mustn't be too hard on them,' said Father Brown gently. 'It's not entirely their fault; but they have no instincts. I mean those things that make a woman refuse to dance with a man or a man to touch an investment. They've been taught that it's all a matter of degree.'

'Anyhow,' cried Flambeau impatiently, 'he's not a patch on my principal; and I shall go through with it. Old Dubosc may be a bit mad, but he's a sort of patriot after all.'

Father Brown continued to consume whitebait.

Something in the stolid way he did so caused Flambeau's fierce black eyes to ramble over his companion afresh. 'What's the matter with you?' Flambeau demanded. 'Dubosc's all right in that way. You don't doubt him?'

'My friend,' said the small priest, laying down his knife and fork in a kind of cold despair, 'I doubt everything. Everything, I mean, that has happened to-day. I doubt the whole story, though it has been acted before my face. I doubt every sight that my eyes have seen since morning. There is something in this business quite different from the ordinary police mystery where one man is more or less lying and the other man more or less telling the truth. Here both men . . . Well! I've told you the only theory I can think of that could satisfy anybody. It doesn't satisfy me.'

'Nor me either,' replied Flambeau frowning, while the other went on eating fish with an air of entire resignation. 'If all you can suggest is that notion of a message conveyed by contraries, I call it uncommonly clever, but . . . well, what would you call it?'

'I should call it thin,' said the priest promptly. 'I should call it uncommonly thin. But that's the queer thing about the whole business. The lie is like a schoolboy's. There are only three versions, Dubosc's and Hirsch's and that fancy of mine. Either that note was written by a French officer to ruin a French official; or it was written by the French official to help German officers; or it was written by the French official to mislead German officers. Very well. You'd expect a secret paper passing between such people, officials or officers, to look quite different from that. You'd expect, probably a cipher, certainly abbreviations; most certainly scientific and strictly professional terms. But this thing's elaborately simple, like a penny dreadful: "In the purple grotto you will find the golden casket." It looks as if . . . as if it were meant to be seen through at once.'

Almost before they could take it in a short figure in French uniform had walked up to their table like the wind, and sat down with a sort of thump.

'I have extraordinary news,' said the Duc de Valognes. 'I have just come from this Colonel of ours. He
is packing up to leave the country, and he asks us to
make his excuses *sur le terrain.*'

'What?' cried Flambeau, with an incredulity quite
frightful – '*apologize?*'

'Yes,' said the Duke gruffly; 'then and there – before
everybody – when the swords are drawn. And you and
I have to do it while he is leaving the country.'

'But what *can* this mean?' cried Flambeau. 'He can't
be afraid of that little Hirsch! Confound it!' he cried, in
a kind of rational rage; 'nobody *could* be afraid of
Hirsch!'

'I believe it's some plot!' snapped Valognes – 'some
plot of the Jews and Freemasons. It's meant to work up
glory for Hirsch . . .'

The face of Father Brown was commonplace, but
curiously contented; it could shine with ignorance as
well as with knowledge. But there was always one flash
when the foolish mask fell, and the wise mask fitted
itself in its place; and Flambeau, who knew his friend,
knew that his friend had suddenly understood. Brown
said nothing, but finished his plate of fish.

'Where did you last see our precious Colonel?' asked
Flambeau, irritably.

'He's round at the Hôtel Saint Louis by the Elysée,
where we drove with him. He's packing up, I tell you.'

'Will he be there still, do you think?' asked Flambeau, frowning at the table.

'I don't think he can get away yet,' replied the Duke;
'he's packing to go a long journey . . .'

'No,' said Father Brown, quite simply, but suddenly
standing up, 'for a very short journey. For one of the
shortest, in fact. But we may still be in time to catch
him if we go there in a motor-cab.'

Nothing more could be got out of him until the cab swept round the corner by the Hôtel Saint Louis, where they got out, and he led the party up a side lane already in deep shadow with the growing dusk. Once, when the Duke impatiently asked whether Hirsch was guilty of treason or not, he answered rather absently: 'No; only of ambition – like Cæsar.' Then he somewhat inconsequently added: 'He lives a very lonely life; he has had to do everything for himself.'

'Well, if he's ambitious, he ought to be satisfied now,' said Flambeau rather bitterly. 'All Paris will cheer him now our cursed Colonel has turned tail.'

'Don't talk so loud,' said Father Brown, lowering his voice; 'your cursed Colonel is just in front.'

The other two started and shrank farther back into the shadow of the wall, for the sturdy figure of their runaway principal could indeed be seen shuffling along in the twilight in front, a bag in each hand. He looked much the same as when they first saw him, except that he had changed his picturesque mountaineering knickers for a conventional pair of trousers. It was clear he was already escaping from the hotel.

The lane down which they followed him was one of those that seem to be at the back of things, and look like the wrong side of the stage scenery. A colourless, continuous wall ran down one flank of it, interrupted at intervals by dull-hued and dirt-stained doors, all shut fast and featureless save for the chalk scribbles of some passing *gamin*. The tops of trees, mostly rather depressing evergreens, showed at intervals over the top of the wall, and beyond them in the grey and purple gloaming could be seen the back of some long terrace of tall Parisian houses, really comparatively close, but somehow looking as inaccessible as a range of marble mountains. On the other side of the lane ran the high gilt railings of a gloomy park.

Flambeau was looking round him in rather a weird way. 'Do you know,' he said, 'there is something about this place that –'

'Hullo!' called out the Duke sharply; 'that fellow's disappeared. Vanished, like a blasted fairy!'

'He has a key,' explained their clerical friend. 'He's only gone into one of these garden doors,' and as he spoke they heard one of the dull wooden doors close again with a click in front of them.

Flambeau strode up to the door thus shut almost in his face, and stood in front of it for a moment, biting his black moustache in a fury of curiosity. Then he threw up his long arms and swung himself aloft like a monkey and stood on the top of the wall, his enormous figure dark against the purple sky, like the dark tree-tops.

The Duke looked at the priest. 'Dubosc's escape is more elaborate than we thought,' he said; 'but I suppose he is escaping from France.'

'He is escaping from everywhere,' answered Father Brown.

Valognes's eyes brightened, but his voice sank. 'Do you mean suicide?' he asked.

'You will not find his body,' replied the other.

A kind of cry came from Flambeau on the wall above. 'My God,' he exclaimed in French, 'I know what this place is now! Why, it's the back of the street where old Hirsch lives. I thought I could recognize the back of a house as well as the back of a man.'

'And Dubosc's gone in there!' cried the Duke, smiting his hip. 'Why, they'll meet after all!' And with sudden Gallic vivacity he hopped up on the wall beside

Flambeau and sat there positively kicking his legs with excitement. The priest alone remained below, leaning against the wall, with his back to the whole theatre of events, and looking wistfully across to the park palings and the twinkling, twilit trees.

The Duke, however stimulated, had the instincts of an aristocrat, and desired rather to stare at the house than to spy on it; but Flambeau, who had the instincts of a burglar (and a detective), had already swung himself from the wall into the fork of a straggling tree from which he could crawl quite close to the only illuminated window in the back of the high dark house. A red blind had been pulled down over the light, but pulled crookedly, so that it gaped on one side, and by risking his neck along a branch that looked as treacherous as a twig, Flambeau could just see Colonel Dubosc walking about in a brilliantly-lighted and luxurious bedroom. But close as Flambeau was to the house, he heard the words of his colleagues by the wall, and repeated them in a low voice.

'Yes, they will meet now after all!'

'They will never meet,' said Father Brown. 'Hirsch was right when he said that in such an affair the principals must not meet. Have you read a queer psychological story by Henry James, of two persons who so perpetually missed meeting each other by accident that they began to feel quite frightened of each other, and to think it was fate? This is something of the kind, but more curious.'

'There are people in Paris who will cure them of such morbid fancies,' said Valognes vindictively. 'They will jolly well have to meet if we capture them and force them to fight.'

'They will not meet on the Day of Judgment,' said the priest. 'If God Almighty held the truncheon of the lists, if St Michael blew the trumpet for the swords to cross – even then, if one of them stood ready, the other would not come.'

'Oh, what does all this mysticism mean?' cried the Duc de Valognes, impatiently; 'why on earth shouldn't they meet like other people?'

'They are the opposite of each other,' said Father Brown, with a queer kind of smile. 'They contradict each other. They cancel out, so to speak.'

He continued to gaze at the darkening trees opposite, but Valognes turned his head sharply at a suppressed exclamation from Flambeau. That investigator, peering into the lighted room, had just seen the Colonel, after a pace or two, proceed to take his coat off. Flambeau's first thought was that this really looked like a fight; but he soon dropped the thought for another. The solidity and squareness of Dubosc's chest and shoulders was all a powerful piece of padding and came off with his coat. In his shirt and trousers he was a comparatively slim gentleman, who walked across the bedroom to the bathroom with no more pugnacious purpose than that of washing himself. He bent over a basin, dried his dripping hands and face on a towel, and turned again so that the strong light fell on his face. His brown complexion had gone, his big black moustache had gone; he was clean-shaven and very pale. Nothing remained of the Colonel but his bright, hawk-like, brown eyes. Under the wall Father Brown was going on in heavy meditation, as if to himself.

'It is all just like what I was saying to Flambeau. These opposites won't do. They don't work. They don't fight. If it's white instead of black, and solid instead of liquid, and so on all along the line – then there's something wrong, Monsieur, there's something wrong. One of these men is fair and the other dark, one stout and the other slim, one strong and the other weak. One has a moustache and no beard, so you can't see his mouth; the other has a beard and no moustache, so you can't see his chin. One has hair cropped to his skull, but a scarf to hide his neck; the other has low shirt-collars, but long hair to hide his skull. It's all too neat and correct, Monsieur, and there's something wrong. Things made so opposite are things that cannot quarrel. Wherever the one sticks out the other sinks in. Like a face and a mask, like a lock and a key . . .'

Flambeau was peering into the house with a visage as white as a sheet. The occupant of the room was standing with his back to him, but in front of a looking-glass, and had already fitted round his face a sort of framework of rank red hair, hanging disordered from the head and clinging round the jaws and chin while leaving the mocking mouth uncovered. Seen thus in the glass the white face looked like the face of Judas laughing horribly and surrounded by capering flames of hell.

For a spasm Flambeau saw the fierce, red-brown eyes dancing, then they were covered with a pair of blue spectacles. Slipping on a loose black coat, the figure vanished towards the front of the house. A few moments later a roar of popular applause from the street beyond announced that Dr Hirsch had once more appeared upon the balcony.

4

The Man in the Passage

Two men appeared simultaneously at the two ends of a sort of passage running along the side of the Apollo Theatre in the Adelphi. The evening daylight in the streets was large and luminous, opalescent and empty. The passage was comparatively long and dark, so each man could see the other as a mere black silhouette at the other end. Nevertheless, each man knew the other, even in that inky outline; for they were both men of striking appearance and they hated each other.

The covered passage opened at one end on one of the steep streets of the Adelphi, and at the other on a terrace overlooking the sunset-coloured river. One side of the passage was a blank wall, for the building it supported was an old unsuccessful theatre restaurant, now shut up. The other side of the passage contained two doors, one at each end. Neither was what was commonly called the stage door; they were a sort of special and private stage doors used by very special performers, and in this case by the star actor and actress in the Shakespearean performance of the day. Persons of that eminence often like to have such private exits and entrances, for meeting friends or avoiding them.

The two men in question were certainly two such friends, men who evidently knew the doors and counted on their opening, for each approached the door at the upper end with equal coolness and confidence. Not, however, with equal speed; but the man who walked fast was the man from the other end of the tunnel, so they both arrived before the secret stage door almost at the same instant. They saluted each other with civility, and waited a moment before one of them, the sharper walker who seemed to have the shorter patience, knocked at the door.

In this and everything else each man was opposite and neither could be called inferior. As private persons both were handsome, capable and popular. As public persons, both were in the first public rank. But everything about them, from their glory to their good looks, was of a diverse and incomparable kind. Sir Wilson Seymour was the kind of man whose importance is known to everybody who knows. The more you mixed with the innermost ring in every polity or profession, the more often you met Sir Wilson Seymour. He was the one intelligent man on twenty unintelligent committees – on every sort of subject, from the reform of the Royal Academy to the project of bimetallism for Greater Britain. In the Arts especially he was omnipotent. He was so unique that nobody could quite decide whether he was a great aristocrat who had taken up Art, or a great artist whom the aristocrats had taken up. But you could not meet him for five minutes without realizing that you had really been ruled by him all your life.

His appearance was 'distinguished' in exactly the same sense; it was at once conventional and unique. Fashion could have found no fault with his high silk hat; yet it was unlike anyone else's hat – a little higher, perhaps, and adding something to his natural height. His tall, slender figure had a slight stoop yet it looked the reverse of feeble. His hair was silver-grey, but he did not look old; it was worn longer than the common yet he did not look effeminate; it was curly but it did not look curled. His carefully pointed beard made him look more manly and militant than otherwise, as it does in those old admirals of Velazquez with whose dark portraits his house was hung. His grey gloves were a shade bluer, his silver-knobbed cane a shade longer than scores of such gloves and canes flapped and flourished about the theatres and the restaurants.

The other man was not so tall, yet would have struck nobody as short, but merely as strong and handsome. His hair also was curly, but fair and cropped close to a strong, massive head – the sort of head you break a door with, as Chaucer said of the Miller's. His military moustache and the carriage of his shoulders showed him a soldier, but he had a pair of those peculiar frank and piercing blue eyes which are more common in sailors. His face was somewhat square, his jaw was square, his shoulders were square, even his jacket was square. Indeed, in the wild school of caricature then current, Mr Max Beerbohm had represented him as a proposition in the fourth book of Euclid.

For he also was a public man, though with quite another sort of success. You did not have to be in the best society to have heard of Captain Cutler, of the siege of Hong-Kong, and the great march across China. You could not get away from hearing of him wherever you were; his portrait was on every other postcard; his maps and battles in every other illustrated paper; songs in his honour in every other music-hall turn or on every other barrel-organ. His fame, though probably more temporary, was ten times more wide, popular and spontaneous than the other man's. In thousands of English homes he appeared enormous above England, like Nelson. Yet he had infinitely less power in England than Sir Wilson Seymour.

The door was opened to them by an aged servant or 'dresser,' whose broken-down face and figure and black shabby coat and trousers contrasted queerly with the glittering interior of the great actress's dressing-room. It was fitted and filled with looking-glasses at every angle of refraction, so that they looked like the hundred facets of one huge diamond – if one could get inside a diamond. The other features of luxury, a few flowers, a few coloured cushions, a few scraps of stage costume, were multiplied by all the mirrors into the madness of the Arabian Nights, and danced and changed places perpetually as the shuffling attendant shifted a mirror outwards or shot one back against the wall.

They both spoke to the dingy dresser by name, calling him Parkinson, and asking for the lady as Miss Aurora Rome. Parkinson said she was in the other room, but he would go and tell her. A shade crossed the brow of both visitors; for the other room was the private room of the great actor with whom Miss Aurora was performing, and she was of the kind that does not inflame admiration without inflaming jealousy. In about half a minute, however, the inner door opened, and she entered as she always did, even in private life, so that the very silence seemed to be a roar of applause, and one well-deserved. She was clad in a somewhat strange garb of peacock green and peacock blue satins, that gleamed like blue and green metals, such as delight children and æsthetes, and her heavy, hot brown hair framed one of those magic faces which are dangerous to all men, but especially to boys and to men growing grey. In company with her male colleague, the great American actor, Isidore Bruno, she was producing a particularly poetical and fantastic interpretation of *Midsummer Night's Dream*: in which the artistic prom-

inence was given to Oberon and Titania, or in other
words to Bruno and herself. Set in dreamy and exquis-
ite scenery, and moving in mystical dances, the green
costume, like burnished beetle-wings, expressed all the
elusive individuality of an elfin queen. But when personally confronted in what was still broad daylight, a
man looked only at the woman's face.

She greeted both men with the beaming and baffling
smile which kept so many males at the same just dangerous distance from her. She accepted some flowers
from Cutler, which were as tropical and expensive as
his victories; and another sort of present from Sir Wilson Seymour, offered later on and more nonchalantly
by that gentleman. For it was against his breeding to
show eagerness, and against his conventional uncon-
ventionality to give anything so obvious as flowers. He
had picked up a trifle, he said, which was rather a curiosity; it was an ancient Greek dagger of the Mycenæan
Epoch, and might well have been worn in the time of
Theseus and Hippolyta. It was made of brass like all
the Heroic weapons, but, oddly enough, sharp enough
to prick anyone still. He had really been attracted to it
by the leaf-like shape; it was as perfect as a Greek vase.
If it was of any interest to Miss Rome or could come in
anywhere in the play, he hoped she would –

The inner door burst open and a big figure appeared,
who was more of a contrast to the explanatory Seymour than even Captain Cutler. Nearly six-foot-six,
and of more than theatrical thews and muscles, Isidore
Bruno, in the gorgeous leopard skin and golden-brown
garments of Oberon, looked like a barbaric god. He
leaned on a sort of hunting-spear, which across a theatre looked a slight, silvery wand, but which in the
small and comparatively crowded room looked as
plain as a pikestaff – and as menacing. His vivid black

eyes rolled volcanically, his bronzed face, handsome as it was, showed at that moment a combination of high cheekbones with set white teeth, which recalled certain American conjectures about his origin in the Southern plantations.

'Aurora,' he began, in that deep voice like a drum of passion that had moved so many audiences, 'will you –'

He stopped indecisively because a sixth figure had suddenly presented itself just inside the doorway – a figure so incongruous in the scene as to be almost comic. It was a very short man in the black uniform of the Roman secular clergy, and looking (especially in such a presence as Bruno's and Aurora's) rather like the wooden Noah out of an ark. He did not, however, seem conscious of any contrast, but said with dull civility: 'I believe Miss Rome sent for me.'

A shrewd observer might have remarked that the emotional temperature rather rose at so unemotional an interruption. The detachment of a professional celibate seemed to reveal to the others that they stood round the woman as a ring of amorous rivals; just as a stranger coming in with frost on his coat will reveal that a room is like a furnace. The presence of the one man who did not care about her increased Miss Rome's sense that everybody else was in love with her, and each in a somewhat dangerous way: the actor with all the appetite of a savage and a spoilt child; the soldier with all the simple selfishness of a man of will rather than mind; Sir Wilson with that daily hardening concentration with which old Hedonists take to a hobby; nay, even the abject Parkinson, who had known her before her triumphs, and who followed her about the room with eyes or feet, with the dumb fascination of a dog.

A shrewd person might also have noted a yet odder

thing. The man like a black wooden Noah (who was not wholly without shrewdness) noted it with a considerable but contained amusement. It was evident that the great Aurora, though by no means indifferent to the admiration of the other sex, wanted at this moment to get rid of all the men who admired her and be left alone with the man who did not – did not admire her in that sense at least; for the little priest did admire and even enjoy the firm feminine diplomacy with which she set about her task. There was, perhaps, only one thing that Aurora Rome was clever about, and that was one half of humanity – the other half. The little priest watched, like a Napoleonic campaign, the swift precision of her policy for expelling all while banishing none. Bruno, the big actor, was so babyish that it was easy to send him off in brute sulks, banging the door. Cutler, the British officer, was pachydermatous to ideas, but punctilious about behaviour. He would ignore all hints, but he would die rather than ignore a definite commission from a lady. As to old Seymour, he had to be treated differently; he had to be left to the last. The only way to move him was to appeal to him in confidence as an old friend, to let him into the secret of the clearance. The priest did really admire Miss Rome as she achieved all these three objects in one selected action.

She went across to Captain Cutler and said in her sweetest manner: 'I shall value all these flowers, because they must be your favourite flowers. But they won't be complete, you know, without *my* favourite flower. *Do* go over to that shop round the corner and get me some lilies-of-the-valley, and then it will be *quite lovely*.'

The first object of her diplomacy, the exit of the enraged Bruno, was at once achieved. He had already handed his spear in a lordly style, like a sceptre, to the piteous Parkinson, and was about to assume one of the cushioned seats like a throne. But at this open appeal to his rival there glowed in his opal eyeballs all the sensitive insolence of the slave; he knotted his enormous brown fists for an instant, and then, dashing open the door, disappeared into his own apartments beyond. But meanwhile Miss Rome's experiment in mobilizing the British Army had not succeeded so simply as seemed probable. Cutler had indeed risen stiffly and suddenly, and walked towards the door, hatless, as if at a word of command. But perhaps there was something ostentatiously elegant about the languid figure of Seymour leaning against one of the looking-glasses that brought him up short at the entrance, turning his head this way and that like a bewildered bulldog.

'I must show this stupid man where to go,' said Aurora in a whisper to Seymour, and ran out to the threshold to speed the parting guest.

Seymour seemed to be listening, elegant and unconscious as was his posture, and he seemed relieved when he heard the lady call out some last instructions to the Captain, and then turn sharply and run laughing down the passage towards the other end, the end on the terrace above the Thames. Yet a second or two after Seymour's brow darkened again. A man in his position has so many rivals, and he remembered that at the other end of the passage was the corresponding entrance to Bruno's private room. He did not lose his dignity; he said some civil words to Father Brown about the revival of Byzantine architecture in the Westminster Cathedral, and then, quite naturally, strolled out himself into the upper end of the passage. Father Brown and Parkinson were left alone, and they were neither of them men with a taste for superfluous conversation. The dresser went round the room, pulling out looking-glasses and pushing them in again, his dingy dark coat and trousers looking all the more dismal since he was still holding the festive fairy spear of King Oberon. Every time he pulled out the frame of a new glass, a new black figure of Father Brown appeared; the absurd glass chamber was full of Father Browns, upside down in the air like angels, turning somersaults like acrobats, turning their backs to everybody like very rude persons.

Father Brown seemed quite unconscious of this cloud of witnesses, but followed Parkinson with an idly attentive eye till he took himself and his absurd spear into the farther room of Bruno. Then he abandoned himself to such abstract meditations as always amused him – calculating the angles of the mirrors, the angles of each refraction, the angle at which each must fit into the wall . . . when he heard a strong but strangled cry.

He sprang to his feet and stood rigidly listening. At the same instant Sir Wilson Seymour burst back into the room, white as ivory. 'Who's that man in the passage?' he cried. 'Where's that dagger of mine?'

Before Father Brown could turn in his heavy boots Seymour was plunging about the room looking for the weapon. And before he could possibly find that weapon or any other, a brisk running of feet broke upon the pavement outside, and the square face of Cutler was thrust into the same doorway. He was still grotesquely grasping a bunch of lilies-of-the-valley. 'What's this?' he cried. 'What's that creature down the passage? Is this some of your tricks?'

'My tricks!' hissed his pale rival, and made a stride towards him.

In the instant of time in which all this happened Father Brown stepped out into the top of the passage,

looked down it, and at once walked briskly towards
what he saw.

At this the other two men dropped their quarrel and
darted after him, Cutler calling out: 'What are you
doing? Who are you?'

'My name is Brown,' said the priest sadly, as he bent
over something and straightened himself again. 'Miss
Rome sent for me, and I came as quickly as I could. I
have come too late.'

The three men looked down, and in one of them at
least the life died in that late light of afternoon. It ran
along the passage like a path of gold, and in the midst
of it Aurora Rome lay lustrous in her robes of green
and gold, with her dead face turned upwards. Her
dress was torn away as in a struggle, leaving the right
shoulder bare, but the wound from which the blood
was welling was on the other side. The brass dagger lay
flat and gleaming a yard or so away.

There was a blank stillness for a measurable time, so
that they could hear far off a flower-girl's laugh outside
Charing Cross, and someone whistling furiously for a
taxicab in one of the streets off the Strand. Then the
Captain, with a movement so sudden that it might
have been passion or play-acting, took Sir Wilson Seymour by the throat.

Seymour looked at him steadily without either fight
or fear. 'You need not kill me,' he said in a voice quite
cold; 'I shall do that on my own account.'

The Captain's hand hesitated and dropped; and the
other added with the same icy candour: 'If I find I
haven't the nerve to do it with that dagger I can do it in
a month with drink.'

'Drink isn't good enough for me,' replied Cutler,
'but I'll have blood for this before I die. Not yours –
but I think I know whose.'

And before the others could appreciate his intention he snatched up the dagger, sprang at the other door at the lower end of the passage, burst it open, bolt and all, and confronted Bruno in his dressing-room. As he did so, old Parkinson tottered in his wavering way out of the door and caught sight of the corpse lying in the passage. He moved shakily towards it; looked at it weakly with a working face; then moved shakily back into the dressing-room again, and sat down suddenly on one of the richly cushioned chairs. Father Brown instantly ran across to him, taking no notice of Cutler and the colossal actor, though the room already rang with their blows and they began to struggle for the dagger. Seymour, who retained some practical sense, was whistling for the police at the end of the passage.

When the police arrived it was to tear the two men from an almost ape-like grapple; and, after a few formal inquiries, to arrest Isidore Bruno upon a charge of murder, brought against him by his furious opponent. The idea that the great national hero of the hour had arrested a wrongdoer with his own hand doubtless had its weight with the police, who are not without elements of the journalist. They treated Cutler with a certain solemn attention, and pointed out that he had got a slight slash on the hand. Even as Cutler bore him back across tilted chair and table, Bruno had twisted the dagger out of his grasp and disabled him just below the wrist. The injury was really slight, but till he was removed from the room the half-savage prisoner stared at the running blood with a steady smile.

'Looks a cannibal sort of chap, don't he?' said the constable confidentially to Cutler.

Cutler made no answer, but said sharply a moment after: 'We must attend to the . . . the death . . .' and his voice escaped from articulation.

'The two deaths,' came in the voice of the priest from the farther side of the room. 'This poor fellow was gone when I got across to him.' And he stood looking down at old Parkinson, who sat in a black huddle on the gorgeous chair. He also had paid his tribute, not without eloquence, to the woman who had died.

The silence was first broken by Cutler, who seemed not untouched by a rough tenderness. 'I wish I was him,' he said huskily. 'I remember he used to watch her wherever she walked more than – anybody. She was his air, and he's dried up. He's just dead.'

'We are all dead,' said Seymour in a strange voice, looking down the road.

They took leave of Father Brown at the corner of the road, with some random apologies for any rudeness they might have shown. Both their faces were tragic, but also cryptic.

The mind of the little priest was always a rabbit-warren of wild thoughts that jumped too quickly for him to catch them. Like the white tail of a rabbit he had the vanishing thought that he was certain of their grief, but not so certain of their innocence.

'We had better all be going,' said Seymour heavily; 'we have done all we can to help.'

'Will you understand my motives,' asked Father Brown quietly, 'if I say you have done all you can to hurt?'

They both started as if guiltily, and Cutler said sharply: 'To hurt whom?'

'To hurt yourselves,' answered the priest. 'I would not add to your troubles if it weren't common justice to warn you. You've done nearly everything you could do to hang yourselves, if this actor should be acquitted. They'll be sure to subpœna me; I shall be bound to say that after the cry was heard each of you rushed into the room in a wild state and began quarrelling about a dagger. As far as my words on oath can go, you might either of you have done it. You hurt yourselves with that; and then Captain Cutler must have hurt himself with the dagger.'

'Hurt myself!' exclaimed the Captain, with contempt. 'A silly little scratch.'

'Which drew blood,' replied the priest, nodding. 'We know there's blood on the brass now. And so we shall never know whether there was blood on it before.'

There was a silence; and then Seymour said, with an emphasis quite alien to his daily accent: 'But I saw a man in the passage.'

'I know you did,' answered the cleric Brown with a face of wood, 'so did Captain Cutler. That's what seems so improbable.'

Before either could make sufficient sense of it even to answer, Father Brown had politely excused himself and gone stumping up the road with his stumpy old umbrella.

As modern newspapers are conducted, the most honest and most important news is the police news. If it be true that in the twentieth century more space is given to murder than to politics, it is for the excellent reason that murder is a more serious subject. But even this would hardly explain the enormous omnipresence and widely distributed detail of 'The Bruno Case,' or 'The Passage Mystery,' in the Press of London and the provinces. So vast was the excitement that for some weeks the Press really told the truth; and the reports of examination and cross-examination, if interminable, even if intolerable are at least reliable. The true reason, of course, was the coincidence of persons. The victim was a popular actress; the accused was a popular actor;

and the accused had been caught red-handed, as it were, by the most popular soldier of the patriotic season. In those extraordinary circumstances the Press was paralysed into probity and accuracy; and the rest of this somewhat singular business can practically be recorded from the reports of Bruno's trial.

The trial was presided over by Mr Justice Monkhouse, one of those who are jeered at as humorous judges, but who are generally much more serious than the serious judges, for their levity comes from a living impatience of professional solemnity; while the serious judge is really filled with frivolity, because he is filled with vanity. All the chief actors being of a worldly importance, the barristers were well balanced; the prosecutor for the Crown was Sir Walter Cowdray, a heavy but weighty advocate of the sort that knows how to seem English and trustworthy, and how to be rhetorical with reluctance. The prisoner was defended by Mr Patrick Butler, K. C., who was mistaken for a mere *flâneur* by those who misunderstood the Irish character – and those who had not been examined by him. The medical evidence involved no contradictions, the doctor whom Seymour had summoned on the spot, agreeing with the eminent surgeon who had later examined the body. Aurora Rome had been stabbed with some sharp instrument such as a knife or dagger; some instrument, at least, of which the blade was short. The wound was just over the heart, and she had died instantly. When the doctor first saw her she could hardly have been dead for twenty minutes. Therefore when Father Brown found her she could hardly have been dead for three.

Some official detective evidence followed, chiefly concerned with the presence or absence of any proof of a struggle; the only suggestion of this was the tearing of the dress at the shoulder, and this did not seem to fit in particularly well with the direction and finality of the blow. When these details had been supplied, though not explained, the first of the important witnesses was called.

Sir Wilson Seymour gave evidence as he did everything else that he did at all – not only well, but perfectly. Though himself much more of a public man than the judge, he conveyed exactly the fine shade of self-effacement before the King's Justice; and though everyone looked at him as they would at the Prime Minister or the Archbishop of Canterbury, they could have said nothing of his part in it but that it was that of a private gentleman, with an accent on the noun. He was also refreshingly lucid, as he was on the committees. He had been calling on Miss Rome at the theatre; he had met Captain Cutler there; they had been joined for a short time by the accused, who had then returned to his own dressing-room; they had then been joined by a Roman Catholic priest, who asked for the deceased lady and said his name was Brown. Miss Rome had then gone just outside the theatre to the entrance of the passage, in order to point out to Captain Cutler a flower-shop at which he was to buy her some more flowers; and the witness had remained in the room, exchanging a few words with the priest. He had then distinctly heard the deceased, having sent the Captain on his errand, turn round laughing and run down the passage towards its other end, where was the prisoner's dressing-room. In idle curiosity as to the rapid movements of his friends, he had strolled out to the head of the passage himself and looked down it towards the prisoner's door. Did he see anything in the passage? Yes; he saw something in the passage.

Sir Walter Cowdray allowed an impressive interval,

during which the witness looked down, and for all his
usual composure seemed to have more than his usual
pallor. Then the barrister said in a lower voice, which
seemed at once sympathetic and creepy: 'Did you see it
distinctly?'

Sir Wilson Seymour, however moved, had his excellent brains in full working-order. 'Very distinctly as
regards its outline, but quite indistinctly, indeed not at
all, as regards the details inside the outline. The passage is of such length that anyone in the middle of it
appears quite black against the light at the other end.'
The witness lowered his steady eyes once more and
added: 'I had noticed the fact before, when Captain
Cutler first entered it.' There was another silence, and
the judge leaned forward and made a note.

'Well,' said Sir Walter patiently, 'what was the outline like? Was it, for instance, like the figure of the
murdered woman?'

'Not in the least,' answered Seymour quietly.

'What did it look like to you?'

'It looked to me,' replied the witness, 'like a tall man.'

Everyone in court kept his eyes riveted on his pen,
or his umbrella-handle, or his book, or his boots or
whatever he happened to be looking at. They seemed
to be holding their eyes away from the prisoner by
main force; but they felt his figure in the dock, and they
felt it as gigantic. Tall as Bruno was to the eye, he
seemed to swell taller and taller when all eyes had been
torn away from him.

Cowdray was resuming his seat with his solemn
face, smoothing his black silk robes, and white silk
whiskers. Sir Wilson was leaving the witness-box, after
a few final particulars to which there were many other
witnesses, when the counsel for the defence sprang up
and stopped him.

'I shall only detain you a moment,' said Mr Butler, who was a rustic-looking person with red eyebrows and an expression of partial slumber. 'Will you tell his lordship how you knew it was a man?'

A faint, refined smile seemed to pass over Seymour's features. 'I'm afraid it is the vulgar test of trousers,' he said. 'When I saw daylight between the long legs I was sure it was a man, after all.'

Butler's sleepy eyes opened as suddenly as some silent explosion. 'After all!' he repeated slowly. 'So you did think at first it was a woman?'

Seymour looked troubled for the first time. 'It is hardly a point of fact,' he said, 'but if his lordship would like me to answer for my impression, of course I shall do so. There was something about the thing that was not exactly a woman and yet was not quite a man; somehow the curves were different. And it had something that looked like long hair.'

'Thank you,' said Mr Butler, K. C., and sat down suddenly, as if he had got what he wanted.

Captain Cutler was a far less plausible and composed witness than Sir Wilson, but his account of the opening incidents was solidly the same. He described the return of Bruno to his dressing-room, the dispatching of himself to buy a bunch of lilies-of-the-valley, his return to the upper end of the passage, the thing he saw in the passage, his suspicion of Seymour, and his struggle with Bruno. But he could give little artistic assistance about the black figure that he and Seymour had seen. Asked about its outline, he said he was no art critic – with a somewhat too obvious sneer at Seymour. Asked if it was a man or a woman, he said it looked more like a beast – with a too obvious snarl at the prisoner. But the man was plainly shaken with sorrow and sincere anger, and Cowdray quickly excused him from confirming facts that were already fairly clear.

The defending counsel also was again brief in his
cross-examination; although (as was his custom) even
in being brief, he seemed to take a long time about it.
'You used a rather remarkable expression,' he said,
looking at Cutler sleepily. 'What do you mean by saying that it looked more like a beast than a man or a
woman?'

Cutler seemed seriously agitated. 'Perhaps I oughtn't
to have said that,' he said; 'but when the brute has
huge humped shoulders like a chimpanzee, and bristles
sticking out of its head like a pig –'

Mr Butler cut short his curious impatience in the
middle. 'Never mind whether its hair was like a pig's,'
he said, 'was it like a woman's?'

'A woman's!' cried the soldier. 'Great Scott, no!'

'The last witness said it was,' commented the counsel, with unscrupulous swiftness. 'And did the figure
have any of those serpentine and semi-feminine curves
to which eloquent allusion has been made? No? No
feminine curves? The figure, if I understand you, was
rather heavy and square than otherwise?'

'He may have been bending forward,' said Cutler, in
a hoarse and rather faint voice.

'Or again, he may not,' said Mr Butler, and sat down
suddenly for the second time.

The third witness called by Sir Walter Cowdray was
the little Catholic clergyman, so little, compared with the
others, that his head seemed hardly to come above
the box, so that it was like cross-examining a child. But
unfortunately Sir Walter had somehow got it into his
head (mostly by some ramifications of his family's religion) that Father Brown was on the side of the prisoner,
because the prisoner was wicked and foreign and even
partly black. Therefore he took Father Brown up
sharply whenever that proud pontiff tried to explain

anything; and told him to answer yes or no, and tell the plain facts without any jesuitry. When Father Brown began, in his simplicity, to say who he thought the man in the passage was, the barrister told him that he did not want his theories.

'A black shape was seen in the passage. And you say you saw the black shape. Well, what shape was it?'

Father Brown blinked as under rebuke; but he had long known the literal nature of obedience. 'The shape,' he said, 'was short and thick, but had two sharp, black projections curved upwards on each side of the head or top, rather like horns, and –'

'Oh! the devil with horns, no doubt,' ejaculated Cowdray, sitting down in triumphant jocularity. 'It was the devil come to eat Protestants.'

'No,' said the priest dispassionately; 'I know who it was.'

Those in court had been wrought up to an irrational, but real sense of some monstrosity. They had forgotten the figure in the dock and thought only of the figure in the passage. And the figure in the passage, described by three capable and respectable men who had all seen it, was a shifting nightmare: one called it a woman, and the other a beast, and the other a devil . . .

The judge was looking at Father Brown with level and piercing eyes. 'You are a most extraordinary witness,' he said; 'but there is something about you that makes me think you are trying to tell the truth. Well, who was the man you saw in the passage?'

'He was myself,' said Father Brown.

Butler, K. C., sprang to his feet in an extraordinary stillness, and said quite calmly: 'Your lordship will allow me to cross-examine?' And then, without stopping, he shot at Brown the apparently disconnected question: 'You have heard about this dagger; you know the experts say the crime was committed with a short blade?'

'A short blade,' assented Brown, nodding solemnly like an owl, 'but a very long hilt.'

Before the audience could quite dismiss the idea that the priest had really seen himself doing murder with a short dagger with a long hilt (which seemed somehow to make it more horrible), he had himself hurried on to explain.

'I mean daggers aren't the only things with short blades. Spears have short blades. And spears catch at the end of the steel just like daggers, if they're that sort of fancy spear they had in theatres; like the spear poor old Parkinson killed his wife with, just when she'd sent for me to settle their family troubles – and I came just too late, God forgive me! But he died penitent – he just died of being penitent. He couldn't bear what he'd done.'

The general impression in court was that the little priest, who was gabbling away, had literally gone mad in the box. But the judge still looked at him with bright and steady eyes of interest; and the counsel for the defence went on with his questions unperturbed.

'If Parkinson did it with that pantomime spear,' said Butler, 'he must have thrust from four yards away. How do you account for signs of struggle, like the dress dragged off the shoulder?' He had slipped into treating this mere witness as an expert; but no one noticed it now.

'The poor lady's dress was torn,' said the witness, 'because it was caught in a panel that slid to just behind her. She struggled to free herself, and as she did so Parkinson came out of the prisoner's room and lunged with the spear.'

'A panel?' repeated the barrister in a curious voice.

'It was a looking-glass on the other side,' explained Father Brown. 'When I was in the dressing-room I noticed that some of them could probably be slid out into the passage.'

There was another vast and unnatural silence, and this time it was the judge who spoke. 'So you really mean that when you looked down that passage, the man you saw was yourself – in a mirror?'

'Yes, my lord; that was what I was trying to say,' said Brown, 'but they asked me for the shape; and our hats have corners just like horns, and so I –'

The judge leaned forward, his old eyes yet more brilliant, and said in specially distinct tones: 'Do you really mean to say that when Sir Wilson Seymour saw that wild what-you-call-him with curves and a woman's hair and a man's trousers, what he saw was Sir Wilson Seymour?'

'Yes, my lord,' said Father Brown.

'And you mean to say that when Captain Cutler saw that chimpanzee with humped shoulders and hog's bristles, he simply saw himself?'

'Yes, my lord.'

The judge leaned back in his chair with a luxuriance in which it was hard to separate the cynicism and the admiration. 'And can you tell us why,' he asked, 'you should know your own figure in a looking-glass, when two such distinguished men don't?'

Father Brown blinked even more painfully than before; then he stammered: 'Really, my lord, I don't know . . . unless it's because I don't look at it so often.'

5

The Mistake of
the Machine

Flambeau and his friend the priest were sitting in the Temple Gardens about sunset; and their neighbourhood or some such accidental influence had turned their talk to matters of legal process. From the problem of the licence in cross-examination, their talk strayed to Roman and mediæval torture, to the examining magistrate in France and the Third Degree in America.

'I've been reading,' said Flambeau, 'of this new psychometric method they talk about so much, especially in America. You know what I mean; they put a pulsometer on a man's wrist and judge by how his heart goes at the pronunciation of certain words. What do you think of it?'

'I think it very interesting,' replied Father Brown; 'it reminds me of that interesting idea in the Dark Ages that blood would flow from a corpse if the murderer touched it.'

'Do you really mean,' demanded his friend, 'that you think the two methods equally valuable?'

'I think them equally valueless,' replied Brown. 'Blood flows, fast or slow, in dead folk or living, for so many more million reasons than we can ever know. Blood will have to flow very funnily; blood will have to flow up the Matterhorn, before I will take it as a sign that I am to shed it.'

'The method,' remarked the other, 'has been guaranteed by some of the greatest American men of science.'

'What sentimentalists men of science are!' exclaimed Father Brown, 'and how much more sentimental must American men of science be! Who but a Yankee would think of proving anything from heart-throbs? Why, they must be as sentimental as a man who thinks a woman is in love with him if she blushes. That's a test from the circulation of the blood, discovered by the immortal Harvey; and a jolly rotten test, too.'

'But surely,' insisted Flambeau, 'it might point pretty straight at something or other.'

'There's a disadvantage in a stick pointing straight,' answered the other. 'What is it? Why, the other end of the stick always points the opposite way. It depends whether you get hold of the stick by the right end. I saw the thing done once and I've never believed in it since.' And he proceeded to tell the story of his disillusionment.

It happened nearly twenty years before, when he was chaplain to his co-religionists in a prison in Chicago – where the Irish population displayed a capacity both for crime and penitence which kept him tolerably busy. The official second-in-command under the Governor was an ex-detective named Greywood Usher, a cadaverous, careful-spoken Yankee philosopher, occasionally varying a very rigid visage with an odd apologetic grimace. He liked Father Brown in a slightly patronizing way; and Father Brown liked him, though he heartily disliked his theories. His theories were extremely complicated and were held with extreme simplicity.

One evening he had sent for the priest, who, according to his custom, took a seat in silence at a table piled and littered with papers, and waited. The official selected from the papers a scrap of newspaper cutting, which he handed across to the cleric, who read it gravely. It appeared to be an extract from one of the pinkest of American Society papers, and ran as follows:

Society's brightest widower is once more on the Freak Dinner stunt. All our exclusive citizens will recall the Perambulator Parade Dinner, in which Last-Trick Todd, at his palatial home at Pilgrim's Pond, caused so many of our prominent *débutantes* to look even younger than their years. Equally elegant and more miscellaneous and large-hearted in social outlook was Last-Trick's show the year previous, the popular Cannibal Crush Lunch, at which the confections handed round were sarcastically moulded in the forms of human arms and legs, and during which more than one of our gayest mental gymnasts was heard offering to eat his partner. The witticism which will inspire this evening is as yet in Mr Todd's pretty reticent intellect, or locked in the jewelled bosoms of our city's gayest leaders; but there is talk of a pretty parody of the simple manners and customs at the other end of Society's scale. This would be all the more telling, as hospitable Todd is entertaining in Lord Falconroy, the famous traveller, a true-blooded aristocrat fresh from England's oak-groves. Lord Falconroy's travels began before his ancient feudal title was resurrected; he was in the Republic in his youth, and fashion murmurs a sly reason for his return. Miss Etta Todd is one of our deep-souled New Yorkers, and comes into an income of nearly twelve hundred million dollars.

'Well,' asked Usher, 'does that interest you?'

'Why, words rather fail me,' answered Father Brown. 'I cannot think at this moment of anything in this world that would interest me less. And, unless the just anger of the Republic is at last going to electrocute journalists for writing like that, I don't quite see why it should interest you either.'

'Ah!' said Mr Usher dryly, and handing across another scrap of newspaper. 'Well, does *that* interest you?'

The paragraph was headed 'Savage Murder of a Warder. Convict Escapes,' and ran: 'Just before dawn this morning a shout for help was heard in the Convict Settlement at Sequah in this State. The authorities, hurrying in the direction of the cry, found the corpse of the warder who patrols the top of the north wall of the prison, the steepest and most difficult exit, for which one man has always been found sufficient. The unfortunate officer had, however, been hurled from the high wall, his brains beaten out as with a club, and his gun was missing. Further inquiries showed that one of the cells was empty; it had been occupied by a rather sullen ruffian giving his name as Oscar Rian. He was only temporarily detained for some comparatively trivial assault; but he gave everyone the impression of a man with a black past and a dangerous future. Finally, when daylight had fully revealed the scene of murder, it was found that he had written on the wall above the body a fragmentary sentence, apparently with a finger dipped in blood: "This was self-defence and he had the gun. I meant no harm to him or any man but one. I am keeping the bullet for Pilgrim's Pond – O. R." A man must have used most fiendish treachery or most savage and amazing bodily daring to have stormed such a wall in spite of an armed man.'

'Well, the literary style is somewhat improved,' admitted the priest cheerfully, 'but still I don't see what I can do for you. I should cut a poor figure, with my short legs, running about this State after an athletic assassin of that sort. I doubt whether anybody could find him. The convict settlement at Sequah is thirty miles from here; the country between is wild and tangled enough, and the country beyond, where he will surely have the sense to go, is a perfect no-man's land tumbling away to the prairies. He may be in any hole or up any tree.'

'He isn't in any hole,' said the governor; 'he isn't up any tree.'

'Why, how do you know?' asked Father Brown, blinking.

'Would you like to speak to him?' inquired Usher.

Father Brown opened his innocent eyes wide. 'He is here?' he exclaimed. 'Why, how did your men get hold of him?'

'I got hold of him myself,' drawled the American, rising and lazily stretching his lanky legs before the fire. 'I got hold of him with the crooked end of a walking-stick. Don't look so surprised. I really did. You know I sometimes take a turn in the country lanes outside this dismal place; well, I was walking early this evening up a steep lane with dark hedges and grey-looking ploughed fields on both sides; and a young moon was up and silvering the road. By the light of it I saw a man running across the field towards the road; running with his body bent and at a good mile-race trot. He appeared to be much exhausted; but when he came to the thick black hedge he went through it as if it were made of spiders' webs; or rather (for I heard the strong branches breaking and snapping like bayonets) as if he himself were made of stone. In the instant in which he appeared up against the moon, crossing the road, I slung my hooked cane at his legs, tripping him and bringing him down. Then I blew my whistle long and loud, and our fellows came running up to secure him.'

'It would have been rather awkward,' remarked

Brown, 'if you had found he was a popular athlete practising a mile race.'

'He was not,' said Usher grimly. 'We soon found out who he was; but I had guessed it with the first glint of the moon on him.'

'You thought it was the runaway convict,' observed the priest simply, 'because you had read in the newspaper cutting that morning that a convict had run away.'

'I had somewhat better grounds,' replied the governor coolly. 'I pass over the first as too simple to be emphasized – I mean that fashionable athletes do not run across ploughed fields or scratch their eyes out in bramble hedges. Nor do they run all doubled up like a crouching dog. There were more decisive details to a fairly well-trained eye. The man was clad in coarse and ragged clothes, but they were something more than merely coarse and ragged. They were so ill-fitting as to be quite grotesque; even as he appeared in black outline against the moonrise, the coat-collar in which his head was buried made him look like a hunchback, and the long loose sleeves looked as if he had no hands. It at once occurred to me that he had somehow managed to change his convict clothes for some confederate's clothes which did not fit him. Second, there was a pretty stiff wind against which he was running; so that I must have seen the streaky look of blowing hair, if the hair had not been very short. Then I remembered that beyond these ploughed fields he was crossing lay Pilgrim's Pond, for which (you will remember) the convict was keeping his bullet; and I sent my walking-stick flying.'

'A brilliant piece of rapid deduction,' said Father Brown; 'but had he got a gun?'

As Usher stopped abruptly in his walk the priest

added apologetically: 'I've been told a bullet is not half so useful without it.'

'He had no gun,' said the other gravely; 'but that was doubtless due to some very natural mischance or change of plans. Probably the same policy that made him change the clothes made him drop the gun; he began to repent the coat he had left behind him in the blood of his victim.'

'Well, that is possible enough,' answered the priest.

'And it's hardly worth speculating on,' said Usher, turning to some other papers, 'for we know it's the man by this time.'

His clerical friend asked faintly: 'But how?' And Greywood Usher threw down the newspapers and took up the two press-cuttings again.

'Well, since you are so obstinate,' he said, 'let's begin at the beginning. You will notice that these two cuttings have only one thing in common, which is the mention of Pilgrim's Pond, the estate, as you know, of the millionaire Ireton Todd. You also know that he is a remarkable character; one of those that rose on stepping-stones –'

'Of our dead selves to higher things,' assented his companion. 'Yes; I know that. Petroleum, I think.'

'Anyhow,' said Usher, 'Last-Trick Todd counts for a great deal in this rum affair.'

He stretched himself once more before the fire and continued talking in his expansive, radiantly explanatory style.

'To begin with, on the face of it, there is no mystery here at all. It is not mysterious, it is not even odd, that a jailbird should take his gun to Pilgrim's Pond. Our people aren't like the English, who will forgive a man for being rich if he throws away money on hospitals or horses. Last-Trick Todd has made himself big by his own considerable abilities; and there's no doubt that many of those on whom he has shown his abilities would like to show theirs on him with a shot-gun. Todd might easily get dropped by some man he'd never even heard of; some labourer he'd locked out, or some clerk in a business he'd busted. Last-Trick is a man of mental endowments and a high public character; but in this country the relations of employers and employed are considerably strained.

'That's how the whole thing looks supposing this Rian made for Pilgrim's Pond to kill Todd. So it looked to me, till another little discovery woke up what I have of the detective in me. When I had my prisoner safe, I picked up my cane again and strolled down the two or three turns of country road that brought me to one of the side entrances of Todd's grounds, the one nearest to the pool or lake after which the place is named. It was some two hours ago, about seven by this time; the moonlight was more luminous, and I could see the long white streaks of it lying on the mysterious mere with its grey, greasy, half-liquid shores in which they say our fathers used to make witches walk until they sank. I'd forgotten the exact tale; but you know the place I mean; it lies north of Todd's house towards the wilderness, and has two queer wrinkled trees, so dismal that they look more like huge fungoids than decent foliage. As I stood peering at this misty pool, I fancied I saw the faint figure of a man moving from the house towards it, but it was all too dim and distant for one to be certain of the fact, and still less of the details. Besides, my attention was very sharply arrested by something much closer. I crouched behind the fence which ran not more than two hundred yards from one wing of the great mansion, and which was fortunately split in places, as if specially for the application of a cautious eye. A door had opened in the dark bulk of the left wing, and a figure appeared black against the illuminated interior – a muffled figure bending forward, evidently peering out into the night. It closed the door behind it, and I saw it was carrying a lantern, which threw a patch of imperfect light on the dress and figure of the wearer. It seemed to be the figure of a woman, wrapped up in a ragged cloak and evidently disguised to avoid notice; there was something very strange both about the rags and the furtiveness in a person coming out of those rooms lined with gold. She took cautiously the curved garden path which brought her within half a hundred yards of me; then she stood up for an instant on the terrace of turf that looks towards the slimy lake, and holding her flaming lantern above her head she deliberately swung it three times to and fro as for a signal. As she swung it the second time a flicker of its light fell for a moment on her own face, a face that I knew. She was unnaturally pale, and her head was bundled in her borrowed plebeian shawl; but I am certain it was Etta Todd, the millionaire's daughter.

'She retraced her steps in equal secrecy and the door closed behind her again. I was about to climb the fence and follow, when I realized that the detective fever that had lured me into the adventure was rather undignified; and that in a more authoritative capacity I already held all the cards in my hand. I was just turning away when a new noise broke on the night. A window was thrown up in one of the upper floors, but just round the corner of the house so that I could not see it; and a voice of terrible distinctness was heard shouting across the dark garden to know where Lord Falconroy was, for he was missing from every room in the house. There was no mistaking that voice. I have heard it on many a political platform or meeting of directors; it was Ireton Todd himself. Some of the others seemed to have gone to the lower windows or on to the steps, and were calling up to him that Falconroy had gone for a stroll down to the Pilgrim's Pond an hour before, and could not be traced since. Then Todd cried "Mighty Murder!" and shut down the window violently; and I could hear him plunging down the stairs inside. Repossessing myself of my former and wiser purpose, I whipped out of the way of the general search that must follow; and returned here not later than eight o'clock.

'I now ask you to recall that little Society paragraph which seemed to you so painfully lacking in interest. If the convict was not keeping the shot for Todd, as he evidently wasn't, it is most likely that he was keeping it for Lord Falconroy; and it looks as if he had delivered the goods. No more handy place to shoot a man than in the curious geological surroundings of that pool, where a body thrown down would sink through thick slime to a depth practically unknown. Let us suppose, then, that our friend with the cropped hair came to kill Falconroy and not Todd. But, as I have pointed out, there are many reasons why people in America might want to kill Todd. There is no reason why anybody in America should want to kill an English lord newly landed, except for the one reason mentioned in the pink paper – that the lord is paying his attentions to the millionaire's daughter. Our crop-haired friend, despite his ill-fitting clothes, must be an aspiring lover.

'I know the notion will seem to you jarring and even comic; but that's because you are English. It sounds to you like saying the Archbishop of Canterbury's daughter will be married in St George's, Hanover Square, to a crossing-sweeper on ticket-of-leave. You don't do justice to the climbing and aspiring power of our more remarkable citizens. You see a good-looking grey-haired man in evening-dress with a sort of authority about him, you know he is a pillar of the State, and you fancy he had a father. You are in error. You do not realize that a comparatively few years ago he may have been in a tenement or (quite likely) in a jail. You don't allow for our national buoyancy and uplift. Many of our most influential citizens have not only risen recently, but risen comparatively late in life. Todd's daughter was fully eighteen when her father first made his pile; so there isn't really anything impossible in her having a hanger-on in low life; or even in her hanging on to him, as I think she must be doing, to judge by the lantern business. If so, the hand that held the lantern may not be unconnected with the hand that held the gun. This case, sir, will make a noise.'

'Well,' said the priest patiently, 'and what did you do next?'

'I reckon you'll be shocked,' replied Greywood Usher, 'as I know you don't cotton to the march of science in these matters. I am given a good deal of discretion here, and perhaps take a little more than I'm given; and I thought it was an excellent opportunity to test that Psychometric Machine I told you about. Now, in my opinion, that machine can't lie.'

'No machine can lie,' said Father Brown; 'nor can it tell the truth.'

'It did in this case, as I'll show you,' went on Usher positively. 'I sat the man in the ill-fitting clothes in a comfortable chair, and simply wrote words on a blackboard; and the machine simply recorded the variations of his pulse; and I simply observed his manner. The trick is to introduce some word connected with the supposed crime in a list of words connected with something quite different, yet a list in which it occurs quite naturally.

Thus I wrote "heron" and "eagle" and "owl", and when I wrote "falcon" he was tremendously agitated; and when I began to make an "r" at the end of the word, that machine just bounded. Who else in this republic has any reason to jump at the name of a newly-arrived Englishman like Falconroy except the man who's shot him? Isn't that better evidence than a lot of gabble from witnesses – the evidence of a reliable machine?'

'You always forget,' observed his companion, 'that the reliable machine always has to be worked by an unreliable machine.'

'Why, what do you mean?' asked the detective.

'I mean Man,' said Father Brown, 'the most unreliable machine I know of. I don't want to be rude; and I don't think you will consider Man to be an offensive or inaccurate description of yourself. You say you observed his manner; but how do you know you observed it right? You say the words have to come in a natural way; but how do you know that you did it naturally? How do you know, if you come to that, that he did not observe your manner? Who is to prove that you were not tremendously agitated? There was no machine tied on to your pulse.'

'I tell you,' cried the American in the utmost excitement, 'I was as cool as a cucumber.'

'Criminals also can be as cool as cucumbers,' said Brown with a smile. 'And almost as cool as you.'

'Well, this one wasn't,' said Usher, throwing the papers about. 'Oh, you make me tired!'

'I'm sorry,' said the other. 'I only point out what seems a reasonable possibility. If you could tell by his manner when the word that might hang him had come, why shouldn't he tell from your manner that the word that might hang him was coming? I should ask for more than words myself before I hanged anybody.'

Usher smote the table and rose in a sort of angry triumph.

'And that,' he cried, 'is just what I'm going to give you. I tried the machine first just in order to test the thing in other ways afterwards and the machine, sir, is right.'

He paused a moment and resumed with less excitement. 'I rather want to insist, if it comes to that, that so far I had very little to go on except the scientific experiment. There was really nothing against the man at all. His clothes were ill-fitting, as I've said, but they were rather better, if anything, than those of the submerged class to which he evidently belonged. Moreover, under all the stains of his plunging through ploughed fields or bursting through dusty hedges, the man was comparatively clean. This might mean, of course, that he had only just broken prison; but it reminded me more of the desperate decency of the comparatively respectable poor. His demeanour was, I am bound to confess, quite in accordance with theirs. He was silent and dignified as they are; he seemed to have a big, but buried, grievance, as they do. He professed total ignorance of the crime and the whole question; and showed nothing but a sullen impatience for something sensible that might come to take him out of his meaningless scrape. He asked me more than once if he could telephone for a lawyer who had helped him a long time ago in a trade dispute, and in every sense acted as you would expect an innocent man to act. There was nothing against him in the world except that little finger on the dial that pointed to the change of his pulse.

'Then, sir, the machine was on its trial; and the machine was right. By the time I came with him out of the private room into the vestibule where all sorts of other people were awaiting examination, I think he had already more or less made up his mind to clear things up by something like a confession. He turned to me and began to say in a low voice: "Oh, I can't stick this any more. If you must know all about me –"

'At the same instant one of the poor women sitting on the long bench stood up, screaming aloud and pointing at him with her finger. I have never in my life heard anything more demoniacally distinct. Her lean finger seemed to pick him out as if it were a pea-shooter. Though the word was a mere howl, every syllable was as clear as a separate stroke on the clock.

' "Drugger Davis!" she shouted. "They've got Drugger Davis!"

'Among the wretched women, mostly thieves and street-walkers, twenty faces were turned, gaping with glee and hate. If I had never heard the words, I should have known by the very shock upon his features that the so-called Oscar Rian had heard his real name. But I'm not quite so ignorant, you may be surprised to hear. Drugger Davis was one of the most terrible and depraved criminals that ever baffled our police. It is certain he had done murder more than once long before his last exploit with the warder. But he was never entirely fixed for it, curiously enough because he did it in the same manner as those milder – or meaner – crimes for which he was fixed pretty often. He was a handsome, well-bred-looking brute, as he still is, to some extent; and he used mostly to go about with bar-maids or shop-girls and do them out of their money. Very often, though, he went a good deal farther; and they were found drugged with cigarettes or chocolates and their whole property missing. Then came one case where the girl was found dead; but deliberation could not quite be proved, and, what was more practical still, the criminal could not be found. I heard a rumour of

his having reappeared somewhere in the opposite character this time, lending money instead of borrowing it;
but still to such poor widows as he might personally
fascinate, and still with the same bad result for them.
Well, there is your innocent man, and there is his innocent record. Even, since then, four criminals and three
warders have identified him and confirmed the story.
Now what have you got to say to my poor little
machine after that? Hasn't the machine done for him?
Or do you prefer to say that the woman and I have
done for him?'

'As to what you've done for him,' replied Father
Brown, rising and shaking himself in a floppy way,
'you've saved him from the electrical chair. I don't
think they can kill Drugger Davis on that old vague
story of the poison; and as for the convict who killed
the warder, I suppose it's obvious that you haven't got
him. Mr Davis is innocent of that crime, at any rate.'

'What do you mean?' demanded the other. 'Why
should he be innocent of that crime?'

'Why, bless us all!' cried the small man in one of his
rare moments of animation, 'why, because he's guilty
of the other crimes! I don't know what you people are
made of. You seem to think that all sins are kept
together in a bag. You talk as if a miser on Monday
were always a spendthrift on Tuesday. You tell me this
man you have here spent weeks and months wheedling
needy women out of small sums of money; that he used
a drug at the best, and a poison at the worst; that he
turned up afterwards as the lowest kind of moneylender, and cheated most poor people in the same
patient and pacific style. Let it be granted – let us
admit, for the sake of argument, that he did all this. If
that is so, I will tell you what he didn't do. He didn't

storm a spiked wall against a man with a loaded gun. He didn't write on the wall with his own hand, to say he had done it. He didn't stop to state that his justification was self-defence. He didn't explain that he had no quarrel with the poor warder. He didn't name the house of the rich man to which he was going with the gun. He didn't write his own initials in a man's blood. Saints alive! Can't you see the whole character is different, in good and evil? Why, you don't seem to be like I am a bit. One would think you'd never had any vices of your own.'

The amazed American had already parted his lips in protest when the door of his private and official room was hammered and rattled in an unceremonious way to which he was totally unaccustomed.

The door flew open. The moment before Greywood Usher had been coming to the conclusion that Father Brown might possibly be mad. The moment after he began to think he was mad himself. There burst and fell into his private room a man in the filthiest rags, with a greasy squash hat still askew on his head, and a shabby green shade shoved up from one of his eyes, both of which were glaring like a tiger's. The rest of his face was almost undiscoverable, being masked with a matted beard and whiskers through which the nose could barely thrust itself, and further buried in a squalid red scarf or handkerchief. Mr Usher prided himself on having seen most of the roughest specimens in the State, but he thought he had never seen such a baboon dressed as a scarecrow as this. But, above all, he had never in all his placid scientific existence heard a man like that speak to him first.

'See here, old man Usher,' shouted the being in the red handkerchief, 'I'm getting tired. Don't you try any of your hide-and-seek on me; I don't get fooled any. Leave go of my guests, and I'll let up on the fancy clockwork. Keep him here for a split instant and you'll feel pretty mean. I reckon I'm not a man with no pull.'

The eminent Usher was regarding the bellowing monster with an amazement which had dried up all other sentiments. The mere shock to his eyes had rendered his ears almost useless. At last he rang a bell with a hand of violence. While the bell was still strong and pealing, the voice of Father Brown fell soft but distinct.

'I have a suggestion to make,' he said, 'but it seems a little confusing. I don't know this gentleman – but – but I think I know him. Now, you know him – you know him quite well – but you don't know him – naturally. Sounds paradoxical, I know.'

'I reckon the Cosmos is cracked,' said Usher, and fell asprawl in his round office chair.

'Now, see here,' vociferated the stranger, striking the table, but speaking in a voice that was all the more mysterious because it was comparatively mild and rational though still resounding. 'I won't let you in. I want –'

'Who in hell are you?' yelled Usher, suddenly sitting up straight.

'I think the gentleman's name is Todd,' said the priest.

Then he picked up the pink slip of newspaper.

'I fear you don't read the Society papers properly,' he said, and began to read out in a monotonous voice, ' "Or locked in the jewelled bosoms of our city's gayest leaders; but there is talk of a pretty parody of the manners and customs of the other end of Society's scale." There's been a big Slum Dinner up at Pilgrim's Pond to-night; and a man, one of the guests, disappeared.

Mr Ireton Todd is a good host, and has tracked him here, without even waiting to take off his fancy-dress.'

'What man do you mean?'

'I mean the man with the comically ill-fitting clothes you saw running across the ploughed field. Hadn't you better go and investigate him? He will be rather impatient to get back to his champagne, from which he ran away in such a hurry, when the convict with the gun hove in sight.'

'Do you seriously mean –' began the official.

'Why, look here, Mr Usher,' said Father Brown quietly, 'you said the machine couldn't make a mistake; and in one sense it didn't. But the other machine did; the machine that worked it. You assumed that the man in rags jumped at the name of Lord Falconroy, because he was Lord Falconroy's murderer. He jumped at the name of Lord Falconroy because he *is* Lord Falconroy.'

'Then why the blazes didn't he say so?' demanded the staring Usher.

'He felt his plight and recent panic were hardly patrician,' replied the priest, 'so he tried to keep the name back at first. But he was just going to tell it you, when' – and Father Brown looked down at his boots – 'when a woman found another name for him.'

'But you can't be so mad as to say,' said Greywood Usher, very white, 'that Lord Falconroy was Drugger Davis.'

The priest looked at him very earnestly, but with a baffling and undecipherable face.

'I am not saying anything about it,' he said. 'I leave all the rest to you. Your pink paper says that the title was recently revived for him; but those papers are very unreliable. It says he was in the States in youth; but the whole story seems very strange. Davis and Falconroy are both pretty considerable cowards, but so are lots of other men. I would not hang a dog on my own opinion about this. But I think,' he went on softly and reflectively, 'I think you Americans are too modest. I think you idealize the English aristocracy – even in assuming it to be so aristocratic. You see a good-looking Englishman in evening-dress; you know he's in the House of Lords; and you fancy he has a father. You don't allow for our national buoyancy and uplift. Many of our most influential noblemen have only risen recently, but –'

'Oh, stop it!' cried Greywood Usher, wringing one lean hand in impatience against a shade of irony in the other's face.

'Don't stay talking to this lunatic!' cried Todd brutally. 'Take me to my friend.'

Next morning Father Brown appeared with the same demure expression, carrying yet another piece of pink newspaper.

'I'm afraid you neglect the fashionable press rather,' he said, 'but this cutting may interest you.'

Usher read the headlines, 'Last-Trick's Strayed Revellers: Mirthful Incident near Pilgrim's Pond.' The paragraph went on: 'A laughable occurrence took place outside Wilkinson's Motor Garage last night. A policeman on duty had his attention drawn by larrikins to a man in prison dress who was stepping with considerable coolness into the steering-seat of a pretty high-toned Panhard; he was accompanied by a girl wrapped in a ragged shawl. On the police interfering, the young woman threw back the shawl, and all recognized Millionaire Todd's daughter, who had just come from the Slum Freak Dinner at the Pond, where all the choicest guests were in a similar *déshabille*. She and the gentleman who had donned prison uniform were going for the customary joy-ride.'

Under the pink slip Mr Usher found a strip of a later paper, headed, 'Astounding Escape of Millionaire's Daughter with Convict. She had Arranged Freak Dinner. Now Safe in –'

Mr Greenwood Usher lifted his eyes, but Father Brown was gone.

6

The Head of Cæsar

There is somewhere in Brompton or Kensington an interminable avenue of tall houses, rich but largely empty, that looks like a terrace of tombs. The very steps up to the dark front doors seem as steep as the side of pyramids; one would hesitate to knock at the door, lest it should be opened by a mummy. But a yet more depressing feature in the grey façade is its telescopic length and changeless continuity. The pilgrim walking down it begins to think he will never come to a break or a corner; but there is one exception – a very small one, but hailed by the pilgrim almost with a shout. There is a sort of mews between two of the tall mansions, a mere slit like the crack of a door by comparison with the street, but just large enough to permit a pigmy ale-house or eating-house, still allowed by the rich to their stable-servants, to stand in the angle. There is something cheery in its very dinginess, and something free and elfin in its very insignificance. At the feet of those grey stone giants it looks like a lighted house of dwarfs.

Anyone passing the place during a certain autumn evening, itself almost fairylike, might have seen a hand pull aside the red half-blind which (along with some large white lettering) half hid the interior from the street, and a face peer out not unlike a rather innocent goblin's. It was, in fact, the face of one with the

harmless human name of Brown, formerly priest of
Cobhole in Essex, and now working in London. His
friend, Flambeau, a semi-official investigator, was sitting opposite him, making his last notes of a case he
had cleared up in the neighbourhood. They were sitting
at a small table, close up to the window, when the priest
pulled the curtain back and looked out. He waited till a
stranger in the street had passed the window, to let the
curtain fall into its place again. Then his round eyes
rolled to the large white lettering on the window above
his head, and then strayed to the next table, at which
sat only a navvy with beer and cheese, and a young girl
with red hair and a glass of milk. Then (seeing his
friend put away the pocket-book), he said softly:

'If you've got ten minutes, I wish you'd follow that
man with the false nose.'

Flambeau looked up in surprise; but the girl with
the red hair also looked up, and with something that
was stronger than astonishment. She was simply and
even loosely dressed in light brown sacking stuff; but
she was a lady, and even, on a second glance, a rather
needlessly haughty one: 'The man with the false nose!'
repeated Flambeau. 'Who's he?'

'I haven't a notion,' answered Father Brown. 'I want
you to find out; I ask it as a favour. He went down
there' – and he jerked his thumb over his shoulder in
one of his undistinguished gestures – 'and can't have
passed three lamp-posts yet. I only want to know the
direction.'

Flambeau gazed at his friend for some time, with an
expression between perplexity and amusement; and
then, rising from the table, squeezed his huge form out
of the little door of the dwarf tavern, and melted into
the twilight.

Father Brown took a small book out of his pocket

and began to read steadily; he betrayed no conscious-
ness of the fact that the red-haired lady had left her
own table and sat down opposite him. At last she
leaned over and said in a low, strong voice: 'Why do
you say that? How do you know it's false?'

He lifted his rather heavy eyelids, which fluttered in
considerable embarrassment. Then his dubious eye
roamed again to the white lettering on the glass front
of the public-house. The young woman's eyes followed
his, and rested there also, but in pure puzzledom.

'No,' said Father Brown, answering her thoughts. 'It
doesn't say "Sela", like the thing in the Psalms; I read it
like that myself when I was wool-gathering just now;
it says "Ales."'

'Well?' inquired the staring young lady. 'What does
it matter what it says?'

His ruminating eye roved to the girl's light canvas
sleeve, round the wrist of which ran a very slight thread
of artistic pattern, just enough to distinguish it from a
working-dress of a common woman and make it more
like the working-dress of a lady art-student. He seemed
to find much food for thought in this; but his reply was
very slow and hesitant. 'You see, madam,' he said,
'from outside the place looks – well, it is a perfectly
decent place – but ladies like you don't – don't generally think so. They never go into such places from
choice, except –'

'Well?' she repeated.

'Except an unfortunate few who don't go in to drink
milk.'

'You are a most singular person,' said the young
lady. 'What is your object in all this?'

'Not to trouble you about it,' he replied, very gently.
'Only to arm myself with knowledge enough to help
you, if ever you freely ask my help.'

'But why should I need help?'

He continued his dreamy monologue. 'You couldn't have come in to see *protégées*, humble friends, that sort of thing, or you'd have gone through into the parlour ... and you couldn't have come in because you were ill, or you'd have spoken to the woman of the place, who's obviously respectable ... besides, you don't look ill in that way, but only unhappy ... This street is the only original long lane that has no turning; and the houses on both sides are shut up ... I could only suppose that you'd seen somebody coming whom you didn't want to meet; and found the public-house was the only shelter in this wilderness of stone ... I don't think I went beyond the licence of a stranger in glancing at the only man who passed immediately after ... And as I thought he looked like the wrong sort ... and you looked like the right sort ... I held myself ready to help if he annoyed you; that is all. As for my friend, he'll be back soon; and he certainly can't find out anything by stumping down a road like this ... I didn't think he could.'

'Then why did you send him out?' she cried, leaning forward with yet warmer curiosity. She had the proud, impetuous face that goes with reddish colouring, and a Roman nose, as it did in Marie Antoinette.

He looked at her steadily for the first time, and said: 'Because I hoped you would speak to me.'

She looked back at him for some time with a heated face, in which there hung a red shadow of anger; then, despite her anxieties, humour broke out of her eyes and the corners of her mouth, and she answered almost grimly: 'Well, if you're so keen on my conversation, perhaps you'll answer my question.' After a pause she added: 'I had the honour to ask you why you thought the man's nose was false.'

'The wax always spots like that just a little in this weather,' answered Father Brown with entire simplicity.

'But it's such a *crooked* nose,' remonstrated the red-haired girl.

The priest smiled in his turn. 'I don't say it's the sort of nose one would wear out of mere foppery,' he admitted. 'This man, I think, wears it because his real nose is so much nicer.'

'But why?' she insisted.

'What is the nursery-rhyme?' observed Brown absent-mindedly. 'There was a crooked man and he went a crooked mile . . . That man, I fancy, has gone a very crooked road – by following his nose.'

'Why, what's he done?' she demanded, rather shakily.

'I don't want to force your confidence by a hair,' said Father Brown, very quietly. 'But I think you could tell me more about that than I can tell you.'

The girl sprang to her feet and stood quite quietly, but with clenched hands, like one about to stride away; then her hands loosened slowly, and she sat down again. 'You are more of a mystery than all the others,' she said desperately; 'but I feel there might be a heart in your mystery.'

'What we all dread most,' said the priest in a low voice, 'is a maze with *no* centre. That is why atheism is only a nightmare.'

'I will tell you everything,' said the red-haired girl doggedly, 'except why I am telling you; and that I don't know.'

She picked at the darned table-cloth and went on: 'You look as if you knew what isn't snobbery as well as what is; and when I say that ours is a good old family, you'll understand it is a necessary part of the story;

indeed, my chief danger is in my brother's high-and-dry notions, *noblesse oblige* and all that. Well, my name is Christabel Carstairs; and my father was that Colonel Carstairs you've probably heard of, who made the famous Carstairs Collection of Roman coins. I could never describe my father to you; the nearest I can say is that he was very like a Roman coin himself. He was as handsome and as genuine and as valuable and as metallic and as out-of-date. He was prouder of his Collection than of his coat-of-arms – nobody could say more than that. His extraordinary character came out most in his will. He had two sons and one daughter. He quarrelled with one son, my brother Giles, and sent him to Australia on a small allowance. He then made a will leaving the Carstairs Collection, actually with a yet smaller allowance, to my brother Arthur. He meant it as a reward, as the highest honour he could offer, in acknowledgment of Arthur's loyalty and rectitude and the distinctions he had already gained in mathematics and economics at Cambridge. He left me practically all his pretty large fortune; and I am sure he meant it in contempt.

'Arthur, you may say, might well complain of this; but Arthur is my father over again. Though he had some differences with my father in early youth, no sooner had he taken over the Collection than he became like a pagan priest dedicated to a temple. He mixed up these Roman halfpence with the honour of the Carstairs family in the same stiff, idolatrous way as his father before him. He acted as if Roman money must be guarded by all the Roman virtues. He took no pleasures; he spent nothing on himself; he lived for the Collection. Often he would not trouble to dress for his simple meals; but pottered about among the corded brown-paper parcels (which no one else was allowed to touch) in an old brown dressing-gown. With its rope and tassel and his pale, thin, refined face, it made him look like an old ascetic monk. Every now and then, though, he would appear dressed like a decidedly fashionable gentleman; but that was only when he went up to the London sales or shops to make an addition to the Carstairs Collection.

'Now, if you've known any young people, you won't be shocked if I say that I got into rather a low frame of mind with all this; the frame of mind in which one begins to say that the Ancient Romans were all very well in their way. I'm not like my brother Arthur; I can't help enjoying enjoyment. I got a lot of romance and rubbish where I got my red hair, from the other side of the family. Poor Giles was the same; and I think the atmosphere of coins might count in excuse for him; though he really did wrong and nearly went to prison. But he didn't behave any worse than I did; as you shall hear.

'I come now to the silly part of the story. I think a man as clever as you can guess the sort of thing that would begin to relieve the monotony for an unruly girl of seventeen placed in such a position. But I am so rattled with more dreadful things that I can hardly read my own feeling; and don't know whether I despise it now as a flirtation or bear it as a broken heart. We lived then at a little seaside watering-place in South Wales, and a retired sea-captain living a few doors off had a son about five years older than myself, who had been a friend of Giles before he went to the Colonies. His name does not affect my tale; but I tell you it was Philip Hawker, because I am telling you everything. We used to go shrimping together, and said and thought we were in love with each other; at least he certainly said he was, and I certainly thought I was. If I tell you he had bronzed curly hair and a falconish sort of face, bronzed by the sea also, it's not for his sake, I assure you, but for the story; for it was the cause of a very curious coincidence.

'One summer afternoon, when I had promised to go shrimping along the sands with Philip, I was waiting rather impatiently in the front drawing-room, watching Arthur handle some packets of coins he had just purchased and slowly shunt them, one or two at a time, into his own dark study and museum which was at the back of the house. As soon as I heard the heavy door close on him finally, I made a bolt for my shrimping-net and tam-o'-shanter and was just going to slip out, when I saw that my brother had left behind him one coin that lay gleaming on the long bench by the window. It was a bronze coin, and the colour, combined with the exact curve of the Roman nose and something in the very lift of the long, wiry neck, made the head of Cæsar on it the almost precise portrait of Philip Hawker. Then I suddenly remembered Giles telling Philip of a coin that was like him, and Philip wishing he had it. Perhaps you can fancy the wild, foolish thoughts with which my head went round; I felt as if I had had a gift from the fairies. It seemed to me that if I could only run away with this, and give it to Philip like a wild sort of wedding-ring, it would be a bond between us for ever; I felt a thousand such things at once. Then there yawned under me, like the pit, the enormous, awful notion of what I was doing; above all, the unbearable thought, which was like touching hot iron, of what Arthur would think of it. A Carstairs a thief; and a thief of the Carstairs treasure! I believe my brother could see me burned like a witch for such a thing. But then, the very thought of such fanatical cruelty heightened my old hatred of his dingy old

antiquarian fussiness and my longing for the youth and
liberty that called to me from the sea. Outside was
strong sunlight with a wind; and a yellow head of some
broom or gorse in the garden rapped against the glass
of the window. I thought of that living and growing
gold calling to me from all the heaths of the world –
and then of that dead, dull gold and bronze and brass
of my brother's growing dustier and dustier as life went
by. Nature and the Carstairs Collection had come to
grips at last.

'Nature is older than the Carstairs Collection. As I
ran down the streets to the sea, the coin clenched tight
in my fist, I felt all the Roman Empire on my back as
well as the Carstairs pedigree. It was not only the old
lion argent that was roaring in my ear, but all the eagles
of the Cæsars seemed flapping and screaming in pursuit of me. And yet my heart rose higher and higher
like a child's kite, until I came over the loose, dry sand-
hills and to the flat, wet sands, where Philip stood
already up to his ankles in the shallow shining water,
some hundred yards out to sea. There was a great red
sunset; and the long stretch of low water, hardly rising
over the ankle for half a mile, was like a lake of ruby
flame. It was not till I had torn off my shoes and stockings and waded to where he stood, which was well
away from the dry land, that I turned and looked
round. We were quite alone in a circle of sea-water and
wet sand; and I gave him the head of Cæsar.

'At the very instant I had a shock of fancy: that a
man far away on the sand-hills was looking at me
intently. I must have felt immediately after that it was
a mere leap of unreasonable nerves; for the man was
only a dark dot in the distance, and I could only just
see that he was standing quite still and gazing, with his
head a little on one side. There was no earthly logical

evidence that he was looking at me; he might have been looking at a ship, or the sunset, or the sea-gulls, or at any of the people who still strayed here and there on the shore between us. Nevertheless, whatever my start sprang from was prophetic; for, as I gazed, he started walking briskly in a bee-line towards us across the wide wet sands. As he drew nearer and nearer I saw that he was dark and bearded, and that his eyes were marked with dark spectacles. He was dressed poorly but respectably in black, from the old black top hat on his head to the solid black boots on his feet. In spite of these he walked straight into the sea without a flash of hesitation, and came on at me with the steadiness of a travelling bullet.

'I can't tell you the sense of monstrosity and miracle I had when he thus silently burst the barrier between land and water. It was as if he had walked straight off a cliff and still marched steadily in mid-air. It was as if a house had flown up into the sky or a man's head had fallen off. He was only wetting his boots; but he seemed to be a demon disregarding a law of Nature. If he had hesitated an instant at the water's edge it would have been nothing. As it was, he seemed to look so much at me alone as not to notice the ocean. Philip was some yards away with his back to me, bending over his net. The stranger came on till he stood within two yards of me, the water washing half-way up to his knees. Then he said, with a clearly modulated and rather mincing articulation: "Would it discommode you to contribute elsewhere a coin with a somewhat different super-scription?"

'With one exception there was nothing definably abnormal about him. His tinted glasses were not really opaque, but of a blue kind common enough, nor were the eyes behind them shifty, but regarded me steadily.

His dark beard was not really long or wild; but he looked rather hairy, because the beard began very high up in his face, just under the cheek-bones. His complexion was neither sallow nor livid, but on the contrary rather clear and youthful; yet this gave a pink-and-white wax look which somehow (I don't know why) rather increased the horror. The only oddity one could fix was that his nose, which was otherwise of a good shape, was just slightly turned sideways at the tip; as if, when it was soft, it had been tapped on one side with a toy hammer. The thing was hardly a deformity; yet I cannot tell you what a living nightmare it was to me. As he stood there in the sunset-stained water he affected me as some hellish sea-monster just risen roaring out of a sea like blood. I don't know why a touch on the nose should affect my imagination so much. I think it seemed as if he could move his nose like a finger. And as if he had just that moment moved it.

' "Any little assistance," he continued with the same queer, priggish accent, "that may obviate the necessity of my communicating with the family."

'Then it rushed over me that I was being black-mailed for the theft of the bronze piece; and all my merely superstitious fears and doubts were swallowed up in one overpowering, practical question. How could he have found out? I had stolen the thing suddenly and on impulse; I was certainly alone; for I always made sure of being unobserved when I slipped out to see Philip in this way. I had not, to all appearance, been followed in the street; and if I had, they could not "X-ray" the coin in my closed hand. The man standing on the sand-hills could no more have seen what I gave Philip than shoot a fly in one eye, like the man in the fairy-tale.

' "Philip," I cried helplessly, "ask this man what he wants."

'When Philip lifted his head at last from mending his net he looked rather red, as if sulky or ashamed; but it may have been only the exertion of stooping and the red evening light; I may have only had another of the morbid fancies that seemed to be dancing about me. He merely said gruffly to the man: "You clear out of this." And, motioning me to follow, set off wading shoreward without paying further attention to him. He stepped on to a stone breakwater that ran out from among the roots of the sand-hills, and so struck homeward, perhaps thinking our incubus would find it less easy to walk on such rough stones, green and slippery with seaweed, than we, who were young and used to it. But my persecutor walked as daintily as he talked; and he still followed me, picking his way and picking his phrases. I heard his delicate, detestable voice appealing to me over my shoulder, until at last, when we had crested the sand-hills, Philip's patience (which was by no means so conspicuous on most occasions) seemed to snap. He turned suddenly, saying, "Go back. I can't talk to you now." And, as the man hovered and opened his mouth, Philip struck him a buffet on it that sent him flying from the top of the tallest sand-hill to the bottom. I saw him crawling out below, covered with sand.

'This stroke comforted me somehow, though it might well increase my peril; but Philip showed none of his usual elation at his own prowess. Though as affectionate as ever, he still seemed cast down; and before I could ask him anything fully, he parted with me at his own gate, with two remarks that struck me as strange. He said that, all things considered, I ought to put the coin back in the Collection; but that he himself would keep it "for the present." And then he added, quite suddenly and irrelevantly: "You know Giles is back from Australia?" '

The door of the tavern opened and the gigantic shadow of the investigator Flambeau fell across the table. Father Brown presented him to the lady in his own slight, persuasive style of speech, mentioning his knowledge and sympathy in such cases; and almost without knowing, the girl was soon reiterating her story to two listeners. But Flambeau, as he bowed and sat down, handed the priest a small slip of paper. Brown accepted it with some surprise and read on it: 'Cab to Wagga Wagga, 379, Mafeking Avenue, Putney.' The girl was going on with her story.

'I went up the steep street to my own house with my head in a whirl; it had not begun to clear when I came to the doorstep, on which I found a milk-can – and the man with the twisted nose. The milk-can told me the servants were all out; for, of course, Arthur, browsing about in his brown dressing-gown in a brown study, would not hear or answer a bell. Thus there was no one to help me in the house, except my brother, whose help must be my ruin. In desperation I thrust two shillings into the horrid thing's hand, and told him to call again in a few days, when I had thought it out. He went off sulking, but more sheepishly than I had expected – perhaps he had been shaken by his fall – and I watched the star of sand splashed on his back receding down the road with a horrid vindictive pleasure. He turned a corner some six houses down.

'Then I let myself in, made myself some tea, and tried to think it out. I sat at the drawing-room window looking on to the garden, which still glowed with the last full evening light. But I was too distracted and dreamy to look at the lawns and flower-pots and flower-beds with any concentration. So I took the shock the more sharply because I'd seen it so slowly.

'The man or monster I'd sent away was standing quite still in the middle of the garden. Oh, we've all read a lot about pale-faced phantoms in the dark; but this was more dreadful than anything of that kind could ever be. Because, though he cast a long evening shadow, he still stood in warm sunlight. And because his face was not pale, but had that waxen bloom still upon it that belongs to a barber's dummy. He stood quite still, with his face towards me; and I can't tell you how horrid he looked among the tulips and all those tall, gaudy, almost hothouse-looking flowers. It looked as if we'd stuck up a wax-work instead of a statue in the centre of our garden.

'Yet almost the instant he saw me move in the window he turned and ran out of the garden by the back gate, which stood open and by which he had undoubtedly entered. This renewed timidity on his part was so different from the impudence with which he had walked into the sea, that I felt vaguely comforted. I fancied, perhaps, that he feared confronting Arthur more than I knew. Anyhow, I settled down at last, and had a quiet dinner alone (for it was against the rules to disturb Arthur when he was rearranging the museum), and, my thoughts, a little released, fled to Philip and lost themselves, I suppose. Anyhow, I was looking blankly, but rather pleasantly than otherwise, at another window, uncurtained, but by this time black as a slate with the final night-fall. It seemed to me that something like a snail was on the outside of the window-pane. But when I stared harder, it was more like a man's thumb pressed on the pane; it had that curled look that a thumb has. With my fear and courage re-awakened together, I rushed at the window and then recoiled with a strangled scream that any man but Arthur must have heard.

'For it was not a thumb, any more than it was a snail. It was the tip of a crooked nose, crushed against the glass; it looked white with the pressure; and the staring face and eyes behind it were at first invisible and afterwards grey like a ghost. I slammed the shutters together somehow, rushed up to my room, and locked myself in. But, even as I passed, I could almost swear I saw a second black window with something on it that was like a snail.

'It might be best to go to Arthur after all. If the thing was crawling close all around the house like a cat, it might have purposes worse even than blackmail. My brother might cast me out and curse me for ever, but he was a gentleman, and would defend me on the spot. After ten minutes' curious thinking, I went down, knocked at the door and then went in: to see the last and worst sight.

'My brother's chair was empty; and he was obviously out. But the man with the crooked nose was sitting waiting for his return, with his hat still insolently on his head, and actually reading one of my brother's books under my brother's lamp. His face was composed and occupied, but his nose-tip still had the air of being the most mobile part of his face, as if it had just turned from left to right like an elephant's proboscis. I had thought him poisonous enough while he was pursuing and watching me; but I think his unconsciousness of my presence was more frightful still.

'I think I screamed loud and long; but that doesn't matter. What I did next does matter: I gave him all the money I had, including a good deal in paper which, though it was mine, I dare say I had no right to touch.

He went off at last, with hateful, tactful regrets all in long words; and I sat down, feeling ruined in every sense. And yet I was saved that very night by a pure accident. Arthur had gone off suddenly to London, as he so often did, for bargains; and returned, late but radiant, having nearly secured a treasure that was an added splendour even to the family Collection. He was so resplendent that I was almost emboldened to confess the abstraction of the lesser gem; but he bore down all other topics with his over-powering projects. Because the bargain might still miss fire any moment, he insisted on my packing at once and going up with him to lodgings he had already taken in Fulham, to be near the curio-shop in question. Thus in spite of myself, I fled from my foe almost in the dead of night – but from Philip also . . . My brother was often at the South Kensington Museum, and, in order to make some sort of secondary life for myself, I paid for a few lessons at the Art Schools. I was coming back from them this evening, when I saw the abomination of desolation walking alive down the long straight street and the rest is as this gentleman has said.

'I've got only one thing to say. I don't deserve to be helped; and I don't question or complain of my punishment; it is just, it ought to have happened. But I still question, with bursting brains, how it can have happened. Am I punished by miracle? or how *can* anyone but Philip and myself know I gave him a tiny coin in the middle of the sea?'

'It is an extraordinary problem,' admitted Flambeau.

'Not so extraordinary as the answer,' remarked Father Brown, rather gloomily. 'Miss Carstairs, will you be at home if we call at your Fulham place in an hour and a half hence?'

The girl looked at him, and then rose and put her

gloves on. 'Yes,' she said, 'I'll be there'; and almost instantly left the place.

That night the detective and the priest were still talking of the matter as they drew near the Fulham house, a tenement strangely mean even for a temporary residence of the Carstairs family.

'Of course the superficial, on reflection,' said Flambeau, 'would think first of this Australian brother who's been in trouble before, who's come back so suddenly and who's just the man to have shabby confederates. But I can't see how he can come into the thing by any process of thought, unless –'

'Well?' asked his companion patiently.

Flambeau lowered his voice. 'Unless the girl's lover comes in, too, and he would be the blacker villain. The Australian chap did know that Hawker wanted the coin. But I can't see how on earth he could know that Hawker had got it, unless Hawker signalled to him or his representative across the shore.'

'That is true,' assented the priest, with respect.

'Have you noted another thing?' went on Flambeau eagerly; 'this Hawker hears his love insulted, but doesn't strike till *he's got to the soft sand-hills*, where he can be victor in a mere sham-fight. If he'd struck amid rocks and sea, he might have hurt his ally.'

'That is true again,' said Father Brown, nodding.

'And now, take it from the start. It lies between few people, but at least three. You want one person for suicide; two people for murder; but at least three people for blackmail.'

'Why?' asked the priest softly.

'Well, obviously,' cried his friend, 'there must be one to be exposed; one to threaten exposure; and one at least whom exposure would horrify.'

After a long ruminant pause, the priest said: 'You miss a logical step. Three persons are needed as ideas. Only two are needed as agents.'

'What can you mean?' asked the other.

'Why shouldn't a blackmailer,' asked Brown, in a low voice, 'threaten his victim with himself? Suppose a wife became a rigid teetotaller *in order* to frighten her husband into concealing *his* pub-frequenting, and then wrote him blackmailing letters in another hand, threatening to tell his wife! Why shouldn't it work? Suppose a father forbade a son to gamble, and then, following him in a good disguise, threatened the boy with his own sham paternal strictness! Suppose – but here we are, my friend.'

'My God!' cried Flambeau; 'you don't mean –'

An active figure ran down the steps of the house and showed under the golden lamplight the unmistakable head that resembled the Roman coin. 'Miss Carstairs,' said Hawker without ceremony, 'wouldn't go in till you came.'

'Well,' observed Brown confidentially, 'don't you think it's the best thing she can do to stop outside – with you to look after her? You see, I rather guess you have guessed it all yourself.'

'Yes,' said the young man, in an undertone, 'I guessed on the sands and now I know; that was why I let him fall soft.'

Taking a latchkey from the girl and the coin from Hawker, Flambeau let himself and his friend into the empty house and passed into the outer parlour. It was empty of all occupants but one. The man whom Father Brown had seen pass the tavern was standing against the wall as if at bay; unchanged, save that he had taken off his black coat and was wearing a brown dressing-gown.

'We have come,' said Father Brown politely, 'to give back this coin to its owner.' And he handed it to the man with the nose.

Flambeau's eyes rolled. 'Is this man a coin-collector?' he asked.

'This man is Mr Arthur Carstairs,' said the priest positively, 'and he is a coin-collector of a somewhat singular kind.'

The man changed colour so horribly that the crooked nose stood out on his face like a separate and comic thing. He spoke, nevertheless, with a sort of despairing dignity. 'You shall see, then,' he said, 'that I have not lost all the family qualities.' And he turned suddenly and strode into an inner room, slamming the door.

'Stop him!' shouted Father Brown, bounding and half falling over a chair; and, after a wrench or two, Flambeau had the door open. But it was too late. In dead silence Flambeau strode across and telephoned for doctor and police.

An empty medicine bottle lay on the floor. Across the table the body of the man in the brown dressing-gown lay amid his burst and gaping brown-paper parcels; out of which poured and rolled, not Roman, but very modern English coins.

The priest held up the bronze head of Cæsar. 'This,' he said, 'was all that was left of the Carstairs Collection.'

After a silence he went on, with more than common gentleness: 'It was a cruel will his wicked father made, and you see he did resent it a little. He hated the Roman money he had, and grew fonder of the real money denied him. He not only sold the Collection bit by bit, but sank bit by bit to the basest ways of making money – even to blackmailing his own family in a disguise. He blackmailed his brother from Australia for his little forgotten crime (that is why he took the cab to Wagga Wagga in Putney), he blackmailed his sister for the theft he alone could have noticed. And that, by the way, is why she had that supernatural guess when he was away on the sand-dunes. Mere figure and gait, however distant, are more likely to remind us of some-body than a well-made-up face quite close.'

There was another silence. 'Well,' growled the detective, 'and so this great numismatist and coin-collector was nothing but a vulgar miser.'

'Is there so great a difference?' asked Father Brown, in the same strange, indulgent tone. 'What is there wrong about a miser that is not often as wrong about a collector? What is wrong, except ... thou shalt not make to thyself any graven image; thou shalt not bow down to them nor serve them, for I ... but we must go and see how the poor young people are getting on.'

'I think,' said Flambeau, 'that, in spite of everything, they are probably getting on very well.'

7

The Purple Wig

Mr Edward Nutt, the industrious editor of the Daily Reformer, sat at his desk, opening letters and marking proofs to the merry tune of a typewriter, worked by a vigorous young lady.

He was a stoutish, fair man, in his shirt-sleeves; his movements were resolute, his mouth firm and his tones final; but his round, rather babyish blue eyes had a bewildered and even wistful look that rather contradicted all this. Nor indeed was the expression altogether misleading. It might truly be said of him, as for many journalists in authority, that his most familiar emotion was one of continuous fear; fear of libel actions, fear of lost advertisements, fear of misprints, fear of the sack.

His life was a series of distracted compromises between the proprietor of the paper (and of him), who was a senile soap-boiler with three ineradicable mistakes in his mind, and the very able staff he had collected to run the paper; some of whom were brilliant and experienced men and (what was even worse) sincere enthusiasts for the political policy of the paper.

A letter from one of these lay immediately before him, and rapid and resolute as he was, he seemed almost to hesitate before opening it. He took up a strip of proof instead, ran down it with a blue eye, and a blue pencil, altered the word 'adultery' to the word 'impropriety,' and the word 'Jew' to the word 'Alien,' rang a bell and sent it flying upstairs.

Then, with a more thoughtful eye, he ripped open the letter from his more distinguished contributor, which bore a postmark of Devonshire, and ran as follows:

DEAR NUTT, – As I see you're working Spooks and Dooks at the same time, what about an article on that rum business of the Eyres of Exmoor; or as the old women call it down here, the Devil's Ear of Eyre? The head of the family, you know, is the Duke of Exmoor; he is one of the few really stiff old Tory aristocrats left, a sound old crusted tyrant it is quite in our line to make trouble about. And I think I'm on the track of a story that will make trouble.

Of course I don't believe in the old legend about James I; and as for you, you don't believe in anything, not even in journalism. The legend, you'll probably remember, was about the blackest business in English history – the poisoning of Overbury by that witch's cat Frances Howard, and the quite mysterious terror which forced the King to pardon the murderers. There was a lot of alleged witchcraft mixed up with it; and the story goes that a man-servant listening at the keyhole heard the truth in a talk between the King and Carr; and the bodily ear with which he heard grew large and monstrous as by magic, so awful was the secret. And though he had to be loaded with lands and gold and made an ancestor of dukes, the elf-shaped ear is still recurrent in the family. Well, you don't believe in black magic; and if you did, you couldn't use it for copy. If a miracle happened in your office, you'd have to hush it up, now so many bishops are agnostics. But that is not the point.

The point is that there really *is* something queer about Exmoor and his family; something quite natural, I dare say, but quite abnormal. And the Ear is in it somehow, I fancy; either a symbol or a delusion or a disease or something. Another tradition says that Cavaliers just after James I began to wear their hair long only to cover the ear of the first Lord Exmoor. This also is no doubt fanciful.

The reason I point it out to you is this: It seems to me that we make a mistake in attacking aristocracy entirely for its champagne and diamonds. Most men rather admire the nobs for having a good time, but I think we surrender too much when we admit that aristocracy has made even the aristocrats happy. I suggest a series of articles pointing out how dreary, how inhuman, how downright diabolist, is the very smell and atmosphere of some of these great houses. There are plenty of instances; but you couldn't begin with a better one than the Ear of the Eyres. By the end of the week I think I can get you the truth about it. – Yours ever, FRANCIS FINN.

Mr Nutt reflected a moment, staring at his left boot; then he called out in a strong, loud and entirely lifeless voice, in which every syllable sounded alike: 'Miss Barlow, take down a letter to Mr Finn, please.

'DEAR FINN, – I think it would do; copy should reach us second post Saturday. – Yours, E. NUTT.'

This elaborate epistle he articulated as if it were all one word; and Miss Barlow rattled it down as if it were all one word. Then he took up another strip of proof and a blue pencil, and altered the word 'supernatural' to the word 'marvellous,' and the expression 'shoot down' to the expression 'repress.'

In such happy, healthful activities did Mr Nutt disport himself, until the ensuing Saturday found him at the same desk, dictating to the same typist, and using the same blue pencil on the first instalment of Mr Finn's revelations. The opening was a sound piece of slashing invective about the evil secrets of princes, and despair in the high places of the earth. Though written violently, it was in excellent English; but the editor, as usual, had given to somebody else the task of breaking it up into sub-headings, which were of a spicier sort, as 'Peeress and Poisons,' and 'The Eerie Ear,' 'The Eyres in their Eyrie,' and so on through a hundred happy changes. Then followed the legend of the Ear, amplified from Finn's first letter, and then the substance of his later discoveries, as follows:

'I know it is the practice of journalists to put the end of the story at the beginning and call it a headline. I know that journalism largely consists in saying "Lord Jones Dead" to people who never knew that Lord Jones was alive. Your present correspondent thinks that this, like many other journalistic customs, is bad journalism; and that the *Daily Reformer* has to set a better example in such things. He proposes to tell his story as it occurred, step by step. He will use the real names of the parties, who in most cases are ready to confirm his testimony. As for the headlines, the sensational proclamations – they will come at the end.

'I was walking along a public path that threads through a private Devonshire orchard and seems to point towards Devonshire cider, when I came suddenly upon just such a place as the path suggested. It was a long, low inn, consisting really of a cottage and two barns; thatched all over with the thatch that looks like brown and grey hair grown before history. But outside the door was a sign which called it the Blue Dragon; and under the sign was one of those long rustic tables that used to stand outside most of the free English inns, before teetotallers and brewers between them destroyed freedom. And at this table sat three gentlemen, who might have lived a hundred years ago.

'Now that I know them all better, there is no difficulty about disentangling the impressions; but just then they looked like three very solid ghosts. The dominant figure, both because he was bigger in all three dimensions, and because he sat centrally in the length of the table, facing me, was a tall, fat man dressed completely in black, with a rubicund, even apoplectic visage, but a rather bald and rather bothered brow. Looking at him again, more strictly, I could not exactly say what it was that gave me the sense of antiquity, except the antique cut of his white clerical necktie and the barred wrinkles across his brow.

'It was even less easy to fix the impression in the case of the man at the right end of the table, who, to say truth, was as commonplace a person as could be seen anywhere, with a round, brown-haired head and a round snub nose, but also clad in clerical black, of a stricter cut. It was only when I saw his broad curved hat lying on the table beside him that I realized why I connected him with anything ancient. He was a Roman Catholic priest.

'Perhaps the third man at the other end of the table, had really more to do with it than the rest, though he was both slighter in physical presence and more inconsiderate in his dress. His lank limbs were clad, I might also say clutched, in very tight grey sleeves and pantaloons; he had a long, sallow, aquiline face which seemed somehow all the more saturnine because his lantern jaws were imprisoned in his collar and neck-cloth more in the style of the old stock; and his hair (which ought to have been dark brown) was of an odd dim, russet colour which, in conjunction with his yellow face, looked rather purple than red. The unobtrusive yet unusual colour was all the more notable because his hair was almost unnaturally healthy and curling, and he wore it full. But, after all analysis, I incline to think that what gave me my first old-fashioned impression was simply a set of tall, old-fashioned wine-glasses, one or two lemons and two churchwarden pipes. And also, perhaps, the old-world errand on which I had come.

'Being a hardened reporter, and it being apparently a public inn, I did not need to summon much of my impudence to sit down at the long table and order some cider. The big man in black seemed very learned, especially about local antiquities; the small man in black, though he talked much less, surprised me with a yet wider culture. So we got on very well together; but the third man, the old gentleman in the tight pantaloons, seemed rather distant and haughty, until I slid into the subject of the Duke of Exmoor and his ancestry.

'I thought the subject seemed to embarrass the other two a little; but it broke the spell of the third man's silence most successfully. Speaking with restraint and with the accent of a highly educated gentleman, and puffing at intervals at his long churchwarden pipe, he proceeded to tell me some of the most horrible stories I have ever heard in my life: how one of the Eyres in the former ages had hanged his own father; and another had his wife scourged at the cart tail through the village; and another had set fire to a church full of children, and so on.

'Some of the tales, indeed, are not fit for public print; such as the story of the Scarlet Nuns, the abominable story of the Spotted Dog, or the thing that was done in the quarry. And all this red roll of impieties came from his thin, genteel lips rather primly than otherwise, as he sat sipping the wine out of his tall, thin glass.

'I could see that the big man opposite me was trying, if anything, to stop him; but he evidently held the old gentleman in considerable respect, and could not venture to do so at all abruptly. And the little priest at the other end of the table, though free from any such air of embarrassment, looked steadily at the table, and seemed to listen to the recital with great pain – as well as he might.

' "You don't seem," I said to the narrator, "to be very fond of the Exmoor pedigree."

'He looked at me a moment, his lips still prim, but whitening and tightening; then he deliberately broke his long pipe and glass on the table and stood up, the very picture of a perfect gentleman with the flaming temper of a fiend.

' "These gentlemen," he said, "will tell you whether I have cause to like it. The curse of the Eyres of old has lain heavy on this country, and many have suffered from it. They know there are none who have suffered from it as I have." And with that he crushed a piece of the fallen glass under his heel, and strode away among the green twilight of the twinkling apple-trees.

' "That is an extraordinary old gentleman," I said to the other two; "do you happen to know what the Exmoor family has done to him? Who is he?"

'The big man in black was staring at me with the wild air of a baffled bull; he did not at first seem to take it in. Then he said at last, "Don't you know who he is?"

'I reaffirmed my ignorance, and there was another silence; then the little priest said, still looking at the table, "That is the Duke of Exmoor."

'Then, before I could collect my scattered senses, he added equally quietly, but with an air of regularizing things: "My friend here is Doctor Mull, the Duke's librarian. My name is Brown."

'"But," I stammered, "if that is the Duke, why does he damn all the old dukes like that?"

'"He seems really to believe," answered the priest called Brown, "that they have left a curse on him." Then he added, with some irrelevance, "That's why he wears a wig."

'It was a few moments before his meaning dawned on me. "You don't mean that fable about the fantastic ear?" I demanded. "I've heard of it, of course, but surely it must be a superstitious yarn spun out of something much simpler. I've sometimes thought it was a wild version of one of those mutilation stories. They used to crop criminals' ears in the sixteenth century."

'"I hardly think it was that," answered the little man thoughtfully, "but it is not outside ordinary science or natural law for a family to have some deformity frequently reappearing – such as one ear bigger than the other."

'The big librarian had buried his big bald brow in his big red hands, like a man trying to think out his duty. "No," he groaned. "You do the man a wrong after all. Understand, I've no reason to defend him, or even keep faith with him. He has been a tyrant to me as to everybody else. Don't fancy because you see him sitting simply here that he isn't a great lord in the worst sense of the word. He would fetch a man a mile to ring a bell a yard off – if it would summon another man three miles to fetch a matchbox three yards off. He must have a footman to carry his walking-stick; a body servant to hold up his opera-glasses –"

'"But not a valet to brush his clothes," cut in the

priest, with a curious dryness, "for the valet would want to brush his wig, too."

'The librarian turned to him and seemed to forget my presence; he was strongly moved and, I think, a little heated with wine. "I don't know how you know it, Father Brown," he said, "but you are right. He lets the whole world do everything for him – except dress him. And that he insists on doing in a literal solitude like a desert. Anybody is kicked out of the house without a character who is so much as found near his dressing-room door."

' "He seems a pleasant old party," I remarked.

' "No," replied Dr Mull quite simply; "and yet that is just what I mean by saying you are unjust to him after all. Gentlemen, the Duke does really feel the bitterness about the curse that he uttered just now. He does, with sincere shame and terror, hide under that purple wig something he thinks it would blast the sons of man to see. I know it is so; and I know it is not a mere natural disfigurement, like a criminal mutilation, or a hereditary disproportion in the features. I know it is worse than that; because a man told me who was present at a scene that no man could invent, where a stronger man than any of us tried to defy the secret, and was scared away from it."

'I opened my mouth to speak, but Mull went on in oblivion of me, speaking out of the cavern of his hands. "I don't mind telling you, Father, because it's really more defending the poor Duke than giving him away. Didn't you ever hear of the time when he very nearly lost all the estates?"

'The priest shook his head; and the librarian proceeded to tell the tale as he had heard it from his predecessor in the same post, who had been his patron and instructor, and whom he seemed to trust implicitly. Up to a certain point it was a common enough tale of the decline of a great family's fortunes – the tale of a family lawyer. This lawyer, however, had the sense to cheat honestly, if the expression explains itself. Instead of using funds he held in trust, he took advantage of the Duke's carelessness to put the family in a financial hole, in which it might be necessary for the Duke to let him hold them in reality.

'The lawyer's name was Isaac Green, but the Duke always called him Elisha; presumably in reference to the fact that he was quite bald, though certainly not more than thirty. He had risen very rapidly, but from very dirty beginnings; being first a "nark" or informer, and then a moneylender: but as solicitor to the Eyres he had the sense, as I say, to keep technically straight until he was ready to deal the final blow. The blow fell at dinner; and the old librarian said he should never forget the very look of the lamp-shades and the decanters, as the little lawyer, with a steady smile, proposed to the great landlord that they should halve the estates between them. The sequel certainly could not be overlooked; for the Duke, in dead silence, smashed a decanter on the man's bald head as suddenly as I had seen him smash the glass that day in the orchard. It left a red triangular scar on the scalp, and the lawyer's eyes altered, but not his smile.

'He rose tottering to his feet, and struck back as such men do strike. "I am glad of that," he said, "for now I can take the whole estate. The law will give it to me."

'Exmoor, it seems, was white as ashes, but his eyes still blazed. "The law will give it you," he said; "but you will not take it ... Why not? Why? because it would mean the crack of doom for me, and if you take it *I shall take off my wig* ... Why, you pitiful plucked fowl, anyone can see your bare head. But no man shall see mine and live."

'Well, you may say what you like and make it mean what you like. But Mull swears it is the solemn fact that the lawyer, after shaking his knotted fists in the air for an instant, simply ran from the room and never reappeared in the countryside; and since then Exmoor has been feared more for a warlock than even for a landlord and a magistrate.

'Now Dr Mull told his story with rather wild theatrical gestures, and with a passion I think at least partisan. I was quite conscious of the possibility that the whole was the extravagance of an old braggart and gossip. But before I end this half of my discoveries, I think it due to Dr Mull to record that my two first inquiries have confirmed his story. I learned from an old apothecary in the village that there was a bald man in evening-dress, giving the name of Green, who came to him one night to have a three-cornered cut on his forehead plastered. And I learnt from the legal records and old newspapers that there was a lawsuit threatened, and at least begun, by one Green against the Duke of Exmoor.'

Mr Nutt, of the *Daily Reformer*, wrote some highly incongruous words across the top of the copy, made some highly mysterious marks down the side of it, and called to Miss Barlow in the same loud, monotonous voice: 'Take down a letter to Mr Finn.

'DEAR FINN, – Your copy will do, but I have had to headline it a bit; and our public would never stand a Romanist priest in the story – you must keep your eye on the suburbs. I've altered him to Mr Brown, a Spiritualist.

Yours,

E. NUTT.'

A day or two afterwards found the active and judicious editor examining, with blue eyes that seemed to grow rounder and rounder, the second instalment of Mr Finn's tale of mysteries in high life. It began with the words:

'I have made an astounding discovery. I freely confess it is quite different from anything I expected to discover, and will give a much more practical shock to the public. I venture to say, without any vanity, that the words I now write will be read all over Europe, and certainly all over America and the Colonies. And yet I heard all I have to tell before I left this same little wooden table in this same little wood of apple-trees.

'I owe it all to the small priest Brown; he is an extraordinary man. The big librarian had left the table, perhaps ashamed of his long tongue, perhaps anxious about the storm in which his mysterious master had vanished: anyway, he betook himself heavily in the Duke's tracks through the trees. Father Brown had picked up one of the lemons and was eyeing it with an odd pleasure.

' "What a lovely colour a lemon is!" he said. "There's one thing I don't like about the Duke's wig – the colour."

' "I don't think I understand," I answered.

' "I dare say he's got good reason to cover his ears, like King Midas," went on the priest, with a cheerful simplicity which somehow seemed rather flippant under the circumstances. "I can quite understand that it's nicer to cover them with hair than with brass plates or leather flaps. But if he wants to use hair, why doesn't he make it look like hair? There never was hair of that colour in this world. It looks more like a sunset-cloud coming through the wood. Why doesn't he conceal the family curse better, if he's really so ashamed of it? Shall

I tell you? It's because he isn't ashamed of it. He's proud of it."

' "It's an ugly wig to be proud of – and an ugly story," I said.

' "Consider," replied this curious little man, "how you yourself really feel about such things. I don't suggest you're either more snobbish or more morbid than the rest of us: but don't you feel in a vague way that a genuine old family curse is rather a fine thing to have? Would you be ashamed, wouldn't you be a little proud, if the heir of the Glamis horror called you his friend? or if Byron's family had confided, to you only, the evil adventures of their race? Don't be too hard on the aristocrats themselves if their heads are as weak as ours would be, and they are snobs about their own sorrows."

' "By Jove!" I cried; "and that's true enough. My own mother's family had a banshee; and, now I come to think of it, it has comforted me in many a cold hour."

' "And think," he went on, "of that stream of blood and poison that spurted from his thin lips the instant you so much as mentioned his ancestors. Why should he show every stranger over such a Chamber of Horrors unless he is proud of it? He doesn't conceal his wig, he doesn't conceal his blood, he doesn't conceal his family curse, he doesn't conceal the family crimes – *but* –"

'The little man's voice changed so suddenly, he shut his hand so sharply, and his eyes so rapidly grew rounder and brighter like a waking owl's, that it had all the abruptness of a small explosion on the table.

' "But," he ended, "*he does really conceal his toilet.*"

'It somehow completed the thrill of my fanciful

nerves that at that instant the Duke appeared again silently among the glimmering trees, with his soft foot and sunset-hued hair, coming round the corner of the house in company with his librarian. Before he came within earshot, Father Brown had added quite composedly, "Why does he really hide the secret of what he does with the purple wig? Because it isn't the sort of secret we suppose."

'The Duke came round the corner and resumed his seat at the head of the table with all his native dignity. The embarrassment of the librarian left him hovering on his hind legs, like a huge bear. The Duke addressed the priest with great seriousness. "Father Brown," he said, "Doctor Mull informs me that you have come here to make a request. I no longer profess an observance of the religion of my fathers; but for their sakes, and for the sake of the days when we met before, I am very willing to hear you. But I presume you would rather be heard in private."

'Whatever I retain of the gentleman made me stand up. Whatever I have attained of the journalist made me stand still. Before this paralysis could pass, the priest had made a momentarily detaining motion. "If," he said, "your Grace will permit me my real petition, or if I retain any right to advise you, I would urge that as many people as possible should be present. All over this country I have found hundreds, even of my own faith and flock, whose imaginations are poisoned by the spell which I implore you to break. I wish we could have all Devonshire here to see you do it."

' "To see me do what?" asked the Duke, arching his eyebrows.

' "To see you take off your wig," said Father Brown.

'The Duke's face did not move; but he looked at his

petitioner with a glassy stare which was the most awful expression I have ever seen on a human face. I could see the librarian's great legs wavering under him like the shadows of stems in a pool; and I could not banish from my own brain the fancy that the trees all around us were filling softly in the silence with devils instead of birds.

'"I spare you," said the Duke in a voice of inhuman pity. "I refuse. If I gave you the faintest hint of the load of horror I have to bear alone, you would lie shrieking at these feet of mine and begging to know no more. I will spare you the hint. You shall not spell the first letter of what is written on the altar of the Unknown God."

'"I know the Unknown God," said the little priest, with an unconscious grandeur of certitude that stood up like a granite tower. "I know his name; it is Satan. The true God was made flesh and dwelt among us. And I say to you, wherever you find men ruled merely by mystery, it is the mystery of iniquity. If the devil tells you something is too fearful to look at, look at it. If he says something is too terrible to hear, hear it. If you think some truth unbearable, bear it. I entreat your Grace to end this nightmare now and here at this table."

'"If I did," said the Duke in a low voice, "you and all you believe, and all by which alone you live, would be the first to shrivel and perish. You would have an instant to know the great Nothing before you died."

'"The Cross of Christ be between me and harm," said Father Brown. "Take off your wig."

'I was leaning over the table in ungovernable excitement; in listening to this extraordinary duel half a thought had come into my head. "Your Grace," I cried, "I call your bluff. Take off that wig or I will knock it off."

'I suppose I can be prosecuted for assault, but I am very glad I did it. When he said, in the same voice of stone, "I refuse," I simply sprang on him. For three long instants he strained against me as if he had all hell to help him; but I forced back his head until the hairy cap fell off it. I admit that, whilst wrestling, I shut my eyes as it fell.

'I was awakened by a cry from Mull, who was also by this time at the Duke's side. His head and mine were both bending over the bald head of the wigless Duke. Then the silence was snapped by the librarian exclaiming: "What can it mean? Why, the man had nothing to hide. His ears are just like everybody else's."

' "Yes," said Father Brown, "that is what he had to hide."

'The priest walked straight up to him, but strangely enough did not even glance at his ears. He stared with an almost comical seriousness at his bald forehead, and pointed to a three-cornered cicatrice, long healed, but still discernible. "Mr Green, I think," he said politely, "and he did get the whole estate after all."

'And now let me tell the readers of the *Daily Reformer* what I think the most remarkable thing in the whole affair. This transformation scene, which will seem to you as wild and purple as a Persian fairy-tale, has been (except for my technical assault) strictly legal and constitutional from its first beginnings. This man with the odd scar and the ordinary ears is not an impostor. Though (in one sense) he wears another man's wig and claims another man's ear, he has not stolen another man's coronet. He really is the one and only Duke of Exmoor. What happened was this. The old Duke really had a slight malformation of the ear, which really was more or less hereditary. He really was morbid about it; and it is likely enough that he did invoke it as a kind of curse in the violent scene (which undoubtedly happened) in which he struck Green with the decanter. But the contest ended very differently. Green pressed his claim and got the estates; the dispossessed nobleman shot himself and died without issue. After a decent interval the beautiful English Government revived the "extinct" peerage of Exmoor, and bestowed it, as is usual, on the most important person, the person who had got the property.

'This man used the old feudal fables – probably, in his snobbish soul, really envied and admired them. So that thousands of poor English people trembled before a mysterious chieftain with an ancient destiny and a diadem of evil stars – when they are really trembling before a guttersnipe who was a pettifogger and a pawnbroker not twelve years ago. I think it very typical of the real case against our aristocracy as it is, and as it will be till God sends us braver men.'

Mr Nutt put down the manuscript and called out with unusual sharpness: 'Miss Barlow, please take down a letter to Mr Finn:

'DEAR FINN, – You must be mad; we can't touch this. I wanted vampires and the bad old days and aristocracy hand-in-hand with superstition. They like that. But you must know the Exmoors would never forgive this. And what would our people say then, I should like to know! Why, Sir Simon is one of Exmoor s greatest pals; and it would ruin that cousin of the Eyres that's standing for us at Bradford. Besides, old Soap-Suds was sick enough at not getting his peerage last year; he'd sack me by wire if I lost him it with such lunacy as this. And what about Duffey? He's doing us some rattling articles on "The Heel of the Norman." And how can he write

about Normans if the man's only a solicitor? Do be
reasonable. – Yours. E. NUTT.'

As Miss Barlow rattled away cheerfully, he crumpled
up the copy and tossed it into the waste-paper basket;
but not before he had, automatically and by mere
force of habit, altered the word 'God' to the word
'circumstances.'

8

The Perishing of
the Pendragons

Father Brown was in no mood for adventures. He had lately fallen ill with over-work, and when he began to recover, his friend Flambeau had taken him on a cruise in a small yacht with Sir Cecil Fanshaw, a young Cornish squire and an enthusiast for Cornish coast scenery. But Brown was still rather weak; he was no very happy sailor; and though he was never of the sort that either grumbles or breaks down, his spirits did not rise above patience and civility. When the other two men praised the ragged violet sunset or the ragged volcanic crags, he agreed with them. When Flambeau pointed out a rock shaped like a dragon, he looked at it and thought it very like a dragon. When Fanshaw more excitedly indicated a rock that was like Merlin, he looked at it, and signified assent. When Flambeau asked whether this rocky gate of the twisted river was not the gate of Fairyland, he said 'Yes.' He heard the most important things and the most trivial with the same tasteless absorption. He heard that the coast was death to all but careful seamen; he also heard that the ship's cat was asleep. He heard that Fanshaw couldn't find his cigar-holder anywhere; he also heard the pilot deliver the oracle 'Both eyes bright, she's all right; one eye winks, down she sinks.' He heard Flambeau say to Fanshaw that no doubt this meant the pilot must keep both eyes open and be spry. And he heard Fanshaw say to Flambeau that, oddly enough, it didn't mean this: it meant that while they saw two of the coast-lights, one near and the other distant, exactly side by side, they were in the right river-channel; but that if one light was hidden behind the other, they were going on the rocks. He heard Fanshaw add that his country was full of such quaint fables and idioms; it was the very home of romance; he even pitted this part of Cornwall against Devonshire, as a claimant to the laurels of Elizabethan seamanship. According to him there had been captains among these coves and islets compared with whom Drake was practically a landsman. He heard Flambeau laugh, and ask if, perhaps, the adventurous title of 'Westward Ho!' only meant that all Devonshire men wished they were living in Cornwall. He heard Fanshaw say there was no need to be silly; that not only had Cornish captains been heroes, but that they were heroes still: that near that very spot there was an old admiral, now retired, who was scarred by thrilling voyages full of adventures; and who had in his youth found the last group of eight Pacific Islands that was added to the chart of the world. This Cecil Fanshaw was, in person, of the kind that commonly urges such crude but pleasing enthusiasms; a very young man, light-haired, high-coloured, with an eager profile; with a boyish bravado of spirits, but an almost girlish delicacy of tint and type. The big shoulders, black brows and black mousquetaire swagger of Flambeau were a great contrast.

All these trivialities Brown heard and saw; but heard them as a tired man hears a tune in the railway wheels, or saw them as a sick man sees the pattern of his wallpaper. No one can calculate the turns of mood in convalescence: but Father Brown's depression must have had a great deal to do with his mere unfamiliarity with the sea. For as the river-mouth narrowed like the neck of a bottle, and the water grew calmer and the air warmer and more earthly, he seemed to wake up and take notice like a baby. They had reached that phase just after sunset when air and water both look bright, but earth and all its growing things look almost black by comparison. About this particular evening, however, there was something exceptional. It was one of those rare atmospheres in which a smoked-glass slide seems to have been slid away from between us and Nature; so that even dark colours on that day look more gorgeous than bright colours on cloudier days. The trampled earth of the river-banks and the peaty stain in the pools did not look drab but glowing umber, and the dark woods astir in the breeze did not look, as usual, dim blue with mere depth or distance, but more like wind-tumbled masses of some vivid violet blossom. This magic clearness and intensity in the colours was further forced on Brown's slowly reviving senses by something romantic and even secret in the very form of the landscape.

The river was still well wide and deep enough for a pleasure boat so small as theirs; but the curves of the country-side suggested that it was closing in on either hand; the woods seemed to be making broken and flying attempts at bridge-building – as if the boat were passing from the romance of a valley to the romance of a hollow and so to the supreme romance of a tunnel. Beyond this mere look of things there was little for Brown's freshening fancy to feed on; he saw no human beings, except some gipsies trailing along the river bank, with faggots and osiers cut in the forest; and one sight no longer unconventional, but in such remote parts still uncommon: a dark-haired lady, bare-headed, and paddling her own canoe. If Father Brown ever attached any importance to either of these, he certainly forgot them at the next turn of the river which brought in sight a singular object.

The water seemed to widen and split, being cloven by the dark wedge of a fish-shaped and wooded islet. With the rate at which they went, the islet seemed to swim towards them like a ship; a ship with a very high prow – or, to speak more strictly, a very high funnel. For at the extreme point nearest them stood up an odd-looking building, unlike anything they could remember or connect with any purpose. It was not specially high, but it was too high for its breadth to be called anything but a tower. Yet it appeared to be built entirely of wood, and that in a most unequal and eccentric way. Some of the planks and beams were of good, seasoned oak; some of such wood cut raw and recent; some again of white pinewood, and a great deal more of the same sort of wood painted black with tar. These black beams were set crooked or criss-cross at all kinds of angles, giving the whole a most patchy and puzzling appearance. There were one or two windows, which appeared to be coloured and leaded in an old-fashioned but more elaborate style. The travellers looked at it with that paradoxical feeling we have when something reminds us of something, and yet we are certain it is something very different.

Father Brown, even when he was mystified, was clever in analysing his own mystification. And he found himself reflecting that the oddity seemed to consist in a particular shape cut out in an incongruous material; as if one saw a top-hat made of tin, or a frock-coat cut out of tartan. He was sure he had seen timbers of different tints arranged like that somewhere, but never in such architectural proportions. The next moment a glimpse through the dark trees told him all he wanted to know, and he laughed. Through a gap in the foliage there appeared for a moment one of those old wooden houses, faced with black beams, which are still to be found here and there in England, but which most of us see imitated in some show called 'Old London' or 'Shakespeare's England.' It was in view only long enough for the priest to see that, however old-fashioned, it was a comfortable and well-kept country-house, with flower-beds in front of it. It had none of the piebald and crazy look of the tower that seemed made out of its refuse.

'What on earth's this?' said Flambeau, who was still staring at the tower.

Fanshaw's eyes were shining, and he spoke trium-phantly. 'Aha! you've not seen a place quite like this before, I fancy; that's why I've brought you here, my friend. Now you shall see whether I exaggerate about the mariners of Cornwall. This place belongs to Old Pendragon, whom we call the Admiral; though he retired before getting the rank. The spirit of Raleigh and Hawkins is a memory with the Devon folk; it's a modern fact with the Pendragons. If Queen Elizabeth were to rise from the grave and come up this river in a gilded barge, she would be received by the Admiral in a house exactly such as she was accustomed to, in every corner and casement, in every panel on the wall or plate on the table. And she would find an English Captain still talking fiercely of fresh lands to be found in little ships, as much as if she had dined with Drake.'

'She'd find a rum sort of thing in the garden,' said Father Brown, 'which would not please her Renais-sance eye. That Elizabethan domestic architecture is charming in its way; but it's against the very nature of it to break out into turrets.'

'And yet,' answered Fanshaw, 'that's the most

romantic and Elizabethan part of the business. It was
built by the Pendragons in the very days of the Spanish
wars; and though it's needed patching and even rebuild-
ing for another reason, it's always been rebuilt in the
old way. The story goes that the lady of Sir Peter Pendragon built it in this place and to this height, because
from the top you can just see the corner where vessels
turn into the river mouth; and she wished to be the first
to see her husband's ship, as he sailed home from the
Spanish Main.'

'For what other reason,' asked Father Brown, 'do
you mean that it has been rebuilt?'

'Oh, there's a strange story about that, too,' said the
young squire with relish. 'You are really in a land of
strange stories. King Arthur was here and Merlin and
the fairies before him. The story goes that Sir Peter
Pendragon, who (I fear) had some of the faults of the
pirates as well as the virtues of the sailor, was bringing
home three Spanish gentlemen in honourable captivity,
intending to escort them to Elizabeth's court. But he
was a man of flaming and tigerish temper, and coming
to high words with one of them, he caught him by
the throat and flung him, by accident or design, into the
sea. A second Spaniard, who was the brother of the
first, instantly drew his sword and flew at Pendragon,
and after a short but furious combat in which both got
three wounds in as many minutes, Pendragon drove his
blade through the other's body and the second Spaniard was accounted for. As it happened the ship had
already turned into the river mouth and was close to
comparatively shallow water. The third Spaniard
sprang over the side of the ship, struck out for the
shore, and was soon near enough to it to stand up to
his waist in water. And turning again to face the ship,
and holding up both arms to Heaven – like a prophet

calling plagues upon a wicked city – he called out to Pendragon in a piercing and terrible voice, that he at least was yet living, that he would go on living, that he would live for ever; and that generation after generation the house of Pendragon should never see him or his, but should know by very certain signs that he and his vengeance were alive. With that he dived under the wave, and was either drowned or swam so long under water that no hair of his head was seen afterwards.'

'There's that girl in the canoe again,' said Flambeau irrelevantly, for good-looking young women would call him off any topic. 'She seems bothered by the queer tower just as we were.'

Indeed, the black-haired young lady was letting her canoe float slowly and silently past the strange islet; and was looking intently up at the strange tower, with a strong glow of curiosity on her oval and olive face.

'Never mind girls,' said Fanshaw impatiently; 'there are plenty of them in the world, but not many things like the Pendragon Tower. As you may easily suppose, plenty of superstitions and scandals have followed in the track of the Spaniard's curse; and no doubt, as you would put it, any accident happening to this Cornish family would be connected with it by rural credulity. But it is perfectly true that this tower has been burnt down two or three times; and the family can't be called lucky, for more than two, I think, of the Admiral's near kin have perished by shipwreck; and one at least, to my own knowledge, on practically the same spot where Sir Peter threw the Spaniard overboard.'

'What a pity!' exclaimed Flambeau. 'She's going.'

'When did your friend the Admiral tell you this family history?' asked Father Brown, as the girl in the canoe paddled off, without showing the least intention of extending her interest from the tower to the yacht, which Fanshaw had already caused to lie alongside the island.

'Many years ago,' replied Fanshaw; 'he hasn't been to sea for some time now, though he is as keen on it as ever. I believe there's a family compact or something. Well, here's the landing-stage; let's come ashore and see the old boy.'

They followed him on to the island, just under the tower, and Father Brown, whether from the mere touch of dry land, or the interest of something on the other bank of the river (which he stared at very hard for some seconds), seemed singularly improved in brisk-ness. They entered a wooded avenue between two fences of thin greyish wood, such as often enclose parks or gardens, and over the top of which the dark trees tossed to and fro like black and purple plumes upon the hearse of a giant. The tower, as they left it behind, looked all the quainter, because such entrances are usually flanked by two towers; and this one looked lopsided. But for this, the avenue had the usual appear-ance of the entrance to a gentleman's grounds; and, being so curved that the house was now out of sight, somehow looked a much larger park than any plantation on such an island could really be. Father Brown was, perhaps, a little fanciful in his fatigue, but he almost thought the whole place must be growing larger, as things do in a nightmare. Anyhow, a mystical monot-ony was the only character of their march, until Fanshaw suddenly stopped, and pointed to something sticking out through the grey fence – something that looked at first rather like the imprisoned horn of some beast. Closer observation showed that it was a slightly curved blade of metal that shone faintly in the fading light.

Flambeau, who like all Frenchmen had been a

soldier, bent over it and said in a startled voice: 'Why, it's a sabre! I believe I know the sort, heavy and curved, but shorter than the cavalry; they used to have them in artillery and the –'

As he spoke the blade plucked itself out of the crack it had made and came down again with a more ponderous slash, splitting the fissiparous fence to the bottom with a rending noise. Then it was pulled out again, flashed above the fence some feet farther along, and again split it halfway down with the first stroke; and after waggling a little to extricate itself (accompanied with curses in the darkness) split it down to the ground with a second. Then a kick of devilish energy sent the whole loosened square of thin wood flying into the pathway, and a great gap of dark coppice gaped in the paling.

Fanshaw peered into the dark opening and uttered an exclamation of astonishment. 'My dear Admiral!' he exclaimed, 'do you – er – do you generally cut out a new front door whenever you want to go for a walk?'

The voice in the gloom swore again, and then broke into a jolly laugh. 'No,' it said; 'I've really got to cut down this fence somehow; it's spoiling all the plants, and no one else here can do it. But I'll only carve another bit off the front door, and then come out and welcome you.'

And sure enough, he heaved up his weapon once more, and, hacking twice, brought down another and similar strip of fence, making the opening about fourteen feet wide in all. Then through this larger forest gateway he came out into the evening light, with a chip of grey wood sticking to his sword-blade.

He momentarily fulfilled all Fanshaw's fable of an old piratical Admiral; though the details seemed afterwards to decompose into accidents. For instance, he wore a broad-brimmed hat as protection against the sun; but the front flap of it was turned up straight to the sky, and the two corners pulled down lower than the ears, so that it stood across his forehead in a crescent like the old cocked hat worn by Nelson. He wore an ordinary dark-blue jacket, with nothing special about the buttons, but the combination of it with white linen trousers somehow had a sailorish look. He was tall and loose, and walked with a sort of swagger, which was not a sailor's roll, and yet somehow suggested it; and he held in his hand a short sabre which was like a navy cutlass, but about twice as big. Under the bridge of the hat his eagle face looked eager, all the more because it was not only clean-shaven, but without eyebrows. It seemed almost as if all the hair had come off his face from his thrusting it through a throng of elements. His eyes were prominent and piercing. His colour was curiously attractive, while partly tropical; it reminded one vaguely of a blood-orange. That is, that while it was ruddy and sanguine, there was a yellow in it that was in no way sickly, but seemed rather to glow like gold apples of the Hesperides. Father Brown thought he had never seen a figure so expressive of all the romances about the countries of the Sun.

When Fanshaw had presented his two friends to their host he fell again into a tone of rallying the latter about his wreckage of the fence and his apparent rage of profanity. The Admiral pooh-poohed it at first as a piece of necessary but annoying garden work; but at length the ring of real energy came back into his laughter, and he cried with a mixture of impatience and good humour:

'Well, perhaps I do go at it a bit rabidly, and feel a kind of pleasure in smashing anything. So would you if your only pleasure was in cruising about to find some new Cannibal Islands, and you had to stick on this muddy little rockery in a sort of rustic pond. When I remember how I've cut down a mile and a half of green poisonous jungle with an old cutlass half as sharp as this; and then remember I must stop here and chop this matchwood, because of some confounded old bargain scribbled in a family Bible, why, I –'

He swung up the heavy steel again; and this time sundered the wall of wood from top to bottom at one stroke.

'I feel like that,' he said laughing, but furiously flinging the sword some yards down the path, 'and now let's go up to the house; you must have some dinner.'

The semicircle of lawn in front of the house was varied by three circular garden beds, one of red tulips, a second of yellow tulips, and the third of some white, waxen-looking blossoms that the visitors did not know and presumed to be exotic. A heavy, hairy and rather sullen-looking gardener was hanging up a heavy coil of garden hose. The corners of the expiring sunset which seemed to cling about the corners of the house gave glimpses here and there of the colours of remoter flower-beds; and in a treeless space on one side of the house opening upon the river stood a tall brass tripod on which was tilted a big brass telescope. Just outside the steps of the porch stood a little painted green garden table, as if someone had just had tea there. The entrance was flanked with two of those half-featured lumps of stone with holes for eyes that are said to be South Sea idols; and on the brown oak beam across the doorway were some confused carvings that looked almost as barbaric.

As they passed indoors, the little cleric hopped suddenly on to the table, and standing on it peered unaffectedly through his spectacles at the mouldings in the oak. Admiral Pendragon looked very much astonished, though not particularly annoyed; while Fanshaw was so amused with what looked like a performing pigmy on his little stand, that he could not control his laughter. But Father Brown was not likely to notice either the laughter or the astonishment.

He was gazing at three carved symbols, which, though very worn and obscure, seemed still to convey some sense to him. The first seemed to be the outline of some tower or other building, crowned with what looked like curly-pointed ribbons. The second was clearer: an old Elizabethan galley with decorative waves beneath it, but interrupted in the middle by a curious jagged rock, which was either a fault in the wood or some conventional representation of the water coming in. The third represented the upper half of a human figure, ending in an escalloped line like the waves; the face was rubbed and featureless, and both arms were held very stiffly up in the air.

'Well,' muttered Father Brown, blinking, 'here is the legend of the Spaniard plain enough. Here he is holding up his arms and cursing in the sea; and here are the two curses: the wrecked ship and the burning of Pendragon Tower.'

Pendragon shook his head with a kind of venerable amusement. 'And how many other things might it not be?' he said. 'Don't you know that that sort of half-man, like a half-lion or half-stag, is quite common in heraldry? Might not that line through the ship be one of those *parti-per-pale* lines, *indented*, I think they call it? And though the third thing isn't so very heraldic, it would be more heraldic to suppose it a tower crowned with laurel than with fire; and it looks just as like it.'

'But it seems rather odd,' said Flambeau, 'that it should exactly confirm the old legend.'

'Ah,' replied the sceptical traveller, 'but you don't know how much of the old legend may have been made up from the old figures. Besides, it isn't the only old legend. Fanshaw, here, who is fond of such things, will tell you there are other versions of the tale, and much more horrible ones. One story credits my unfortunate ancestor with having had the Spaniard cut in two; and that will fit the pretty picture also. Another obligingly credits our family with the possession of a tower full of snakes and explains those little, wriggly things in that way. And a third theory supposes the crooked line on the ship to be a conventionalized thunderbolt; but that alone, if seriously examined, would show what a very little way these unhappy coincidences really go.'

'Why, how do you mean?' asked Fanshaw.

'It so happens,' replied his host coolly, 'that there was no thunder and lightning at all in the two or three shipwrecks I know of in our family.'

'Oh!' said Father Brown, and jumped down from the little table.

There was another silence in which they heard the continuous murmur of the river; then Fanshaw said, in a doubtful and perhaps disappointed tone: 'Then you don't think there is anything in the tales of the tower in flames?'

'There are the tales, of course,' said the Admiral, shrugging his shoulders; 'and some of them, I don't deny, on evidence as decent as one ever gets for such things. Someone saw a blaze hereabout, don't you know, as he walked home through a wood; someone keeping sheep on the uplands inland thought he saw a flame hovering over Pendragon Tower. Well, a damp dab of mud like this confounded island seems the last place where one would think of fires.'

'What is that fire over there?' asked Father Brown with a gentle suddenness, pointing to the woods on the left river-bank. They were all thrown a little off their balance, and the more fanciful Fanshaw had even some difficulty in recovering his, as they saw a long, thin stream of blue smoke ascending silently into the end of the evening light.

Then Pendragon broke into a scornful laugh again. 'Gipsies!' he said; 'they've been camping about here for a week. Gentlemen, you want your dinner,' and he turned as if to enter the house.

But the antiquarian superstition in Fanshaw was still quivering, and he said hastily: 'But, Admiral, what's that hissing noise quite near the island? It's very like fire.'

'It's more like what it is,' said the Admiral, laughing as he led the way; 'it's only some canoe going by.'

Almost as he spoke, the butler, a lean man in black, with very black hair and a very long, yellow face, appeared in the doorway and told him that dinner was served.

The dining-room was as nautical as the cabin of a ship; but its note was rather that of the modern than the Elizabethan captain. There were, indeed, three antiquated cutlasses in a trophy over the fireplace, and one brown sixteenth-century map with Tritons and little ships dotted about a curly sea. But such things were less prominent on the white panelling than some cases of quaint-coloured South American birds, very scientifically stuffed, fantastic shells from the Pacific, and several instruments so rude and queer in shape that savages might have used them either to kill their enemies or to cook them. But the alien colour culminated in the fact that, besides the butler, the Admiral's only servants were two negroes, somewhat quaintly clad in tight uniforms of yellow. The priest's instinctive trick of analysing his own impressions told him that the colour and the little neat coat-tails of these bipeds had suggested the word 'Canary,' and so by a mere pun connected them with southward travel. Towards the end of the dinner they took their yellow clothes and black faces out of the room, leaving only the black clothes and yellow face of the butler.

'I'm rather sorry you take this so lightly,' said Fanshaw to the host; 'for the truth is, I've brought these friends of mine with the idea of their helping you, as they know a good deal of these things. Don't you really believe in the family story at all?'

'I don't believe in anything,' answered Pendragon very briskly, with a bright eye cocked at a red tropical bird. 'I'm a man of science.'

Rather to Flambeau's surprise, his clerical friend, who seemed to have entirely woken, took up the digression and talked natural history with his host with a flow of words and much unexpected information, until the dessert and decanters were set down and the last of the servants vanished. Then he said, without altering his tone:

'Please don't think me impertinent, Admiral Pendragon. I don't ask for curiosity, but really for my guidance and your convenience. Have I made a bad shot if I guess you don't want these old things talked of before your butler?'

The Admiral lifted the hairless arches over his eyes and exclaimed: 'Well, I don't know where you got it, but the truth is I can't stand the fellow, though I've no excuse for discharging a family servant. Fanshaw, with his fairy tales, would say my blood moved against men with that black, Spanish-looking hair.'

Flambeau struck the table with his heavy fist. 'By Jove!' he cried; 'and so had that girl!'

'I hope it'll all end to-night,' continued the Admiral, 'when my nephew comes back safe from his ship. You looked surprised. You won't understand, I suppose, unless I tell you the story. You see, my father had two sons; I remained a bachelor, but my elder brother married, and had a son who became a sailor like all the rest of us, and will inherit the proper estate. Well, my father was a strange man; he somehow combined Fanshaw's superstition with a good deal of my scepticism; they were always fighting in him; and after my first voyages, he developed a notion which he thought somehow would settle finally whether the curse was truth or trash. If all the Pendragons sailed about anyhow, he thought there would be too much chance of natural catastrophes to prove anything. But if we went to sea one at a time in strict order of succession to the property, he thought it might show whether any connected fate followed the family as a family. It was a silly notion, I think, and I quarrelled with my father pretty heartily; for I was an ambitious man and was left to the last, coming, by succession, after my own nephew.'

'And your father and brother,' said the priest, very gently, 'died at sea, I fear.'

'Yes,' groaned the Admiral; 'by one of those brutal accidents on which are built all the lying mythologies of mankind, they were both shipwrecked. My father, coming up this coast out of the Atlantic, was washed up on these Cornish rocks. My brother's ship was sunk, no one knows where, on the voyage home from Tasmania. His body was never found. I tell you it was from perfectly natural mishap; lots of other people besides Pendragons were drowned; and both disasters are discussed in a normal way by navigators. But, of course, it set this forest of superstition on fire; and men saw the flaming tower everywhere. That's why I say it will be all right when Walter returns. The girl he's engaged to was coming to-day; but I was so afraid of some chance delay frightening her that I wired her not to come till she heard from me. But he's practically sure to be here some time to-night, and then it'll all end in smoke – tobacco smoke. We'll crack that old lie when we crack a bottle of this wine.'

'Very good wine,' said Father Brown, gravely lifting his glass, 'but, as you see, a very bad wine-bibber. I most sincerely beg your pardon': for he had spilt a small spot of wine on the table-cloth. He drank and put down the glass with a composed face; but his hand had started at the exact moment when he became conscious of a face looking in through the garden window just behind the Admiral – the face of a woman, swarthy, with southern hair and eyes, and young, but like a mask of tragedy.

After a pause the priest spoke again in his mild manner. 'Admiral,' he said, 'will you do me a favour? Let me, and my friends if they like, stop in that tower of yours just for to-night? Do you know that in my business you're an exorcist almost before anything else?'

Pendragon sprang to his feet and paced swiftly to and fro across the window, from which the face had instantly vanished. 'I tell you there is nothing in it,' he cried, with ringing violence. 'There is one thing I know about this matter. You may call me an atheist. I am an atheist.' Here he swung round and fixed Father Brown with a face of frightful concentration. 'This business is perfectly natural. There is no curse in it at all.'

Father Brown smiled. 'In that case,' he said, 'there can't be any objection to my sleeping in your delightful summer-house.'

'The idea is utterly ridiculous,' replied the Admiral, beating a tattoo on the back of his chair.

'Please forgive me for everything,' said Brown in his most sympathetic tone, 'including spilling the wine. But it seems to me you are not quite so easy about the flaming tower as you try to be.'

Admiral Pendragon sat down again as abruptly as he had risen; but he sat quite still, and when he spoke again it was in a lower voice. 'You do it at your own peril,' he said; 'but wouldn't *you* be an atheist to keep sane in all this devilry?'

Some three hours afterwards Fanshaw, Flambeau and the priest were still dawdling about the garden in the dark; and it began to dawn on the other two that Father Brown had no intention of going to bed either in the tower or the house.

'I think the lawn wants weeding,' said he dreamily. 'If I could find a spud or something I'd do it myself.'

They followed him, laughing and half remonstrating; but he replied with the utmost solemnity, explaining to them, in a maddening little sermon, that one can always find some small occupation that is helpful to others. He did not find a spud; but he found an old broom made of twigs, with which he began energetically to brush the fallen leaves off the grass.

'Always some little thing to be done,' he said with idiotic cheerfulness; 'as George Herbert says: "Who sweeps an Admiral's garden in Cornwall as for Thy laws makes that and the action fine." And now,' he added, suddenly slinging the broom away, 'let's go and water the flowers.'

With the same mixed emotions they watched him uncoil some considerable lengths of the large garden hose, saying with an air of wistful discrimination: 'The red tulips before the yellow, I think. Look a bit dry, don't you think?'

He turned the little tap on the instrument, and the water shot out straight and solid as a long rod of steel.

'Look out, Samson,' cried Flambeau; 'why, you've cut off the tulip's head.'

Father Brown stood ruefully contemplating the decapitated plant.

'Mine does seem to be a rather kill or cure sort of watering,' he admitted, scratching his head. 'I suppose it's a pity I didn't find the spud. You should have seen me with the spud! Talking of tools, you've got that swordstick, Flambeau, you always carry? That's right; and Sir Cecil could have that sword the Admiral threw away by the fence here. How grey everything looks!'

'The mist's rising from the river,' said the staring Flambeau.

Almost as he spoke the huge figure of the hairy gardener appeared on a higher ridge of the trenched and terraced lawn, hailing them with a brandished rake and a horribly bellowing voice. 'Put down that hose,' he shouted; 'put down that hose and go to your –'

'I am fearfully clumsy,' replied the reverend gentleman weakly; 'do you know, I upset some wine at dinner.' He made a wavering half-turn of apology towards the gardener, with the hose still spouting in his hand. The gardener caught the cold crash of the water full in his face like the crash of a cannon-ball; staggered, slipped and went sprawling with his boots in the air.

'How very dreadful!' said Father Brown, looking round in a sort of wonder. 'Why, I've hit a man!'

He stood with his head forward for a moment as if looking or listening; and then set off at a trot towards the tower, still trailing the hose behind him. The tower was quite close, but its outline was curiously dim.

'Your river mist,' he said, 'has a rum smell.'

'By the Lord it has,' cried Fanshaw, who was very white. 'But you can't mean –'

'I mean,' said Father Brown, 'that one of the Admiral's scientific predictions is coming true to-night. This story is going to end in smoke.'

As he spoke a most beautiful rose-red light seemed to burst into blossom like a gigantic rose; but accompanied with a crackling and rattling noise that was like the laughter of devils.

'My God! what is this?' cried Sir Cecil Fanshaw.

'The sign of the flaming tower,' said Father Brown, and sent the driving water from his hose into the heart of the red patch.

'Lucky we hadn't gone to bed!' ejaculated Fanshaw. 'I suppose it can't spread to the house.'

'You may remember,' said the priest quietly, 'that the wooden fence that might have carried it was cut away.'

Flambeau turned electrified eyes upon his friend, but Fanshaw only said rather absently: 'Well, nobody can be killed, anyhow.'

'This is rather a curious kind of tower,' observed Father Brown; 'when it takes to killing people, it always kills people who are somewhere else.'

At the same instant the monstrous figure of the gardener with the streaming beard stood again on the green ridge against the sky, waving others to come on; but now waving not a rake but a cutless. Behind him came the two negroes, also with the old crooked cutlasses out of the trophy. But in the blood-red glare, with their black faces and yellow figures, they looked like devils carrying instruments of torture. In the dim garden behind them a distant voice was heard calling out brief directions. When the priest heard the voice, a terrible change came over his countenance.

But he remained composed; and never took his eye off the patch of flame which had begun by spreading, but now seemed to shrink a little as it hissed under the torch of the long silver spear of water. He kept his finger along the nozzle of the pipe to ensure the aim, and attended to no other business, knowing only by the noise and that semi-conscious corner of the eye, the exciting incidents that began to tumble themselves about the island garden. He gave two brief directions to his friends. One was: 'Knock these fellows down somehow and tie them up, whoever they are; there's rope down by those faggots. They want to take away my nice hose.' The other was: 'As soon as you get a chance, call out to that canoeing girl; she's over on the bank with the gipsies. Ask her if they could get some buckets across and fill them from the river.' Then he closed his mouth and continued to water the new red flower as ruthlessly as he had watered the red tulip.

He never turned his head to look at the strange fight that followed between the foes and friends of the mysterious fire. He almost felt the island shake when Flambeau collided with the huge gardener; he merely imagined how it would whirl round them as they wrestled. He heard the crashing fall; and his friend's gasp of triumph as he dashed on to the first negro; and the cries of both the blacks as Flambeau and Fanshaw bound them. Flambeau's enormous strength more than redressed the odds in the fight, especially as the fourth man still hovered near the house, only a shadow and a voice. He heard also the water broken by the paddles of a canoe; the girl's voice giving orders, the voices of gipsies answering and coming nearer, the plumping and sucking noise of empty buckets plunged into a full stream; and finally the sound of many feet around the fire. But all this was less to him than the fact that the red rent, which had lately once more increased, had once more slightly diminished.

Then came a cry that very nearly made him turn his head. Flambeau and Fanshaw, now reinforced by some of the gipsies, had rushed after the mysterious man by the house; and he heard from the other end of the garden the Frenchman's cry of horror and astonishment. It was echoed by a howl not to be called human, as the being broke from their hold and ran along the garden. Three times at least it raced round the whole island, in a way that was as horrible as the chase of a lunatic, both in the cries of the pursued and the ropes carried by the pursuers; but was more horrible still, because it somehow suggested one of the chasing games of children in a garden. Then, finding them closing in on every side, the figure sprang upon one of the higher river banks and disappeared with a splash into the dark and driving river.

'You can do no more, I fear,' said Brown in a voice cold with pain. 'He has been washed down to the rocks by now, where he has sent so many others. He knew the use of a family legend.'

'Oh, don't talk in these parables,' cried Flambeau impatiently. 'Can't you put it simply in words of one syllable?'

'Yes,' answered Brown, with his eye on the hose. ' "Both eyes bright, she's all right; one eye blinks, down she sinks." '

The fire hissed and shrieked more and more, like a strangled thing, as it grew narrower and narrower under the flood from the pipe and buckets, but Father Brown still kept his eye on it as he went on speaking:

'I thought of asking this young lady, if it were morning yet, to look through that telescope at the river mouth and the river. She might have seen something to

interest her: the sign of the ship, or Mr Walter Pendragon coming home, and perhaps even the sign of the
half-man, for though he is certainly safe by now, he
may very well have waded ashore. He has been within
a shave of another shipwreck; and would never have
escaped it, if the lady hadn't had the sense to suspect
the old Admiral's telegram and come down to watch
him. Don't let's talk about the old Admiral. Don't let's
talk about anything. It's enough to say that whenever
this tower, with its pitch and resin-wood, really caught
fire, the spark on the horizon always looked like the
twin light to the coast light-house.'

'And that,' said Flambeau, 'is how the father and
brother died. The wicked uncle of the legends very
nearly got his estate after all.'

Father Brown did not answer; indeed, he did not
speak again, save for civilities, till they were all safe
round a cigar-box in the cabin of the yacht. He saw that
the frustrated fire was extinguished; and then refused to
linger, though he actually heard young Pendragon,
escorted by an enthusiastic crowd, come tramping up
the river bank; and might (had he been moved by
romantic curiosities) have received the combined thanks
of the man from the ship and the girl from the canoe.
But his fatigue had fallen on him once more, and he
only started once, when Flambeau abruptly told him he
had dropped cigar-ash on his trousers.

'That's no cigar-ash,' he said rather wearily. 'That's
from the fire, but you don't think so because you're all
smoking cigars. That's just the way I got my first faint
suspicion about the chart.'

'Do you mean Pendragon's chart of his Pacific
Islands?' asked Fanshaw.

'You thought it was a chart of the Pacific Islands,'
answered Brown. 'Put a feather with a fossil and a bit

of coral and everyone will think it's a specimen. Put the same feather with a ribbon and an artificial flower and everyone will think it's for a lady's hat. Put the same feather with an ink-bottle, a book and a stack of writing-paper, and most men will swear they've seen a quill pen. So you saw that map among tropic birds and shells and thought it was a map of Pacific Islands. It was the map of this river.'

'But how do you know?' asked Fanshaw.

'I saw the rock you thought was like a dragon, and the one like Merlin, and –'

'You seem to have noticed a lot as we came in,' cried Fanshaw. 'We thought you were rather abstracted.'

'I was sea-sick,' said Father Brown simply. 'I felt simply horrible. But feeling horrible has nothing to do with not seeing things.' And he closed his eyes.

'Do you think most men would have seen that?' asked Flambeau. He received no answer: Father Brown was asleep.

9

The God of the Gongs

It was one of those chilly and empty afternoons in early winter, when the daylight is silver rather than gold and pewter rather than silver. If it was dreary in a hundred bleak offices and yawning drawing-rooms, it was drearier still along the edges of the flat Essex coast, where the monotony was the more inhuman for being broken at very long intervals by a lamp-post that looked less civilized than a tree, or a tree that looked more ugly than a lamp-post. A light fall of snow had half-melted into a few strips, also looking leaden rather than silver, when it had been fixed again by the seal of frost; no fresh snow had fallen, but a ribbon of the old snow ran along the very margin of the coast, so as to parallel the pale ribbon of the foam.

The line of the sea looked frozen in the very vividness of its violet-blue, like the vein of a frozen finger. For miles and miles, forward and back, there was no breathing soul, save two pedestrians, walking at a brisk pace, though one had much longer legs and took much longer strides than the other.

It did not seem a very appropriate place or time for a holiday, but Father Brown had few holidays, and had to take them when he could, and he always preferred, if possible, to take them in company with his old friend Flambeau, ex-criminal and ex-detective. The priest had had a fancy for visiting his old parish at Cobhole, and was going northeastward along the coast.

After walking a mile or two farther, they found that the shore was beginning to be formally embanked, so as to form something like a parade; the ugly lamp-posts became less few and far between and more ornamental, though quite equally ugly. Half a mile farther on Father Brown was puzzled first by little labyrinths of flowerless flower-pots, covered with the low, flat, quiet-coloured plants that look less like a garden than a tessellated pavement, between weak curly paths studded with seats with curly backs. He faintly sniffed the atmosphere of a certain sort of seaside town that he did not specially care about, and, looking ahead along the parade by the sea, he saw something that put the matter beyond a doubt. In the grey distance the big bandstand of a watering-place stood up like a giant mushroom with six legs.

'I suppose,' said Father Brown, turning up his coat-collar and drawing a woollen scarf rather closer round his neck, 'that we are approaching a pleasure resort.'

'I fear,' answered Flambeau, 'a pleasure resort to which few people just now have the pleasure of resorting. They try to revive these places in the winter, but it never succeeds except with Brighton and the old ones. This must be Seawood, I think – Lord Pooley's experiment; he had the Sicilian Singers down at Christmas, and there's talk about holding one of the great glove-fights here. But they'll have to chuck the rotten place into the sea; it's as dreary as a lost railway-carriage.'

They had come under the big bandstand, and the priest was looking up at it with a curiosity that had something rather odd about it, his head a little on one side, like a bird's. It was the conventional, rather tawdry kind of erection for its purpose: a flattened dome or canopy, gilt here and there, and lifted on six slender pillars of painted wood, the whole being raised about five feet above the parade on a round wooden platform like a drum. But there was something fantastic about the snow combined with something artificial about the gold that haunted Flambeau as well as his friend with some association he could not capture, but which he knew was at once artistic and alien.

'I've got it,' he said at last. 'It's Japanese. It's like those fanciful Japanese prints, where the snow on the mountain looks like sugar, and the gilt on the pagodas is like gilt on gingerbread. It looks just like a little pagan temple.'

'Yes,' said Father Brown. 'Let's have a look at the god.' And with an agility hardly to be expected of him, he hopped up on to the raised platform.

'Oh, very well,' said Flambeau, laughing; and the next instant his own towering figure was visible on that quaint elevation.

Slight as was the difference of height, it gave in those level wastes a sense of seeing yet farther and farther across land and sea. Inland the little wintry gardens faded into a confused grey copse; beyond that, in the distance, were long low barns of a lonely farmhouse, and beyond that nothing but the long East Anglian plains. Seawards there was no sail or sign of life save a few seagulls: and even they looked like the last snowflakes, and seemed to float rather than fly.

Flambeau turned abruptly at an exclamation behind him. It seemed to come from lower down than might have been expected, and to be addressed to his heels rather than his head. He instantly held out his hand, but he could hardly help laughing at what he saw. For some reason or other the platform had given way under Father Brown, and the unfortunate little man had dropped through to the level of the parade. He was just tall enough, or short enough, for his head alone to stick out of the hole in the broken wood, looking like St John the Baptist's head on a charger. The face wore a disconcerted expression, as did, perhaps, that of St John the Baptist.

In a moment he began to laugh a little. 'This wood must be rotten,' said Flambeau. 'Though it seems odd it should bear me, and you go through the weak place. Let me help you out.'

But the little priest was looking rather curiously at the corners and edges of the wood alleged to be rotten, and there was a sort of trouble on his brow.

'Come along,' cried Flambeau impatiently, still with his big brown hand extended. 'Don't you want to get out?'

The priest was holding a splinter of the broken wood between his finger and thumb, and did not immediately reply. At last he said thoughtfully: 'Want to get out? Why, no. I rather think I want to get in.' And he dived into the darkness under the wooden floor so abruptly as to knock off his big curved clerical hat and leave it lying on the boards above, without any clerical head in it.

Flambeau looked once more inland and out to sea, and once more could see nothing but seas as wintry as the snow, and snows as level as the sea.

There came a scurrying noise behind him, and the little priest came scrambling out of the hole faster than he had fallen in. His face was no longer disconcerted, but rather resolute, and, perhaps only through the reflections of the snow, a trifle paler than usual.

'Well?' asked his tall friend. 'Have you found the god of the temple?'

'No,' answered Father Brown. 'I have found what was sometimes more important. The Sacrifice.'

'What the devil do you mean?' cried Flambeau, quite alarmed.

Father Brown did not answer. He was staring, with a knot in his forehead, at the landscape; and he suddenly pointed at it. 'What's that house over there?' he asked.

Following his finger, Flambeau saw for the first time the corners of a building nearer than the farmhouse, but screened for the most part with a fringe of trees. It was not a large building, and stood well back from the shore; but a glint of ornament on it suggested that it was part of the same watering-place scheme of decoration as the bandstand, the little gardens and the curly-backed iron seats.

Father Brown jumped off the bandstand, his friend following; and as they walked in the direction indicated the trees fell away to right and left, and they saw a small, rather flashy hotel, such as is common in resorts – the hotel of the Saloon Bar rather than the Bar Parlour. Almost the whole frontage was of gilt plaster and figured glass, and between that grey seascape and the grey, witch-like trees, its gimcrack quality had something spectral in its melancholy. They both felt vaguely that if any food or drink were offered at such a hostelry, it would be the pasteboard ham and empty mug of the pantomime.

In this, however, they were not altogether confirmed. As they drew nearer and nearer to the place they saw in front of the buffet, which was apparently closed, one of the iron garden-seats with curly backs that had adorned the gardens, but much longer, running almost the whole length of the frontage. Presumably, it was placed so that visitors might sit there and look at the sea, but one hardly expected to find anyone doing it in such weather.

Nevertheless, just in front of the extreme end of the iron seat stood a small round restaurant table, and on this stood a small bottle of Chablis and a plate of almonds and raisins. Behind the table and on the seat sat a dark-haired young man, bareheaded, and gazing at the sea in a state of almost astonishing immobility.

But though he might have been a waxwork when they were within four yards of him, he jumped up like a jack-in-the-box when they came within three, and said in a deferential, though not undignified, manner: 'Will you step inside, gentlemen? I have no staff at present, but I can get you anything simple myself.'

'Much obliged,' said Flambeau. 'So you are the proprietor?'

'Yes,' said the dark man, dropping back a little into his motionless manner. 'My waiters are all Italians, you see, and I thought it only fair they should see their countryman beat the black, if he really can do it. You know the great fight between Malvoli and Nigger Ned is coming off after all?'

'I'm afraid we can't wait to trouble your hospitality seriously,' said Father Brown. 'But my friend would be glad of a glass of sherry, I'm sure, to keep out the cold and drink success to the Latin champion.'

Flambeau did not understand the sherry, but he did not object to it in the least. He could only say amiably: 'Oh, thank you very much.'

'Sherry, sir – certainly,' said their host, turning to his hostel. 'Excuse me if I detain you a few minutes. As I told you, I have no staff –' And he went towards the black windows of his shuttered and unlighted inn.

'Oh, it doesn't really matter,' began Flambeau, but the man turned to reassure him.

'I have the keys,' he said. 'I could find my way in the dark.'

'I didn't mean –' began Father Brown.

He was interrupted by a bellowing human voice that came out of the bowels of the uninhabited hotel. It thundered some foreign name loudly but inaudibly, and the hotel proprietor moved more sharply towards it than he had done for Flambeau's sherry. As instant evidence proved, the proprietor had told, then and after, nothing but the literal truth. But both Flambeau and Father Brown have often confessed that, in all their (often outrageous) adventures, nothing had so chilled their blood as that voice of an ogre, sounding suddenly out of a silent and empty inn.

'My cook!' cried the proprietor hastily. 'I had forgotten my cook. He will be starting presently. Sherry, sir?'

And, sure enough, there appeared in the doorway a big white bulk with white cap and white apron, as befits a cook, but with the needless emphasis of a black face. Flambeau had often heard that negroes made good cooks. But somehow something in the contrast of colour and caste increased his surprise that the hotel proprietor should answer the call of the cook, and not the cook the call of the proprietor. But he reflected that head cooks are proverbially arrogant; and, besides, the host had come back with the sherry, and that was the great thing.

'I rather wonder,' said Father Brown, 'that there are so few people about the beach, when this big fight is coming on after all. We only met one man for miles.'

The hotel proprietor shrugged his shoulders. 'They come from the other end of the town, you see – from the station, three miles from here. They are only interested in the sport, and will stop in hotels for the night only. After all, it is hardly weather for basking on the shore.'

'Or on the seat,' said Flambeau, and pointed to the little table.

'I have to keep a look-out,' said the man with the motionless face. He was a quiet, well-featured fellow, rather sallow; his dark clothes had nothing distinctive about them, except that his black necktie was worn rather high, like a stock, and secured by a gold pin with some grotesque head to it. Nor was there anything notable in the face, except something that was probably a mere nervous trick – a habit of opening one eye more narrowly than the other, giving the impression that the other was larger, or was, perhaps, artificial.

The silence that ensued was broken by their host saying quietly: 'Whereabouts did you meet the one man on your march?'

'Curiously enough,' answered the priest, 'close by here – just by that bandstand.'

Flambeau, who had sat on the long iron seat to finish his sherry, put it down and rose to his feet, staring at his friend in amazement. He opened his mouth to speak, and then shut it again.

'Curious,' said the dark-haired man thoughtfully. 'What was he like?'

'It was rather dark when I saw him,' began Father Brown, 'but he was –'

As has been said, the hotel-keeper can be proved to have told the precise truth. His phrase that the cook was starting presently was fulfilled to the letter, for the cook came out, pulling his gloves on, even as they spoke.

But he was a very different figure from the confused mass of white and black that had appeared for an instant in the doorway. He was buttoned and buckled up to his bursting eyeballs in the most brilliant fashion. A tall black hat was tilted on his broad black head – a hat of the sort that the French wit has compared to eight mirrors. But somehow the black man was like the black hat. He also was black, and yet his glossy skin flung back the light at eight angles or more. It is needless to say that he wore white spats and a white slip inside his waistcoat. The red flower stood up in his buttonhole aggressively, as if it had suddenly grown there. And in the way he carried his cane in one hand and his cigar in the other there was a certain attitude – an attitude we must always remember when we talk of racial prejudices: something innocent and insolent – the cake walk.

'Sometimes,' said Flambeau, looking after him, 'I'm not surprised that they lynch them.'

'I am never surprised,' said Father Brown, 'at any work of hell. But as I was saying,' he resumed, as the negro, still ostentatiously pulling on his yellow gloves, betook himself briskly towards the watering-place, a queer music-hall figure against that grey and frosty scene – 'as I was saying, I couldn't describe the man very minutely, but he had a flourish and old-fashioned whiskers and moustachios, dark or dyed, as in the pictures of foreign financiers, round his neck was wrapped a long purple scarf that thrashed out in the wind as he walked. It was fixed at the throat rather in the way that nurses fix children's comforters with a safety-pin. Only this,' added the priest, gazing placidly out to sea, 'was not a safety-pin.'

The man sitting on the long iron bench was also gazing placidly out to sea. Now he was once more in repose, Flambeau felt quite certain that one of his eyes was naturally larger than the other. Both were now well opened, and he could almost fancy the left eye grew larger as he gazed.

'It was a very long gold pin, and had the carved

head of a monkey or some such thing,' continued the cleric; 'and it was fixed in a rather odd way – he wore pince-nez and a broad black –'

The motionless man continued to gaze at the sea, and the eyes in his head might have belonged to two different men. Then he made a movement of blinding swiftness.

Father Brown had his back to him, and in that flash might have fallen dead on his face. Flambeau had no weapon, but his large brown hands were resting on the end of the long iron seat. His shoulders abruptly altered their shape, and he heaved the whole huge thing high over his head, like a headsman's axe about to fall. The mere height of the thing, as he held it vertical, looked like a long iron ladder by which he was inviting men to climb towards the stars. But the long shadow, in the level evening light, looked like a giant brandishing the Eiffel Tower. It was the shock of that shadow, before the shock of the iron crash, that made the stranger quail and dodge, and then dart into his inn, leaving the flat and shining dagger he had dropped exactly where it had fallen.

'We must get away from here instantly,' cried Flambeau, flinging the huge seat away with furious indifference on the beach. He caught the little priest by the elbow and ran him down a grey perspective of barren back garden, at the end of which there was a closed back garden door. Flambeau bent over it an instant in violent silence, and then said: 'The door is locked.'

As he spoke a black feather from one of the ornamental firs fell, brushing the brim of his hat. It startled him more than the small and distant detonation that had come just before. Then came another distant detonation, and the door he was trying to open shook under the bullet buried in it. Flambeau's shoulders again filled out and altered suddenly. Three hinges and a lock burst at the same instant, and he went out into the empty path behind, carrying the great garden door with him, as Samson carried the gates of Gaza.

Then he flung the garden door over the garden wall, just as a third shot picked up a spurt of snow and dust behind his heel. Without ceremony he snatched up the little priest, slung him astraddle on his shoulders, and went racing towards Seawood as fast as his long legs could carry him. It was not until nearly two miles farther on that he set his small companion down. It had hardly been a dignified escape, in spite of the classic model of Anchises, but Father Brown's face only wore a broad grin.

'Well,' said Flambeau, after an impatient silence, as they resumed their more conventional tramp through the streets on the edge of the town, where no outrage need be feared, 'I don't know what all this means, but I take it I may trust my own eyes that you never met the man you have so accurately described.'

'I did meet him in a way,' Brown said, biting his finger rather nervously – 'I did really. And it was too dark to see him properly, because it was under that bandstand affair. But I'm afraid I didn't describe him so very accurately after all, for his pince-nez was broken under him, and the long gold pin wasn't stuck through his purple scarf but through his heart.'

'And I suppose,' said the other in a lower voice, 'that glass-eyed guy had something to do with it.'

'I had hoped he had only a little,' answered Brown in a rather troubled voice, 'and I may have been wrong in what I did. I acted on impulse. But I fear this business has deep roots and dark.'

They walked on through some streets in silence. The

yellow lamps were beginning to be lit in the cold blue twilight, and they were evidently approaching the more central parts of the town. Highly coloured bills announcing the glove-fight between Nigger Ned and Malvoli were slapped about the walls.

'Well,' said Flambeau, 'I never murdered anyone, even in my criminal days, but I can almost sympathize with anyone doing it in such a dreary place. Of all God-forsaken dustbins of Nature, I think the most heart-breaking are places like that bandstand, that were meant to be festive and are forlorn. I can fancy a morbid man feeling he must kill his rival in the solitude and irony of such a scene. I remember once taking a tramp in your glorious Surrey hills, thinking of nothing but gorse and skylarks, when I came out on a vast circle of land, and over me lifted a vast, voiceless structure, tier above tier of seats, as huge as a Roman amphitheatre and as empty as a new letter-rack. A bird sailed in heaven over it. It was the Grand Stand at Epsom. And I felt that no one would ever be happy there again.'

'It's odd you should mention Epsom,' said the priest. 'Do you remember what was called the Sutton Mystery, because two suspected men – ice-cream men, I think – happened to live at Sutton? They were eventually released. A man was found strangled, it was said, on the Downs round that part. As a fact, I know (from an Irish policeman who is a friend of mine) that he was found close up to the Epsom Grand Stand – in fact, only hidden by one of the lower doors being pushed back.'

'That is queer,' assented Flambeau. 'But it rather confirms my view that such pleasure places look awfully lonely out of season, or the man wouldn't have been murdered there.'

'I'm not so sure he –' began Brown, and stopped.

'Not so sure he was murdered?' queried his companion.

'Not so sure he was murdered out of the season,' answered the little priest, with simplicity. 'Don't you think there's something rather tricky about this solitude, Flambeau? Do you feel sure a wise murderer would always *want* the spot to be lonely? It's very, very seldom a man is *quite* alone. And, short of that, the more alone he is, the more certain he is to be seen. No; I think there must be some other – Why, here we are at the Pavilion or Palace, or whatever they call it.'

They had emerged on a small square, brilliantly lighted, of which the principal building was gay with gilding, gaudy with posters, and flanked with two giant photographs of Malvoli and Nigger Ned.

'Hallo!' cried Flambeau in great surprise, as his clerical friend stumped straight up the broad steps. 'I didn't know pugilism was your latest hobby. Are you going to see the fight?'

'I don't think there will be any fight,' replied Father Brown.

They passed rapidly through ante-rooms and inner rooms; they passed through the hall of combat itself, raised, roped, and padded with innumerable seats and boxes, and still the cleric did not look round or pause till he came to a clerk at a desk outside a door marked 'Committee.' There he stopped and asked to see Lord Pooley.

The attendant observed that his lordship was very busy, as the fight was coming on soon, but Father Brown had a good-tempered tedium of reiteration for which the official mind is generally not prepared. In a few moments the rather baffled Flambeau found himself in the presence of a man who was still shouting directions to another man going out of the room. 'Be

careful, you know, about the ropes after the fourth –
Well, and what do you want, I wonder!'

Lord Pooley was a gentleman, and, like most of the
few remaining to our race, was worried – especially
about money. He was half grey and half flaxen, and he
had the eyes of fever and a high-bridged, frost-bitten
nose.

'Only a word,' said Father Brown. 'I have come to
prevent a man being killed.'

Lord Pooley bounded off his chair as if a spring had
flung him from it. 'I'm damned if I'll stand any more of
this!' he cried. 'You and your committees and parsons
and petitions! Weren't there parsons in the old days,
when they fought without gloves? Now they're fighting with the regulation gloves, and there's not the rag
of a possibility of either of the boxers being killed.'

'I didn't mean either of the boxers,' said the little
priest.

'Well, well, well!' said the nobleman, with a touch
of frosty humour. 'Who's going to be killed? The
referee?'

'I don't know who's going to be killed,' replied
Father Brown, with a reflective stare. 'If I did I shouldn't
have to spoil your pleasure. I could simply get him to
escape. I never could see anything wrong about prize-
fights. As it is, I must ask you to announce that the
fight is off for the present.'

'Anything else?' jeered the gentleman with feverish
eyes. 'And what do you say to the two thousand people
who have come to see it?'

'I say there will be one thousand nine hundred and
ninety-nine of them left alive when they have seen it,'
said Father Brown.

Lord Pooley looked at Flambeau. 'Is your friend
mad?' he asked.

'Far from it,' was the reply.

'And look here,' resumed Pooley in his restless way, 'it's worse than that. A whole pack of Italians have turned up to back Malvoli – swarthy, savage fellows of some country, anyhow. You know what these Mediterranean races are like. If I send out word that it's off we shall have Malvoli storming in here at the head of a whole Corsican clan.'

'My lord, it is a matter of life and death,' said the priest. 'Ring your bell. Give your message. And see whether it is Malvoli who answers.'

The nobleman struck the bell on the table with an odd air of new curiosity. He said to the clerk who appeared almost instantly in the doorway: 'I have a serious announcement to make to the audience shortly. Meanwhile, would you kindly tell the two champions that the fight will have to be put off.'

The clerk stared for some seconds as if at a demon and vanished.

'What authority have you for what you say?' asked Lord Pooley abruptly. 'Whom did you consult?'

'I consulted a bandstand,' said Father Brown, scratching his head. 'But, no, I'm wrong; I consulted a book, too. I picked it up on a bookstall in London – very cheap, too.'

He had taken out of his pocket a small, stout, leather-bound volume, and Flambeau, looking over his shoulder, could see that it was some book of old travels, and had a leaf turned down for reference.

' "The only form in which Voodoo –" ' began Father Brown, reading aloud.

'In which what?' inquired his lordship.

' "In which Voodoo," ' repeated the reader, almost with relish, ' "is widely organized outside Jamaica itself is in the form known as the Monkey, or the God of the Gongs, which is powerful in many parts of the two American continents, especially among half-breeds, many of whom look exactly like white men. It differs from most other forms of devil-worship and human sacrifice in the fact that the blood is not shed formally on the altar, but by a sort of assassination among the crowd. The gongs beat with a deafening din as the doors of the shrine open and the monkey-god is revealed; almost the whole congregation rivet ecstatic eyes on him. But after –"'

The door of the room was flung open, and the fashionable negro stood framed in it, his eyeballs rolling, his silk hat still insolently tilted on his head. 'Huh!' he cried, showing his apish teeth. 'What this? Huh! Huh! You steal a coloured gentleman's prize – prize his already – yo' think yo' jes' save that white 'Talian trash –'

'The matter is only deferred,' said the nobleman quietly. 'I will be with you to explain in a minute or two.'

'Who you to –' shouted Nigger Ned, beginning to storm.

'My name is Pooley,' replied the other, with a creditable coolness. 'I am the organizing secretary, and I advise you just now to leave the room.'

'Who this fellow?' demanded the dark champion, pointing to the priest disdainfully.

'My name is Brown,' was the reply. 'And I advise you just now to leave the country.'

The prize-fighter stood glaring for a few seconds, and then, rather to the surprise of Flambeau and the others, strode out, sending the door to with a crash behind him.

'Well,' asked Father Brown, rubbing his dusty hair

up, 'what do you think of Leonardo da Vinci? A beautiful Italian head.'

'Look here,' said Lord Pooley, 'I've taken a considerable responsibility on your bare word. I think you ought to tell me more about this.'

'You are quite right, my lord,' answered Brown. 'And it won't take long to tell.' He put the little leather book in his overcoat pocket. 'I think we know all that this can tell us, but you shall look at it to see if I'm right. That negro who has just swaggered out is one of the most dangerous men on earth, for he has the brains of a European, with the instincts of a cannibal. He has turned what was clean, common-sense butchery among his fellow-barbarians into a very modern and scientific secret society of assassins. He doesn't know I know it, nor, for the matter of that, that I can't prove it.'

There was a silence, and the little man went on.

'But if I want to murder somebody, will it really be the best plan to make sure I'm alone with him?'

Lord Pooley's eyes recovered their frosty twinkle as he looked at the little clergyman. He only said: 'If you *want* to murder somebody, I should advise it.'

Father Brown shook his head, like a murderer of much riper experience. 'So Flambeau said,' he replied, with a sigh. 'But consider. The more a man feels lonely the less he can be sure he is alone. It must mean empty spaces round him, and they are just what make him obvious. Have you never seen one ploughman from the heights, or one shepherd from the valleys? Have you never walked along a cliff, and seen one man walking along the sands? Didn't you know when he'd killed a crab, and wouldn't you have known if it had been a creditor? No! No! No! For an intelligent murderer, such as you or I might be, it is an impossible plan to make sure that nobody is looking at you.'

'But what other plan is there?'

'There is only one,' said the priest. 'To make sure that everybody is looking at something else. A man is throttled close by the big stand at Epsom. Anybody might have seen it done while the stand stood empty – any tramp under the hedges or motorist among the hills. But nobody would have seen it when the stand was crowded and the whole ring roaring, when the favourite was coming in first – or wasn't. The twisting of a neck-cloth, the thrusting of a body behind a door could be done in an instant – so long as it was *that* instant. It was the same, of course,' he continued turning to Flambeau, 'with that poor fellow under the bandstand. He was dropped through the hole (it wasn't an accidental hole) just at some very dramatic moment of the entertainment, when the bow of some great violinist or the voice of some great singer opened or came to its climax. And here, of course, when the knock-out blow came – it would not be the only one. That is the little trick Nigger Ned has adopted from his old God of Gongs.'

'By the way, Malvoli –' Pooley began.

'Malvoli,' said the priest, 'has nothing to do with it. I dare say he has some Italians with him, but our amiable friends are not Italians. They are octoroons and African half-bloods of various shades, but I fear we English think all foreigners are much the same so long as they are dark and dirty. Also,' he added, with a smile, 'I fear the English decline to draw any fine distinction between the moral character produced by my religion and that which blooms out of Voodoo.'

The blaze of the spring season had burst upon Seawood, littering its foreshore with families and bathing-machines, with nomadic preachers and nigger minstrels, before the two friends saw it again, and long before the storm of pursuit after the strange secret society had died away. Almost on every hand the secret of their purpose perished with them. The man of the hotel was found drifting dead on the sea like so much seaweed; his right eye was closed in peace, but his left eye was wide open, and glistened like glass in the moon. Nigger Ned had been overtaken a mile or two away, and murdered three policemen with his closed left hand. The remaining officer was surprised – nay, pained – and the negro got away. But this was enough to set all the English papers in a flame, and for a month or two the main purpose of the British Empire was to prevent the buck nigger (who was so in both senses) escaping by any English port. Persons of a figure remotely reconcilable with his were subjected to quite extraordinary inquisitions, made to scrub their faces before going on board ship, as if each white complexion were made up like a mask of grease-paint. Every negro in England was put under special regulations and made to report himself; the outgoing ships would no more have taken a nigger than a basilisk. For people had found out how fearful and vast and silent was the force of the savage secret society, and by the time Flambeau and Father Brown were leaning on the parade parapet in April, the Black Man meant in England almost what he once meant in Scotland.

'He must be still in England,' observed Flambeau, 'and horridly well hidden, too. They must have found him at the ports if he had only whitened his face.'

'You see, he is really a clever man,' said Father Brown apologetically. 'And I'm sure he wouldn't whiten his face.'

'Well, but what would he do?'

'I think,' said Father Brown, 'he would blacken his face.'

Flambeau, leaning motionless on the parapet, laughed and said: 'My dear fellow!'

Father Brown, also leaning motionless on the parapet, moved one finger for an instant into the direction of the soot-masked niggers singing on the sands.

10

The Salad of Colonel Cray

Father Brown was walking home from Mass on a white weird morning when the mists were slowly lifting – one of those mornings when the very element of light appears as something mysterious and new. The scattered trees outlined themselves more and more out of the vapour, as if they were first drawn in grey chalk and then in charcoal. At yet more distant intervals appeared the houses upon the broken fringe of the suburb; their outlines became clearer and clearer until he recognized many in which he had chance acquaintances, and many more the names of whose owners he knew. But all the windows and doors were sealed; none of the people were of the sort that would be up at such a time, or still less on such an errand. But as he passed under the shadow of one handsome villa with verandas and wide ornate gardens, he heard a noise that made him almost involuntarily stop. It was the unmistakable noise of a pistol or carbine or some light firearm discharged; but it was not this that puzzled him most. The first full noise was immediately followed by a series of fainter noises – as he counted them, about six. He supposed it must be the echo; but the odd thing was that the echo was not in the least like the original sound. It was not like anything else that he could think of; the three things nearest to it seemed to be the noise made by siphons of soda-water, one of the many noises made

by an animal, and the noise made by a person attempt-
ing to conceal laughter. None of which seemed to make
much sense.

Father Brown was made of two men. There was a
man of action, who was as modest as a primrose and
as punctual as a clock; who went his small round of
duties and never dreamed of altering it. There was also
a man of reflection, who was much simpler but much
stronger, who could not easily be stopped; whose
thought was always (in the only intelligent sense of the
words) free thought. He could not help, even uncon-
sciously, asking himself all the questions that there
were to be asked, and answering as many of them as he
could; all that went on like his breathing or circulation.
But he never consciously carried his actions outside the
sphere of his own duty; and in this case the two attitudes were aptly tested. He was just about to resume
his trudge in the twilight, telling himself it was no
affair of his, but instinctively twisting and untwisting
twenty theories about what the odd noises might mean.
Then the grey sky-line brightened into silver, and in the
broadening light he realized that he had been to the
house which belonged to an Anglo-Indian Major
named Putnam; and that the Major had a native cook
from Malta who was of his communion. He also began
to remember that pistol-shots are sometimes serious
things; accompanied with consequences with which he
was legitimately concerned. He turned back and went
in at the garden gate, making for the front door.

Half-way down one side of the house stood out a
projection like a very low shed; it was, as he afterwards
discovered, a large dustbin. Round the corner of this
came a figure, at first a mere shadow in the haze, apparently bending and peering about. Then, coming nearer,
it solidified into a figure that was, indeed, rather

unusually solid. Major Putnam was a bald-headed, bull-necked man, short and very broad, with one of those rather apoplectic faces that are produced by a prolonged attempt to combine the oriental climate with the occidental luxuries. But the face was a good-humoured one, and even now, though evidently puzzled and inquisitive, wore a kind of innocent grin. He had a large palm-leaf hat on the back of his head (suggesting a halo that was by no means appropriate to the face), but otherwise he was clad only in a very vivid suit of striped scarlet and yellow pyjamas; which, though glowing enough to behold, must have been, on a fresh morning, pretty chilly to wear. He had evidently come out of his house in a hurry, and the priest was not surprised when he called out without further ceremony: 'Did you hear that noise?'

'Yes,' answered Father Brown; 'I thought I had better look in, in case anything was the matter.'

The Major looked at him rather queerly with his good-humoured gooseberry eyes. 'What do you think the noise was?' he asked.

'It sounded like a gun or something,' replied the other, with some hesitation; 'but it seemed to have a singular sort of echo.'

The Major was still looking at him quietly, but with protruding eyes, when the front door was flung open, releasing a flood of gaslight on the face of the fading mist; and another figure in pyjamas sprang or tumbled out into the garden. The figure was much longer, leaner, and more athletic; the pyjamas, though equally tropical, were comparatively tasteful, being of white with a light lemon-yellow stripe. The man was haggard, but handsome, more sunburned than the other; he had an aquiline profile and rather deep-sunken eyes, and a slight air of oddity arising from the combination of coal-black hair with a much lighter moustache. All this Father Brown absorbed in detail more at leisure. For the moment he only saw one thing about the man; which was the revolver in his hand.

'Cray!' exclaimed the Major, staring at him; 'did you fire that shot?'

'Yes, I did,' retorted the black-haired gentleman hotly; 'and so would you in my place. If you were chased everywhere by devils and nearly –'

The Major seemed to intervene rather hurriedly. 'This is my friend Father Brown,' he said. And then to Brown: 'I don't know whether you've met Colonel Cray of the Royal Artillery.'

'I have heard of him, of course,' said the priest innocently. 'Did you – did you hit anything?'

'I thought so,' answered Cray with gravity.

'Did he –' asked Major Putnam in a lowered voice, 'did he fall or cry out, or anything?'

Colonel Cray was regarding his host with a strange and steady stare. 'I'll tell you exactly what he did,' he said. 'He sneezed.'

Father Brown's hand went half-way to his head, with the gesture of a man remembering somebody's name. He knew now what it was that was neither soda-water nor the snorting of a dog.

'Well,' ejaculated the staring Major, 'I never heard before that a service revolver was a thing to be sneezed at.'

'Nor I,' said Father Brown faintly. 'It's lucky you didn't turn your artillery on him or you might have given him quite a bad cold.' Then, after a bewildered pause, he said: 'Was it a burglar?'

'Let us go inside,' said Major Putnam, rather sharply, and led the way into his house.

The interior exhibited a paradox often to be marked

in such morning hours: that the rooms seemed brighter than the sky outside; even after the Major had turned out the one gaslight in the front hall. Father Brown was surprised to see the whole dining-table set out as for a festive meal, with napkins in their rings, and wine-glasses of some six unnecessary shapes set beside every plate. It was common enough, at that time of the morning, to find the remains of a banquet over-night; but to find it freshly spread so early was unusual.

While he stood wavering in the hall Major Putnam rushed past him and sent a raging eye over the whole oblong of the tablecloth. At last he spoke, spluttering: 'All the silver gone!' he gasped. 'Fish-knives and forks gone. Old cruet-stand gone. Even the old silver cream-jug gone. And now, Father Brown, I am ready to answer your question of whether it was a burglar.'

'They're simply a blind,' said Cray stubbornly. 'I know better than you why people persecute this house; I know better than you why –'

The Major patted him on the shoulder with a gesture almost peculiar to the soothing of a sick child, and said: 'It was a burglar. Obviously it was a burglar.'

'A burglar with a bad cold,' observed Father Brown, 'that might assist you to trace him in the neighbourhood.'

The Major shook his head in a sombre manner. 'He must be far beyond tracing now, I fear,' he said.

Then, as the restless man with the revolver turned again towards the door into the garden, he added in a husky, confidential voice: 'I doubt whether I should send for the police, for fear my friend here has been a little too free with his bullets, and got on the wrong side of the law. He's lived in very wild places; and, to be frank with you, I think he sometimes fancies things.'

'I think you once told me,' said Brown, 'that he believes some Indian secret society is pursuing him.'

Major Putnam nodded, but at the same time shrugged his shoulders.

'I suppose we'd better follow him outside,' he said. 'I don't want any more – shall we say, sneezing?'

They passed out into the morning light, which was now even tinged with sunshine, and saw Colonel Cray's tall figure bent almost double, minutely examining the condition of gravel and grass. While the Major strolled unobtrusively towards him, the priest took an equally indolent turn, which took him round the next corner of the house to within a yard or two of the projecting dustbin.

He stood regarding this dismal object for some minute and a half; then he stepped towards it, lifted the lid and put his head inside. Dust and other discolouring matter shook upwards as he did so; but Father Brown never observed his own appearance, whatever else he observed. He remained thus for a measurable period, as if engaged in some mysterious prayers. Then he came out again, with some ashes on his hair, and walked unconcernedly away.

By the time he came round to the garden door again he found a group there which seemed to roll away morbidities as the sunlight had already rolled away the mists. It was in no way rationally reassuring; it was simply broadly comic, like a cluster of Dickens's characters. Major Putnam had managed to slip inside and plunge into a proper shirt and trousers, with a crimson cummerbund, and a light square jacket over all; thus normally set off, his red festive face seemed bursting with a commonplace cordiality. He was indeed emphatic, but then he was talking to his cook – the swarthy son of Malta, whose lean, yellow and rather careworn face contrasted quaintly with his snow-white cap and costume. The cook might well be careworn, for cookery was the Major's hobby. He was one of those amateurs who always know more than the professional. The only other person he even admitted to be a judge of an omelette was his friend Cray – and as Brown remembered this, he turned to look for the other officer. In the new presence of daylight and people clothed and in their right mind, the sight of him was rather a shock. The taller and more elegant man was still in his night-garb, with tousled black hair, and now crawling about the garden on his hands and knees, still looking for traces of the burglar; and now and again, to all appearance, striking the ground with his hand in anger at not finding him. Seeing him thus quadrupedal in the grass, the priest raised his eyebrows rather sadly; and for the first time guessed that 'fancies things' might be an euphemism.

The third item in the group of the cook and the epicure was also known to Father Brown; it was Audrey Watson, the Major's ward and housekeeper; and at this moment, to judge by her apron, tucked-up sleeves and resolute manner, much more the housekeeper than the ward.

'It serves you right,' she was saying: 'I always told you not to have that old-fashioned cruet-stand.'

'I prefer it,' said Putnam, placably. 'I'm old-fashioned myself; and the things keep together.'

'And vanish together, as you see,' she retorted. 'Well, if you are not going to bother about the burglar, I shouldn't bother about the lunch. It's Sunday, and we can't send for vinegar and all that in the town; and you Indian gentlemen can't enjoy what you call a dinner without a lot of hot things. I wish to goodness now you hadn't asked Cousin Oliver to take me to the musical service. It isn't over till half-past twelve, and the Colonel has to leave by then. I don't believe you men can manage alone.'

'Oh yes, we can, my dear,' said the Major, looking at her very amiably. 'Marco has all the sauces; and we've often done ourselves well in very rough places, as you might know by now. And it's time you had a treat, Audrey; you mustn't be a housekeeper every hour of the day; and I know you want to hear the music.'

'I want to go to church,' she said, with rather severe eyes.

She was one of those handsome women who will always be handsome, because the beauty is not in an air or a tint, but in the very structure of the head and features. But though she was not yet middle-aged and her auburn hair was of a Titianesque fullness in form and colour, there was a look in her mouth and around her eyes which suggested that some sorrows wasted her, as winds waste at last the edges of a Greek temple. For indeed the little domestic difficulty of which she was now speaking so decisively was rather comic than tragic. Father Brown gathered, from the course of the conversation, that Cray the other *gourmet*, had to leave before the usual lunch-time; but that Putnam, his host, not to be done out of a final feast with an old crony, had arranged for a special *déjeuner* to be set out and consumed in the course of the morning, while Audrey and other graver persons were at morning service. She was going there under the escort of a relative and old friend of hers, Dr Oliver Oman, who, though a scientific man of a somewhat bitter type, was enthusiastic for music, and would go even to church to get it. There was nothing in all this that could conceivably concern the tragedy in Miss Watson's face; and by a half conscious instinct, Father Brown turned again to the seeming lunatic grubbing about in the grass.

When he strolled across to him, the black, unbrushed head was lifted abruptly, as if in some surprise at his continued presence. And indeed, Father Brown, for reasons best known to himself, had lingered much longer than politeness required; or even, in the ordinary sense, permitted.

'Well!' cried Cray, with wild eyes. 'I suppose you think I'm mad, like the rest?'

'I have considered the thesis,' answered the little man, composedly. 'And I incline to think you are not.'

'What do you mean?' snapped Cray quite savagely.

'Real madmen,' explained Father Brown, 'always encourage their own morbidity. They never strive against it. But you are trying to find traces of the burglar; even when there aren't any. You are struggling against it. You want what no madman ever wants.'

'And what is that?'

'You want to be proved wrong,' said Brown.

During the last words Cray had sprung or staggered to his feet and was regarding the cleric with agitated eyes. 'By hell, but that is a true word!' he cried. 'They are all at me here that the fellow was only after the silver – as if I shouldn't be only too pleased to think so! *She's* been at me,' and he tossed his tousled black head towards Audrey, but the other had no need of the direction, 'she's been at me to-day about how cruel I was to shoot a poor harmless house-breaker, and how I have the devil in me against poor harmless natives. But I was a good-natured man once – as good-natured as Putnam.'

After a pause he said: 'Look here, I've never seen you before; but you shall judge of the whole story. Old Putnam and I were friends in the same mess; but, owing to some accidents on the Afghan border, I got my command much sooner than most men; only we were both invalided home for a bit. I was engaged to Audrey out there; and we all travelled back together. But on the journey back things happened. Curious things. The result of them was that Putnam wants it broken off, and even Audrey keeps it hanging on – and I know what they mean. I know what they think I am. So do you.

'Well, these are the facts. The last day we were in an Indian city I asked Putnam if I could get some Trichinopoli cigars; he directed me to a little place opposite his lodgings. I have since found he was quite right; but "opposite" is a dangerous word when one decent house stands opposite five or six squalid ones; and I must have mistaken the door. It opened with difficulty, and then only on darkness; but as I turned back, the door behind me sank back and settled into its place with a noise as of innumerable bolts. There was nothing to do but to walk forward; which I did through passage after passage, pitch-dark. Then I came to a flight of steps, and then to a blind door, secured by a latch of elaborate Eastern ironwork, which I could only trace by touch, but which I loosened at last. I came out again upon gloom, which was half turned into a greenish twilight by a multitude of small but steady lamps below. They showed merely the feet or fringes of some huge and empty architecture. Just in front of me was something that looked like a mountain. I confess I nearly fell on the great stone platform on which I had emerged, to realize that it was an idol. And worst of all, an idol with its back to me.

'It was hardly half human, I guessed; to judge by the small squat head, and still more by a thing like a tail or extra limb turned up behind and pointing, like a loathsome large finger, at some symbol graven in the centre of the vast stone back. I had begun, in the dim light, to guess at the hieroglyphic, not without horror, when a more horrible thing happened. A door opened silently in the temple wall behind me and a man came out, with a brown face and a black coat. He had a carved smile on his face, of copper flesh and ivory teeth; but I think the most hateful thing about him was that he was in European dress. I was prepared, I think, for shrouded priests or naked fakirs. But this seemed to say that the devilry was over all the earth. As indeed I found it to be.

' "If you had only seen the Monkey's Feet," he said, smiling steadily, and without other preface, "we should have been very gentle – you would only be tortured and die. If you had seen the Monkey's Face, still we should be very moderate, very tolerant – you would only be tortured and live. But as you have seen the Monkey's Tail, we must pronounce the worst sentence. Which is – Go Free."

'When he said the words I heard the elaborate iron latch with which I had struggled, automatically unlock itself: and then, far down the dark passages I had passed, I heard the heavy street-door shifting its own bolts backwards.

' "It is vain to ask for mercy; you must go free," said the smiling man. "Henceforth a hair shall slay you like a sword, and a breath shall bite you like an adder; weapons shall come against you out of nowhere; and you shall die many times." And with that he was swallowed once more in the wall behind; and I went out into the street.'

Cray paused; and Father Brown unaffectedly sat down on the lawn and began to pick daisies.

Then the soldier continued: 'Putnam, of course,

with his jolly common sense, pooh-poohed all my fears; and from that time dates his doubt of my mental balance. Well, I'll simply tell you, in the fewest words, the three things that have happened since; and you shall judge which of us is right.

'The first happened in an Indian village on the edge of the jungle, but hundreds of miles from the temple, or town, or type of tribes and customs where the curse had been put on me. I woke in black midnight, and lay thinking of nothing in particular, when I felt a faint tickling thing, like a thread or a hair, trailed across my throat. I shrank back out of its way, and could not help thinking of the words in the temple. But when I got up and sought lights and a mirror, the line across my neck was a line of blood.

'The second happened in a lodging in Port Said, later, on our journey home together. It was a jumble of tavern and curiosity-shop; and though there was nothing there remotely suggesting the cult of the Monkey, it is, of course, possible that some of its images or talismans were in such a place. Its curse was there, anyhow. I woke again in the dark with a sensation that could not be put in colder or more literal words than that a breath bit like an adder. Existence was an agony of extinction; I dashed my head against walls until I dashed it against a window; and fell rather than jumped into the garden below. Putnam, poor fellow, who had called the other thing a chance scratch, was bound to take seriously the fact of finding me half insensible on the grass at dawn. But I fear it was my mental state he took seriously; and not my story.

'The third happened in Malta. We were in a fortress there; and as it happened our bedrooms overlooked the open sea, which almost came up to our window-sills, save for a flat white outer wall as bare as the sea.

I woke up again; but it was not dark. There was a full moon, as I walked to the window; I could have seen a bird on the bare battlement, or a sail on the horizon. What I did see was a sort of stick or branch circling, self-supported, in the empty sky. It flew straight in at my window and smashed the lamp beside the pillow I had just quitted. It was one of those queer-shaped war-clubs some Eastern tribes use. But it had come from no human hand.'

Father Brown threw away a daisy-chain he was making, and rose with a wistful look. 'Has Major Putnam,' he asked, 'got any Eastern curios, idols, weapons and so on, from which one might get a hint?'

'Plenty of those, though not much use, I fear,' replied Cray; 'but by all means come into his study.'

As they entered they passed Miss Watson buttoning her gloves for church, and heard the voice of Putnam downstairs still giving a lecture on cookery to the cook. In the Major's study and den of curios they came suddenly on a third party, silk-hatted and dressed for the street, who was poring over an open book on the smoking-table – a book which he dropped rather guiltily, and turned.

Cray introduced him civilly enough, as Dr Oman, but he showed such disfavour in his very face that Brown guessed the two men, whether Audrey knew it or not, were rivals. Nor was the priest wholly unsympathetic with the prejudice. Dr Oman was a very well-dressed gentleman indeed; well-featured, though almost dark enough for an Asiatic. But Father Brown had to tell himself sharply that one should be in charity even with those who wax their pointed beards, who have small gloved hands, and who speak with perfectly modulated voices.

Cray seemed to find something specially irritating in

the small prayer-book in Oman's dark-gloved hand. 'I didn't know that was in your line,' he said rather rudely.

Oman laughed mildly, but without offence. 'This is more so, I know,' he said, laying his hand on the big book he had dropped, 'a dictionary of drugs and such things. But it's rather too large to take to church.' Then he closed the larger book, and there seemed again the faintest touch of hurry and embarrassment.

'I suppose,' said the priest, who seemed anxious to change the subject, 'all these spears and things are from India?'

'From everywhere,' answered the doctor. 'Putnam is an old soldier, and has been in Mexico and Australia, and the Cannibal Islands for all I know.'

'I hope it was not in the Cannibal Islands,' said Brown, 'that he learnt the art of cookery.' And he ran his eyes over the stew-pots or other strange utensils on the wall.

At this moment the jolly subject of their conversation thrust his laughing, lobsterish face into the room. 'Come along, Cray,' he cried. 'Your lunch is just coming in. And the bells are ringing for those who want to go to church.'

Cray slipped upstairs to change; Dr Oman and Miss Watson betook themselves solemnly down the street, with a string of other churchgoers; but Father Brown noticed that the doctor twice looked back and scrutinized the house; and even came back to the corner of the street to look at it again.

The priest looked puzzled. '*He* can't have been at the dustbin,' he muttered. 'Not in those clothes. Or was he there earlier to-day?'

Father Brown, touching other people, was as sensitive as a barometer; but to-day he seemed about as sensitive as a rhinoceros. By no social law, rigid or implied, could he be supposed to linger round the lunch of the Anglo-Indian friends; but he lingered, covering his position with torrents of amusing but quite needless conversation. He was the more puzzling because he did not seem to want any lunch. As one after another of the most exquisitely balanced kedgerees of curries, accompanied with their appropriate vintages, were laid before the other two, he only repeated that it was one of his fast-days, and munched a piece of bread and sipped and then left untasted a tumbler of cold water. His talk, however, was exuberant.

'I'll tell you what I'll do for you,' he cried; 'I'll mix you a salad! I can't eat it, but I'll mix it like an angel! You've got a lettuce there.'

'Unfortunately it's the only thing we have got,' answered the good-humoured Major. 'You must remember that mustard, vinegar, oil and so on vanished with the cruet and the burglar.'

'I know,' replied Brown, rather vaguely. 'That's what I've always been afraid would happen. That's why I always carry a cruet-stand about with me. I'm so fond of salads.'

And to the amazement of the two men he took a pepper-pot out of his waistcoat pocket and put it on the table.

'I wonder why the burglar wanted mustard, too,' he went on, taking a mustard-pot from another pocket. 'A mustard plaster, I suppose. And vinegar' – producing that condiment – 'haven't I heard something about vinegar and brown paper? As for oil, which I think I put in my left –'

His garrulity was an instant arrested; for lifting his eyes, he saw what no one else saw – the black figure of Dr Oman standing on the sunlit lawn and looking steadily into the room. Before he could quite recover himself Cray had cloven in.

'You're an astounding card,' he said, staring. 'I shall come and hear your sermons, if they're as amusing as your manners.' His voice changed a little, and he leaned back in his chair.

'Oh, there are sermons in a cruet-stand, too,' said Father Brown, quite gravely. 'Have you heard of faith like a grain of mustard-seed; or charity that anoints with oil? And as for vinegar, can any soldiers forget that solitary soldier, who, when the sun was darkened –'

Colonel Cray leaned forward a little and clutched the table-cloth.

Father Brown, who was making the salad, tipped two spoonfuls of the mustard into the tumbler of water beside him; stood up and said in a new, loud and sudden voice – 'Drink that!'

At the same moment the motionless doctor in the garden came running, and bursting open a window cried: 'Am I wanted? Has he been poisoned?'

'Pretty near,' said Brown, with the shadow of a smile; for the emetic had very suddenly taken effect. And Cray lay in a deck-chair, gasping as for life, but alive.

Major Putnam had sprung up, his purple face mottled. 'A crime!' he cried hoarsely. 'I will go for the police!'

The priest could hear him dragging down his palm-leaf hat from the peg and tumbling out of the front door; he heard the garden gate slam. But he only stood looking at Cray; and after a silence said quietly:

'I shall not talk to you much; but I will tell you what you want to know. There is no curse on you. The Temple of the Monkey was either a coincidence or a part of the trick; the trick was the trick of a white man. There is only one weapon that will bring blood with that mere feathery touch: a razor held by a white man. There is one way of making a common room full of invisible, overpowering poison: turning on the gas – the crime of a white man. And there is only one kind of club that can be thrown out of a window, turn in mid-air and come back to the window next to it: the Australian boomerang. You'll see some of them in the Major's study.'

With that he went outside and spoke for a moment to the doctor. The moment after, Audrey Watson came rushing into the house and fell on her knees beside Cray's chair. He could not hear what they said to each other; but their faces moved with amazement, not unhappiness. The doctor and the priest walked slowly towards the garden gate.

'I suppose the Major was in love with her, too,' he said with a sigh; and when the other nodded observed: 'You were very generous, doctor. You did a fine thing. But what made you suspect?'

'A very small thing,' said Oman; 'but it kept me restless in church till I came back to see that all was well. That book on his table was a work on poisons; and was put down open at the place where it stated that a certain Indian poison, though deadly and difficult to trace, was particularly easily reversible by the use of the commonest emetics. I suppose he read that at the last moment –'

'And remembered that there were emetics in the cruet-stand,' said Father Brown. 'Exactly. He threw the cruet in the dustbin – where I found it, along with other silver – for the sake of a burglary blind. But if you look at that pepper-pot I put on the table, you'll see a small hole. That's where Cray's bullet struck, shaking up the pepper and making the criminal sneeze.'

There was a silence. Then Dr Oman said grimly: 'The Major is a long time looking for the police.'

'Or the police in looking for the Major?' said the priest. 'Well, good-bye.'

11

The Strange Crime of
John Boulnois

Mr Calhoun Kidd was a very young gentleman with a
very old face, a face dried up with its own eagerness,
framed in blue-black hair and a black butterfly tie. He
was the emissary in England of the colossal American
daily called the Western Sun – also humorously
described as the 'Rising Sunset.' This was in allusion to
a great journalistic declaration (attributed to Mr Kidd
himself) that 'he guessed the sun would rise in the west
yet, if American citizens did a bit more hustling.'
Those, however, who mock American journalism from
the standpoint of somewhat mellower traditions forget
a certain paradox which partly redeems it. For while
the journalism of the States permits a pantomimic vul-
garity long past anything English, it also shows a real
excitement about the most earnest mental problems, of
which English papers are innocent, or rather incapable. The Sun was full of the most solemn matters
treated in the most farcical way. William James figured
there as well as 'Weary Willie,' and pragmatists alter-
nated with pugilists in the long procession of its
portraits.

Thus, when a very unobtrusive Oxford man named
John Boulnois wrote in a very unreadable review called
the *Natural Philosophy Quarterly* a series of articles
on alleged weak points in Darwinian evolution, it fluttered no corner of the English papers; though Boulnois's

theory (which was that of a comparatively stationary universe visited occasionally by convulsions of change) had some rather faddy fashionableness at Oxford, and got so far as to be named 'Catastrophism.' But many American papers seized on the challenge as a great event; and the *Sun* threw the shadow of Mr Boulnois quite gigantically across its pages. By the paradox already noted, articles of valuable intelligence and enthusiasm were presented with headlines apparently written by an illiterate maniac; headlines such as 'Darwin Chews Dirt; Critic Boulnois says He Jumps the Shocks' – or 'Keep Catastrophic, says Thinker Boulnois.' And Mr Calhoun Kidd, of the *Western Sun*, was bidden to take his butterfly tie and lugubrious visage down to the little house outside Oxford where Thinker Boulnois lived in happy ignorance of such a title.

That fated philosopher had consented, in a somewhat dazed manner, to receive the interviewer, and had named the hour of nine that evening. The last of a summer sunset clung about Cumnor and the low wooded hills; the romantic Yankee was both doubtful of his road and inquisitive about his surroundings; and seeing the door of a genuine feudal old-country inn, The Champion Arms, standing open, he went in to make inquiries.

In the bar parlour he rang the bell, and had to wait some little time for a reply to it. The only other person present was a lean man with close red hair and loose, horsey-looking clothes, who was drinking very bad whisky, but smoking a very good cigar. The whisky, of course, was the choice brand of The Champion Arms; the cigar he had probably brought with him from London. Nothing could be more different than his cynical *négligé* from the dapper dryness of the young American; but something in his pencil and open notebook, and perhaps in the expression of his alert blue eye, caused Kidd to guess, correctly, that he was a brother journalist.

'Could you do me the favour,' asked Kidd, with the courtesy of his nation, 'of directing me to the Grey Cottage, where Mr Boulnois lives, as I understand?'

'It's a few yards down the road,' said the red-haired man, removing his cigar; 'I shall be passing it myself in a minute, but I'm going on to Pendragon Park to try and see the fun.'

'What is Pendragon Park?' asked Calhoun Kidd.

'Sir Claude Champion's place – haven't you come down for that, too?' asked the other pressman, looking up. 'You're a journalist, aren't you?'

'I have come to see Mr Boulnois,' said Kidd.

'I've come to see Mrs Boulnois,' replied the other. 'But I shan't catch her at home.' And he laughed rather unpleasantly.

'Are you interested in Catastrophism?' asked the wondering Yankee.

'I'm interested in catastrophes; and there are going to be some,' replied his companion gloomily. 'Mine's a filthy trade, and I never pretend it isn't.'

With that he spat on the floor; yet somehow in the very act and instant one could realize that the man had been brought up as a gentleman.

The American pressman considered him with more attention. His face was pale and dissipated, with the promise of formidable passions yet to be loosed; but it was a clever and sensitive face; his clothes were coarse and careless, but he had a good seal ring on one of his long, thin fingers. His name, which came out in the course of talk, was James Dalroy; he was the son of a bankrupt Irish landlord, and attached to a pink paper which he heartily despised, called *Smart Society*, in the capacity of reporter and of something painfully like spy.

Smart Society, I regret to say, felt none of that interest in Boulnois on Darwin which was such a credit to the head and hearts of the *Western Sun*. Dalroy had come down, it seemed, to snuff up the scent of a scandal which might very well end in the Divorce Court, but which was at present hovering between Grey Cottage and Pendragon Park.

Sir Claude Champion was known to the readers of the *Western Sun* as well as Mr Boulnois. So were the Pope and the Derby Winner; but the idea of their intimate acquaintanceship would have struck Kidd as equally incongruous. He had heard of (and written about, nay, falsely pretended to know) Sir Claude Champion, as 'one of the brightest and wealthiest of England's Upper Ten'; as the great sportsman who raced yachts round the world; as the great traveller who wrote books about the Himalayas, as the politician who swept constituencies with a startling sort of Tory Democracy, and as the great dabbler in art, music, literature, and, above all, acting. Sir Claude was really rather magnificent in other than American eyes. There was something of the Renascence Prince about his omnivorous culture and restless publicity; he was not only a great amateur, but an ardent one. There was in him none of that antiquarian frivolity that we convey by the word 'dilettante.'

That faultless falcon profile with purple-black Italian eye, which had been snap-shotted so often both for *Smart Society* and the *Western Sun*, gave everyone the impression of a man eaten by ambition as by a fire, or even a disease. But though Kidd knew a great deal about Sir Claude – a great deal more, in fact, than there was to know – it would never have crossed his wildest dreams to connect so showy an aristocrat with the newly-unearthed founder of Catastrophism, or to guess that Sir Claude Champion and John Boulnois could be intimate friends. Such, according to Dalroy's account, was nevertheless the fact. The two had hunted in couples at school and college, and, though their social destinies had been very different (for Champion was a great landlord and almost a millionaire, while Boulnois was a poor scholar and, until just lately, an unknown one), they still kept in very close touch with each other. Indeed, Boulnois's cottage stood just outside the gates of Pendragon Park.

But whether the two men could be friends much longer was becoming a dark and ugly question. A year or two before, Boulnois had married a beautiful and not unsuccessful actress, to whom he was devoted in his own shy and ponderous style; and the proximity of the household to Champion's had given that flighty celebrity opportunities for behaving in a way that could not but cause painful and rather base excitement. Sir Claude had carried the arts of publicity to perfection; and he seemed to take a crazy pleasure in being equally ostentatious in an intrigue that could do him no sort of honour. Footmen from Pendragon were perpetually leaving bouquets for Mrs Boulnois; carriages and motor-cars were perpetually calling at the cottage for Mrs Boulnois; balls and masquerades perpetually filled the grounds in which the baronet paraded Mrs Boulnois, like the Queen of Love and Beauty at a tournament. That very evening, marked by Mr Kidd for the exposition of Catastrophism, had been marked by Sir Claude Champion for an open-air rendering of *Romeo and Juliet*, in which he was to play Romeo to a Juliet it was needless to name.

'I don't think it can go on without a smash,' said the young man with red hair, getting up and shaking himself. 'Old Boulnois may be squared – or he may be square. But if he's square he's thick – what you might call cubic. But I don't believe it's possible.'

'He is a man of grand intellectual powers,' said Calhoun Kidd in a deep voice.

'Yes,' answered Dalroy; 'but even a man of grand intellectual powers can't be such a blighted fool as all that. Must you be going on? I shall be following myself in a minute or two.'

But Calhoun Kidd, having finished a milk and soda, betook himself smartly up the road towards the Grey Cottage, leaving his cynical informant to his whisky and tobacco. The last of the daylight had faded; the skies were of a dark, green-grey, like slate, studded here and there with a star, but lighter on the left side of the sky, with the promise of a rising moon.

The Grey Cottage, which stood entrenched, as it were, in a square of stiff, high thorn-hedges, was so close under the pines and palisades of the Park that Kidd at first mistook it for the Park Lodge. Finding the name on the narrow wooden gate, however, and seeing by his watch that the hour of the 'Thinker's' appointment had just struck, he went in and knocked at the front door. Inside the garden hedge, he could see that the house, though unpretentious enough, was larger and more luxurious than it looked at first, and was quite a different kind of place from a porter's lodge. A dog-kennel and a beehive stood outside, like symbols of old English country-life; the moon was rising behind a plantation of prosperous pear trees; the dog that came out of the kennel was reverend-looking and reluctant to bark; and the plain, elderly manservant who opened the door was brief but dignified.

'Mr Boulnois asked me to offer his apologies, sir,' he said, 'but he has been obliged to go out suddenly.'

'But see here, I had an appointment,' said the interviewer, with a rising voice. 'Do you know where he went to?'

'To Pendragon Park, sir,' said the servant, rather sombrely, and began to close the door.

Kidd started a little.

'Did he go with Mrs – with the rest of the party?' he asked rather vaguely.

'No, sir,' said the man shortly; 'he stayed behind, and then went out alone.' And he shut the door, brutally, but with an air of duty not done.

The American, that curious compound of impudence and sensitiveness, was annoyed. He felt a strong desire to hustle them all along a bit and teach them business habits; the hoary old dog and the grizzled, heavy-faced old butler with his prehistoric shirt-front, and the drowsy old moon, and above all the scatterbrained old philosopher who couldn't keep an appointment.

'If that's the way he goes on he deserves to lose his wife's purest devotion,' said Mr Calhoun Kidd. 'But perhaps he's gone over to make a row. In that case I reckon a man from the *Western Sun* will be on the spot.'

And turning the corner by the open lodge-gates, he set off, stumping up the long avenue of black pinewoods that pointed in abrupt perspective towards the inner gardens of Pendragon Park. The trees were as black and orderly as plumes upon a hearse; there were still a few stars. He was a man with more literary than direct natural associations; the word 'Ravenswood' came into his head repeatedly. It was partly the raven colour of the pine-woods; but partly also an indescribable atmosphere almost described in Scott's great tragedy; the smell of something that died in the eight-eenth century; the smell of dank gardens and broken urns, of wrongs that will never now be righted; of something that is none the less incurably sad because it is strangely unreal.

More than once, as he went up that trim, black road of tragic artifice, he stopped startled, thinking he heard steps in front of him. He could see nothing in front but the twin sombre walls of pine and the wedge of starlit sky above them. At first he thought he must have fan-cied it or been mocked by a mere echo of his own tramp. But as he went on he was more and more inclined to conclude, with the remains of his reason, that there really were other feet upon the road. He thought hazily of ghosts; and was surprised how swiftly he could see the image of an appropriate and local ghost, one with a face as white as Pierrot's, but patched with black. The apex of the triangle of dark-blue sky was growing brighter and bluer, but he did not realize as yet that this was because he was coming nearer to the lights of the great house and garden. He only felt that the atmosphere was growing more intense; there was in the sadness more violence and secrecy – more – he hesitated for the word, and then said it with a jerk of laughter – Catastrophism.

More pines, more pathway slid past him, and then he stood rooted as by a blast of magic. It is vain to say that he felt as if he had got into a dream; but this time he felt quite certain that he had got into a book. For we human beings are used to inappropriate things; we are accustomed to the clatter of the incongruous; it is a tune to which we can go to sleep. If one appropriate thing happens, it wakes us up like the pang of a perfect chord. Something happened such as would have hap-pened in such a place in a forgotten tale.

Over the black pinewood came flying and flashing in the moon a naked sword – such a slender and sparkling rapier as may have fought many an unjust duel in that ancient park. It fell on the pathway far in front of him and lay there glistening like a large needle. He ran like a hare and bent to look at it. Seen at close quarters it had rather a showy look: the big red jewels in the hilt and guard were a little dubious. But there were other red drops upon the blade which were not dubious.

He looked round wildly in the direction from which the dazzling missile had come, and saw that at this point the sable façade of fir and pine was interrupted by a smaller road at right angles; which, when he turned it, brought him in full view of the long, lighted house, with a lake and fountains in front of it. Nevertheless, he did not look at this, having something more interesting to look at.

Above him, at the angle of the steep green bank of the terraced garden, was one of those small picturesque surprises common in the old landscape gardening; a kind of small round hill or dome of grass, like a giant mole-hill, ringed and crowned with three concentric fences of roses, and having a sundial in the highest point in the centre. Kidd could see the finger of the dial stand up dark against the sky like the dorsal fin of a shark, and the vain moonlight clinging to that idle clock. But he saw something else clinging to it also, for one wild moment – the figure of a man.

Though he saw it there only for a moment, though it was outlandish and incredible in costume, being clad from neck to heel in tight crimson, with glints of gold, yet he knew in one flash of moonlight who it was. That white face flung up to heaven, clean-shaven and so unnaturally young, like Byron with a Roman nose, those black curls already grizzled – he had seen the thousand public portraits of Sir Claude Champion. The wild red figure reeled an instant against the sundial; the next it had rolled down the steep bank and lay at the American's feet, faintly moving one arm. A gaudy, unnatural gold ornament on the arm suddenly reminded Kidd of *Romeo and Juliet*; of course the tight crimson suit was part of the play. But there was a long red stain down the bank from which the man had rolled – that was no part of the play. He had been run through the body.

Mr Calhoun Kidd shouted and shouted again. Once more he seemed to hear phantasmal footsteps, and started to find another figure already near him. He knew the figure, and yet it terrified him. The dissipated youth who had called himself Dalroy had a horribly quiet way with him; if Boulnois failed to keep appointments that had been made, Dalroy had a sinister air of keeping appointments that hadn't. The moonlight discoloured everything; against Dalroy's red hair his wan face looked not so much white as pale green.

All this morbid impressionism must be Kidd's excuse for having cried out, brutally and beyond all reason: 'Did you do this, you devil?'

James Dalroy smiled his unpleasing smile; but before he could speak, the fallen figure made another movement of the arm, waving vaguely towards the place where the sword fell; then came a moan, and then it managed to speak.

'Boulnois . . . Boulnois, I say . . . Boulnois did it . . . jealous of me . . . he was jealous, he was, he was . . .'

Kidd bent his head down to hear more, and just managed to catch the words:

'Boulnois . . . with my own sword . . . he threw it . . .'

Again the failing hand waved towards the sword,

and then fell rigid with a thud. In Kidd rose from its depth all that acrid humour that is the strange salt of the seriousness of his race.

'See here,' he said sharply and with command, 'you must fetch a doctor. This man's dead.'

'And a priest, too, I suppose,' said Dalroy in an undecipherable manner. 'All these Champions are papists.'

The American knelt down by the body, felt the heart, propped up the head and used some last efforts at restoration; but before the other journalist reappeared, followed by a doctor and a priest, he was already prepared to assert they were too late.

'Were you too late also?' asked the doctor, a solid prosperous-looking man, with conventional moustache and whiskers, but a lively eye, which darted over Kidd dubiously.

'In one sense,' drawled the representative of the *Sun*. 'I was too late to save the man, but I guess I was in time to hear something of importance. I heard the dead man denounce his assassin.'

'And who was the assassin?' asked the doctor, drawing his eyebrows together.

'Boulnois,' said Calhoun Kidd, and whistled softly.

The doctor stared at him gloomily with a reddening brow; but he did not contradict. Then the priest, a shorter figure in the background, said mildly: 'I understood that Mr Boulnois was not coming to Pendragon Park this evening.'

'There again,' said the Yankee grimly, 'I may be in a position to give the old country a fact or two. Yes, *sir*, John Boulnois was going to stay in all this evening; he fixed up a real good appointment there with me. But John Boulnois changed his mind; John Boulnois left his home abruptly and all alone, and came over to this derned Park an hour or so ago. His butler told me so. I think we hold what the all-wise police call a clue – have you sent for them?'

'Yes,' said the doctor; 'but we haven't alarmed anyone else yet.'

'Does Mrs Boulnois know?' asked James Dalroy; and again Kidd was conscious of an irrational desire to hit him on his curling mouth.

'I have not told her,' said the doctor gruffly; 'but here come the police.'

The little priest had stepped out into the main avenue, and now returned with the fallen sword, which looked ludicrously large and theatrical when attached to his dumpy figure, at once clerical and commonplace. 'Just before the police come,' he said apologetically, 'has anyone got a light?'

The Yankee journalist took an electric torch from his pocket, and the priest held it close to the middle part of the blade, which he examined with blinking care. Then, without glancing at the point or pommel, he handed the long weapon to the doctor.

'I fear I'm no use here,' he said, with a brief sigh. 'I'll say good night to you, gentlemen.' And he walked away up the dark avenue towards the house, his hands clasped behind him and his big head bent in cogitation.

The rest of the group made increased haste towards the lodge-gates, where an inspector and two constables could already be seen in consultation with the lodge-keeper. But the little priest only walked slower and slower in the dim cloister of pine, and at last stopped dead, on the steps of the house. It was his silent way of acknowledging an equally silent approach; for there came towards him a presence that might have satisfied even Calhoun Kidd's demands for a lovely and aristocratic ghost. It was a young woman in silvery satins of a

Renascence design; she had golden hair in two long shining ropes, and a face so startlingly pale between them that she might have been chryselephantine – made, that is, like some old Greek statues, out of ivory and gold. But her eyes were very bright, and her voice, though low, was confident.

'Father Brown?' she said.

'Mrs Boulnois?' he replied gravely. Then he looked at her and immediately said: 'I see you know about Sir Claude.'

'How do you know I know?' she asked steadily.

He did not answer the question, but asked another: 'Have you seen your husband?'

'My husband is at home,' she said. 'He has nothing to do with this.'

Again he did not answer; and the woman drew nearer to him, with a curiously intense expression on her face.

'Shall I tell you something more?' she said, with a rather fearful smile. 'I don't think he did it, and *you* don't either.'

Father Brown returned her gaze with a long, grave stare, and then nodded, yet more gravely.

'Father Brown,' said the lady, 'I am going to tell you all I know, but I want you to do me a favour first. Will you tell me *why* you haven't jumped to the conclusion of poor John's guilt, as all the rest have done? Don't mind what you say: I – I know about the gossip and the appearances that are against him.'

Father Brown looked honestly embarrassed, and passed his hand across his forehead. 'Two very little things,' he said. 'At least, one's very trivial and the other very vague. But such as they are, they don't fit in with Mr Boulnois being the murderer.'

He turned his blank, round face up to the stars and

continued absentmindedly: 'To take the vague idea first. I attach a good deal of importance to vague ideas. All those things that "aren't evidence" are what convince me. I think a moral impossibility the biggest of all impossibilities. I know your husband only slightly, but I think this crime of his, as generally conceived, something very like a moral impossibility. Please do not think I mean that Boulnois could not be so wicked. Anybody can be wicked – as wicked as he chooses. We can direct our moral wills; but we can't generally change our instinctive tastes and ways of doing things. Boulnois might commit a murder, but not this murder. He would not snatch Romeo's sword from its romantic scabbard; or slay his foe on the sundial as on a kind of altar; or leave his body among the roses; or fling the sword away among the pines. If Boulnois killed anyone he'd do it quietly and heavily, as he'd do any other doubtful thing – take a tenth glass of port, or read a loose Greek poet. No, the romantic setting is not like Boulnois. It's more like Champion.'

'Ah!' she said, and looked at him with eyes like diamonds.

'And the trivial thing was this,' said Brown. 'There were fingerprints on that sword; fingerprints can be detected quite a time after they are made if they're on some polished surface like glass or steel. These were on a polished surface. They were half-way down the blade of the sword. Whose prints they were I have no earthly clue; but why should anybody hold a sword half-way down? It was a long sword, but length is an advantage in lunging at an enemy. At least, at most enemies. At all enemies except one.'

'Except one!' she repeated.

'There is only one enemy,' said Father Brown, 'whom it is easier to kill with a dagger than a sword.'

'I know,' said the woman. 'Oneself.'

There was a long silence, and then the priest said quietly but abruptly: 'Am I right, then? Did Sir Claude kill himself?'

'Yes,' she said, with a face like marble. 'I saw him do it.'

'He died,' said Father Brown, 'for love of you?'

An extraordinary expression flashed across her face, very different from pity, modesty, remorse, or anything her companion had expected: her voice became suddenly strong and full. 'I don't believe,' she said, 'he ever cared about me a rap. He hated my husband.'

'Why?' asked the other, and turned his round face from the sky to the lady.

'He hated my husband because . . . it is so strange I hardly know how to say it . . . because . . .'

'Yes?' said Brown patiently.

'Because my husband wouldn't hate him.'

Father Brown only nodded, and seemed still to be listening; he differed from most detectives in fact and fiction in a small point – he never pretended not to understand when he understood perfectly well.

Mrs Boulnois drew near once more with the same contained glow of certainty. 'My husband,' she said, 'is a great man. Sir Claude Champion was not a great man: he was a celebrated and successful man. My husband has never been celebrated or successful; and it is the solemn truth that he has never dreamed of being so. He no more expects to be famous for thinking than for smoking cigars. On all that side he has a sort of splendid stupidity. He has never grown up. He still liked Champion exactly as he liked him at school; he admired him as he would admire a conjuring trick done at the dinner-table. But he couldn't be got to conceive the notion of *envying* Champion. *And Champion wanted to be envied*. He went mad and killed himself for that.'

'Yes,' said Father Brown; 'I think I begin to understand.'

'Oh, don't you see?' she cried; 'the whole picture is made for that – the place is planned for it. Champion put John in a little house at his very door, like a dependant – to make him *feel* a failure. He never felt it. He thinks no more about such things than – than an absent-minded lion. Champion would burst in on John's shabbiest hours or homeliest meals with some dazzling present or announcement or expedition that made it like the visit of Haroun Alraschid, and John would accept or refuse amiably with one eye off, so to speak, like one lazy schoolboy agreeing or disagreeing with another. After five years of it John had not turned a hair; and Sir Claude Champion was a monomaniac.'

'And Haman began to tell them,' said Father Brown, 'of all the things wherein the king had honoured him; and he said: "All these things profit me nothing while I see Mordecai the Jew sitting in the gate."'

'The crisis came,' Mrs Boulnois continued, 'when I persuaded John to let me take down some of his speculations and send them to a magazine. They began to attract attention, especially in America, and one paper wanted to interview him. When Champion (who was interviewed nearly every day) heard of this late little crumb of success falling to his unconscious rival, the last link snapped that held back his devilish hatred. Then he began to lay that insane siege to my own love and honour which has been the talk of the shire. You will ask me why I allowed such atrocious attentions. I answer that I could not have declined them except by explaining to my husband, and there are some things the soul cannot do, as the body cannot fly. Nobody could have explained to my husband. Nobody could do it now. If you said to him in so many words, "Champion is stealing your wife," he would think the joke a little vulgar: that it could be anything but a joke – that notion could find no crack in his great skull to get in by. Well, John was to come and see us act this evening, but just as we were starting he said he wouldn't; he had got an interesting book and a cigar. I told this to Sir Claude, and it was his death-blow. The monomaniac suddenly saw despair. He stabbed himself, crying out like a devil that Boulnois was slaying him; he lies there in the garden dead of his own jealousy to produce jealousy; and John is sitting in the dining-room reading a book.'

There was another silence, and then the little priest said: 'There is only one weak point, Mrs Boulnois, in all your very vivid account. Your husband is not sitting in the dining-room reading a book. That American reporter told me he had been to your house, and your butler told him Mr Boulnois had gone to Pendragon Park after all.'

Her bright eyes widened to an almost electric glare; and yet it seemed rather bewilderment than confusion or fear. 'Why, what *can* you mean?' she cried. 'All the servants were out of the house, seeing the theatricals. And we don't keep a butler, thank goodness!'

Father Brown started and spun half round like an absurd teetotum. 'What, what?' he cried seeming galvanized into sudden life. 'Look here – I say – can I make your husband hear if I go to the house?'

'Oh, the servants will be back by now,' she said, wondering.

'Right, right!' rejoined the cleric energetically, and set off scuttling up the path towards the Park gates. He turned once to say: 'Better get hold of that Yankee, or

"Crime of John Boulnois" will be all over the Republic in large letters.'

'You don't understand,' said Mrs Boulnois. 'He wouldn't mind. I don't think he imagines that America really is a place.'

When Father Brown reached the house with the bee-hive and the drowsy dog, a small and neat maid-servant showed him into the dining-room, where Boulnois sat reading by a shaded lamp, exactly as his wife described him. A decanter of port and a wineglass were at his elbow; and the instant the priest entered he noted the long ash stand out unbroken on his cigar.

'He has been here for half an hour at least,' thought Father Brown. In fact, he had the air of sitting where he had sat when his dinner was cleared away.

'Don't get up, Mr Boulnois,' said the priest in his pleasant, prosaic way. 'I shan't interrupt you a moment. I fear I break in on some of your scientific studies.'

'No,' said Boulnois; 'I was reading "The Bloody Thumb."' He said it with neither frown nor smile, and his visitor was conscious of a certain deep and virile indifference in the man which his wife had called great-ness. He laid down a gory yellow 'shocker' without even feeling its incongruity enough to comment on it humorously. John Boulnois was a big, slow-moving man with a massive head, partly grey and partly bald, and blunt, burly features. He was in shabby and very old-fashioned evening-dress, with a narrow triangular opening of shirt-front: he had assumed it that evening in his original purpose of going to see his wife act Juliet.

'I won't keep you long from "The Bloody Thumb" or any other catastrophic affairs,' said Father Brown, smiling. 'I only came to ask you about the crime you committed this evening.'

Boulnois looked at him steadily, but a red bar began to show across his broad brow; and he seemed like one discovering embarrassment for the first time.

'I know it was a strange crime,' assented Brown in a low voice. 'Stranger than murder perhaps – to you. The little sins are sometimes harder to confess than the big ones – but that's why it's so important to confess them. Your crime is committed by every fashionable hostess six times a week: and yet you find it stick to your tongue like a nameless atrocity.'

'It makes one feel,' said the philosopher slowly, 'such a damned fool.'

'I know,' assented the other, 'but one often has to choose between feeling a damned fool and being one.'

'I can't analyse myself well,' went on Boulnois; 'but sitting in that chair with that story I was as happy as a schoolboy on a half-holiday. It was security, eternity – I can't convey it . . . the cigars were within reach . . . the matches were within reach . . . the *Thumb* had four more appearances to . . . it was not only a peace, but a plenitude. Then that bell rang, and I thought for one long, mortal minute that I couldn't get out of that chair – literally, physically, muscularly couldn't. Then I did it like a man lifting the world, because I knew all the servants were out. I opened the front door, and there was a little man with his mouth open to speak and his notebook open to write in. I remembered the Yankee interviewer I had forgotten. His hair was parted in the middle, and I tell you that murder –'

'I understand,' said Father Brown. 'I've seen him.'

'I didn't commit murder,' continued the Catastrophist mildly, 'but only perjury. I said I had gone across to Pendragon Park and shut the door in his face. That is my crime, Father Brown, and I don't know what penance you would inflict for it.'

'I shan't inflict any penance,' said the clerical gentleman, collecting his heavy hat and umbrella with an air of some amusement; 'quite the contrary. I came here specially to let you off the little penance which would otherwise have followed your little offence.'

'And what,' asked Boulnois, smiling, 'is the little penance I have so luckily been let off?'

'Being hanged,' said Father Brown.

12

The Fairy Tale of
Father Brown

The picturesque city and state of Heiligwaldenstein was one of those toy kingdoms of which certain parts of the German Empire still consist. It had come under the Prussian hegemony quite late in history – hardly fifty years before the fine summer day when Flambeau and Father Brown found themselves sitting in its gardens and drinking its beer. There had been not a little of war and wild justice there within living memory, as soon will be shown. But in merely looking at it one could not dismiss that impression of childishness which is the most charming side of Germany – those little pantomime, paternal monarchies in which a king seems as domestic as a cook. The German soldiers by the innumerable sentry-boxes looked strangely like German toys, and the clean-cut battlements of the castle, gilded by the sunshine, looked the more like the gilt gingerbread. For it was brilliant weather. The sky was as Prussian a blue as Potsdam itself could require, but it was yet more like that lavish and glowing use of the colour which a child extracts from a shilling paint-box. Even the grey-ribbed trees looked young, for the pointed buds on them were still pink, and in a pattern against the strong blue looked like innumerable childish figures.

Despite his prosaic appearance and generally practical walk of life, Father Brown was not without a certain streak of romance in his composition, though he generally kept his day-dreams to himself, as many children do. Amid the brisk, bright colours of such a day, and in the heraldic framework of such a town, he did feel rather as if he had entered a fairy tale. He took a childish pleasure, as a younger brother might, in the formidable sword-stick which Flambeau always flung as he walked, and which now stood upright beside his tall mug of Munich. Nay, in his sleepy irresponsibility, he even found himself eyeing the knobbed and clumsy head of his own shabby umbrella, with some faint memories of the ogre's club in a coloured toy-book. But he never composed anything in the form of fiction, unless it be the tale that follows:

'I wonder,' he said, 'whether one would have real adventures in a place like this, if one put oneself in the way? It's a splendid back-scene for them, but I always have a kind of feeling that they would fight you with pasteboard sabres more than real, horrible swords.'

'You are mistaken,' said his friend. 'In this place they not only fight with swords, but kill without swords. And there's worse than that.'

'Why, what do you mean?' asked Father Brown.

'Why,' replied the other, 'I should say this was the only place in Europe where a man was ever shot without firearms.'

'Do you mean a bow and arrow?' asked Brown in some wonder.

'I mean a bullet in the brain,' replied Flambeau. 'Don't you know the story of the late Prince of this place? It was one of the great police mysteries about twenty years ago. You remember, of course, that this place was forcibly annexed at the time of Bismarck's very earliest schemes of consolidation – forcibly, that is, but not at all easily. The empire (or what wanted to be one) sent Prince Otto of Grossenmark to rule the place in the Imperial interests. We saw his portrait in the gallery there – a handsome old gentleman if he'd had any hair or eyebrows, and hadn't been wrinkled all over like a vulture; but he had things to harass him, as I'll explain in a minute. He was a soldier of distinguished skill and success, but he didn't have altogether an easy job with this little place. He was defeated in several battles by the celebrated Arnhold brothers – the three guerrilla patriots to whom Swinburne wrote a poem, you remember:

> Wolves with the hair of the ermine,
> Crows that are crowned and kings –
> These things be many as vermin,
> Yet Three shall abide these things.

Or something of that kind. Indeed, it is by no means certain that the occupation would ever have been successful had not one of the three brothers, Paul, despicably, but very decisively declined to abide these things any longer, and, by surrendering all the secrets of the insurrection, ensured its overthrow and his own ultimate promotion to the post of chamberlain to Prince Otto. After this, Ludwig, the one genuine hero among Mr Swinburne's heroes, was killed, sword in hand, in the capture of the city; and the third, Heinrich, who, though not a traitor, had always been tame and even timid compared with his active brothers, retired into something like a hermitage, became converted to a Christian quietism which was almost Quakerish, and never mixed with men except to give nearly all he had to the poor. They tell me that not long ago he could still be seen about the neighbourhood occasionally, a man in a black cloak, nearly blind, with very wild, white hair, but a face of astonishing softness.'

'I know,' said Father Brown. 'I saw him once.'

His friend looked at him in some surprise. 'I didn't know you'd been here before,' he said. 'Perhaps you know as much about it as I do. Anyhow, that's the story of the Arnholds, and he was the last survivor of them. Yes, and of all the men who played parts in that drama.'

'You mean that the Prince, too, died long before?'

'Died,' repeated Flambeau, 'and that's about as much as we can say. You must understand that towards the end of his life he began to have those tricks of the nerves not uncommon with tyrants. He multiplied the ordinary daily and nightly guard round his castle till there seemed to be more sentry-boxes than houses in the town, and doubtful characters were shot without mercy. He lived almost entirely in a little room that was in the very centre of the enormous labyrinth of all the other rooms, and even in this he erected another sort of central cabin or cupboard, lined with steel, like a safe or a battleship. Some say that under the floor of this again was a secret hole in the earth, no more than large enough to hold him, so that, in his anxiety to avoid the grave, he was willing to go into a place pretty much like it. But he went further yet. The populace had been supposed to be disarmed ever since the suppression of the revolt, but Otto now insisted, as governments very seldom insist, on an absolute and literal disarmament. It was carried out, with extraordinary thoroughness and severity, by very well-organized officials over a small and familiar area, and, so far as human strength and science can be absolutely certain of anything, Prince Otto was absolutely certain that nobody could introduce so much as a toy pistol into Heiligwaldenstein.'

'Human science can never be quite certain of things like that,' said Father Brown, still looking at the red budding of the branches over his head, 'if only because of the difficulty about definition and connotation. What is a *weapon*? People have been murdered with the mildest domestic comforts; certainly with tea-kettles, probably with tea-cosies. On the other hand, if you showed an Ancient Briton a revolver, I doubt if he would know it was a weapon – until it was fired into him, of course. Perhaps somebody introduced a firearm so new that it didn't even look like a firearm. Perhaps it looked like a thimble or something. Was the bullet at all peculiar?'

'Not that I ever heard of,' answered Flambeau; 'but all my information is fragmentary, and only comes from my old friend Grimm. He was a very able detective in the German service, and he tried to arrest me; I arrested him instead, and we had many interesting chats. He was in charge here of the inquiry about Prince Otto, but I forgot to ask him anything about the bullet. According to Grimm, what happened was this.' He paused a moment to drain the greater part of his dark lager at a draught, and then resumed:

'On the evening in question, it seems, the Prince was expected to appear in one of the outer rooms, because he had to receive certain visitors whom he really wished to meet. They were geological experts sent to investigate the old question of the alleged supply of gold from the rocks round here, upon which (as it was said) the small city-state had so long maintained its credit and been able to negotiate with its neighbours even under the ceaseless bombardment of bigger armies. Hitherto it had never been found by the most exacting inquiry which could –'

'Which could be quite certain of discovering a toy pistol,' said Father Brown with a smile. 'But what about the brother who ratted? Hadn't he anything to tell the Prince?'

'He always asseverated that he did not know,' replied Flambeau; 'that this was the one secret his brothers had not told him. It is only right to say that it received some support from fragmentary words spoken by the great Ludwig in the hour of death, when he looked at Heinrich but pointed at Paul, and said, "You have not told *him* . . ." and was soon afterwards incapable of speech. Anyhow, the deputation of distinguished geologists and mineralogists from Paris and Berlin were there in the most magnificent and appropriate dress, for there are no men who like wearing their decorations so much as the men of science – as anybody knows who has ever been to a soirée of the Royal Society. It was a brilliant gathering, but very late, and gradually the Chamberlain – you saw his portrait, too: a man with black eyebrows, serious eyes, and a meaningless sort of smile underneath – the Chamberlain, I say, discovered there was everything there except the Prince himself. He searched all the outer *salons*; then, remembering the man's mad fits of fear, hurried to the inmost chamber. That also was empty, but the steel turret or cabin erected in the middle of it took some time to open. When it did open it was empty, too. He went and looked into the hole in the ground, which seemed deeper and somehow all the more like a grave – this is his account, of course. And even as he did so he heard a burst of cries and tumult in the long rooms and corridors without.

'First it was a distant din and thrill of something unthinkable on the horizon of the crowd, even beyond the castle. Next it was a wordless clamour startlingly close, and loud enough to be distinct if each word had not killed the other. Next came words of a terrible clearness, coming nearer, and next one man, rushing into the room and telling the news as briefly as such news is told.

'Otto, Prince of Heiligwaldenstein and Grossen-mark, was lying in the dews of the darkening twilight in the woods beyond the castle, with his arms flung out and his face flung up to the moon. The blood still pulsed from his shattered temple and jaw, but it was the only part of him that moved like a living thing. He was clad in his full white and yellow uniform, as to receive his guests within, except that the sash or scarf had been unbound and lay rather crumpled by his side. Before he could be lifted he was dead. But, dead or alive, he was a riddle – he who had always hidden in the inmost chamber out there in the wet woods, unarmed and alone.'

'Who found his body?' asked Father Brown.

'Some girl attached to the Court named Hedwig von something or other,' replied his friend, 'who had been out in the wood picking wild flowers.'

'Had she picked any?' asked the priest, staring rather vacantly at the veil of the branches above him.

'Yes,' replied Flambeau. 'I particularly remember that the Chamberlain, or old Grimm or somebody, said how horrible it was, when they came up at her call, to see a girl holding spring flowers and bending over that – that bloody collapse. However, the main point is that before help arrived he was dead, and the news, of course, had to be carried back to the castle. The consternation it created was something beyond even that natural in a Court at the fall of a potentate. The foreign visitors, especially the mining experts, were in the wildest doubt and excitement, as well as many important Prussian officials, and it soon began to be clear that the scheme for finding the treasure bulked much bigger in the business than people had supposed. Experts and officials had been promised great prizes or international advantages, and some even said that the Prince's secret apartments and strong military protection were due less to fear of the populace than to the pursuit of some private investigation of –'

'Had the flowers got long stalks?' asked Father Brown.

Flambeau stared at him. 'What an odd person you are!' he said. 'That's exactly what old Grimm said. He said the ugliest part of it, he thought – uglier than the blood and bullet – was that the flowers were quite short, plucked close under the head.'

'Of course,' said the priest, 'when a grown up girl is *really* picking flowers, she picks them with plenty of stalk. If she just pulled their heads off, as a child does, it looks as if –' And he hesitated.

'Well?' inquired the other.

'Well, it looks rather as if she had snatched them nervously, to make an excuse for being there after – well, after she was there.'

'I know what you're driving at,' said Flambeau rather gloomily. 'But that and every other suspicion breaks down on the one point – the want of a weapon. He could have been killed, as you say, with lots of other things – even with his own military sash; but we have to explain not how he was killed, but how he was shot. And the fact is we can't. They had the girl most ruthlessly searched; for, to tell the truth, she was a little suspect, though the niece and ward of the wicked old Chamberlain, Paul Arnhold. But she was very romantic, and was suspected of sympathy with the old revolutionary enthusiasm in her family. All the same, however romantic you are, you can't imagine a big bullet into a man's jaw or brain without using a gun or pistol. And there was no pistol, though there were two pistol shots. I leave it to you, my friend.'

'How do you know there were two shots?' asked the little priest.

'There was only one in his head,' said his companion, 'but there was another bullet-hole in the sash.'

Father Brown's smooth brow became suddenly constricted. 'Was the other bullet found?' he demanded.

Flambeau started a little. 'I don't think I remember,' he said.

'Hold on! Hold on! Hold on!' cried Brown, frowning more and more, with a quite unusual concentration of curiosity. 'Don't think me rude. Let me think this out for a moment.'

'All right,' said Flambeau, laughing, and finished his beer. A slight breeze stirred the budding trees and blew up into the sky cloudlets of white and pink that seemed to make the sky bluer and the whole coloured scene more quaint. They might have been cherubs flying home to the casements of a sort of celestial nursery. The oldest tower of the castle, the Dragon Tower, stood up as grotesque as the ale-mug, but as homely. Only beyond the tower glimmered the wood in which the man had lain dead.

'What became of this Hedwig eventually?' asked the priest at last.

'She is married to General Schwartz,' said Flambeau. 'No doubt you've heard of his career, which was rather romantic. He had distinguished himself even before his exploits at Sadowa and Gravelotte; in fact, he rose from the ranks, which is very unusual even in the smallest of the German –'

Father Brown sat up suddenly.

'Rose from the ranks!' he cried, and made a mouth as if to whistle. 'Well, well, what a queer story! What a queer way of killing a man; but I suppose it was the only one possible. But to think of hate so patient –'

'What do you mean?' demanded the other. 'In what way did they kill the man?'

'They killed him with the sash,' said Brown carefully; and then, as Flambeau protested: 'Yes, yes, I know about the bullet. Perhaps I ought to say he died of having a sash. I know it doesn't sound like having a disease.'

'I suppose,' said Flambeau, 'that you've got some notion in your head, but it won't easily get the bullet out of his. As I explained before, he *might* easily have been strangled. But he *was* shot. By whom? By what?'

'He was shot by his own orders,' said the priest.

'You mean he committed suicide?'

'I didn't say by his own wish,' replied Father Brown. 'I said by his own orders.'

'Well, anyhow, what is your theory?'

Father Brown laughed. 'I am only on my holiday,' he said. 'I haven't got any theories. Only this place reminds me of fairy stories, and, if you like, I'll tell you a story.'

The little pink clouds, that looked rather like sweetstuff, had floated up to crown the turrets of the gilt gingerbread castle, and the pink baby fingers of the budding trees seemed spreading and stretching to reach them; the blue sky began to take a bright violet of evening, when Father Brown suddenly spoke again:

'It was on a dismal night, with rain still dropping from the trees and dew already clustering, that Prince Otto of Grossenmark stepped hurriedly out of a side door of the castle and walked swiftly into the wood. One of the innumerable sentries saluted him, but he did not notice it. He had no wish to be specially noticed himself. He was glad when the great trees, grey and already greasy with rain, swallowed him up like a swamp. He had deliberately chosen the least frequented side of his palace, but even that was more frequented than he liked. But there was no particular chance of officious or diplomatic pursuit, for his exit had been a sudden impulse. All the full-dressed diplomatists he left behind were unimportant. He had realized suddenly that he could do without them.

'His great passion was not the much nobler dread of death, but the strange desire of gold. For this legend of the gold he had left Grossenmark and invaded Heiligwaldenstein. For this and only this he had bought the traitor and butchered the hero, for this he had long questioned and cross-questioned the false Chamberlain, until he had come to the conclusion that, touching his ignorance, the renegade really told the truth. For this he had, somewhat reluctantly, paid and promised money on the chance of gaining the larger amount; and for this he had stolen out of his palace like a thief in the rain, for he had thought of another way to get the desire of his eyes, and to get it cheap.

'Away at the upper end of a rambling mountain path to which he was making his way, among the pillared rocks along the ridge that hangs above the town, stood the hermitage, hardly more than a cavern fenced with thorn, in which the third of the great brethren had long hidden himself from the world. He, thought Prince Otto, could have no real reason for refusing to give up the gold. He had known its place for years, and made no effort to find it, even before his new ascetic creed had cut him off from property or pleasures. True, he had been an enemy, but he now professed a duty of having no enemies. Some concession to his cause, some appeal to his principles, would probably get the mere money secret out of him. Otto was no coward, in spite of his network of military precautions, and, in any case, his avarice was stronger than his fears. Nor was there much cause for fear. Since he was certain there were no private arms in the whole principality, he was a hundred times more certain there were none in the Quaker's little hermitage on the hill, where he lived on herbs, with two old rustic servants, and with no other voice of man for year after year. Prince Otto looked down with something of a grim smile at the bright, square labyrinths of the lamp-lit city below him. For as far as the eye could see there ran the rifles of his friends, and not one pinch of powder for his enemies. Rifles ranked so close even to that mountain path that a cry from him would bring the soldiers rushing up the hill, to say nothing of the fact that the wood and ridge were patrolled at regular intervals; rifles so far away, in the dim woods, dwarfed by distance, beyond the river, that an enemy could not slink into the town by any detour. And round the palace rifles at the west door and the east door, at the north door and the south, and all along the four façades linking them. He was safe.

'It was all the more clear when he had crested the ridge and found how naked was the nest of his old enemy. He found himself on a small platform of rock, broken abruptly by the three corners of precipice. Behind was the black cave, masked with green thorn, so low that it was hard to believe that a man could enter it. In front was the fall of the cliffs and the vast but cloudy vision of the valley. On the small rock platform stood an old bronze lectern or reading-stand, groaning under a great German Bible. The bronze or copper of it had grown green with the eating airs of that exalted place, and Otto had instantly the thought,

"Even if they had arms, they must be rusted by now."
Moonrise had already made a deathly dawn behind the
crests and crags, and the rain had ceased.

'Behind the lectern, and looking across the valley,
stood a very old man in a black robe that fell as straight
as the cliffs around him, but whose white hair and
weak voice seemed alike to waver in the wind. He was
evidently reading some daily lesson as part of his reli-
gious exercises. "They trust in their horses . . ."

' "Sir," said the Prince of Heiligwaldenstein, with
quite unusual courtesy, "I should like only one word
with you."

' ". . . and in their chariots," went on the old man
weakly, "but we will trust in the name of the Lord of
Hosts . . ." His last words were inaudible, but he closed
the book reverently and, being nearly blind, made a
groping movement and gripped the reading-stand.
Instantly his two servants slipped out of the low-
browed cavern and supported him. They wore dull-black
gowns like his own, but they had not the frosty silver
on the hair, nor the frost-bitten refinement of the features. They were peasants, Croat or Magyar, with
broad, blunt visages and blinking eyes. For the first
time something troubled the Prince, but his courage
and diplomatic sense stood firm.

' "I fear we have not met," he said, "since that awful
cannonade in which your poor brother died."

' "All my brothers died," said the old man, still
looking across the valley. Then, for one instant turning
on Otto his drooping, delicate features, and the wintry
hair that seemed to drip over his eyebrows like icicles,
he added: "You see, I am dead, too."

' "I hope you'll understand," said the Prince, con-
trolling himself almost to a point of conciliation, "that
I do not come here to haunt you, as a mere ghost of

those great quarrels. We will not talk about who was right or wrong in that, but at least there was one point on which we were never wrong, because you were always right. Whatever is to be said of the policy of your family, no one for one moment imagines that you were moved by the mere gold; you have proved yourself above the suspicion that –"

'The old man in the old black gown had hitherto continued to gaze at him with watery blue eyes and a sort of weak wisdom in his face. But when the word "gold" was said he held out his hand as if in arrest of something, and turned away his face to the mountains.

' "He has spoken of gold," he said. "He has spoken of things not lawful. Let him cease to speak."

'Otto had the vice of his Prussian type and tradition, which is to regard success not as an incident but as a quality. He conceived himself and his like as perpetually conquering peoples who were perpetually being conquered. Consequently, he was ill acquainted with the emotion of surprise, and ill prepared for the next movement, which startled and stiffened him. He had opened his mouth to answer the hermit, when the mouth was stopped and the voice strangled by a strong, soft gag suddenly twisted round his head like a tourniquet. It was fully forty seconds before he even realized that the two Hungarian servants had done it, and that they had done it with his own military scarf.

'The old man went again weakly to his great brazen-supported Bible, turned over the leaves, with a patience that had something horrible about it, till he came to the Epistle of St James, and then began to read: "The tongue is a little member, but –"

'Something in the very voice made the Prince turn suddenly and plunge down the mountain-path he had climbed. He was half-way towards the gardens of the palace before he even tried to tear the strangling scarf from his neck and jaws. He tried again and again, and it was impossible; the men who had knotted that gag knew the difference between what a man can do with his hands in front of him and what he can do with his hands behind his head. His legs were free to leap like an antelope on the mountains, his arms were free to use any gesture or wave any signal, but he could not speak. A dumb devil was in him.

'He had come close to the woods that walled in the castle before he had quite realized what his wordless state meant and was meant to mean. Once more he looked down grimly at the bright, square labyrinths of the lamplit city below him, and he smiled no more. He felt himself repeating the phrases of his former mood with a murderous irony. Far as the eye could see ran the rifles of his friends, every one of whom would shoot him dead if he could not answer the challenge. Rifles were so near that the wood and ridge could be patrolled at regular intervals; therefore it was useless to hide in the wood till morning. Rifles were ranked so far away that an enemy could not slink into the town by any detour; therefore it was vain to return to the city by any remote course. A cry from him would bring his soldiers rushing up the hill. But from him no cry would come.

'The moon had risen in strengthening silver, and the sky showed in stripes of bright, nocturnal blue between the black stripes of the pines about the castle. Flowers of some wide and feathery sort – for he had never noticed such things before – were at once made luminous and discoloured by the moonshine, and seemed indescribably fantastic as they clustered, as if crawling about the roots of the trees. Perhaps his reason had been suddenly unseated by the unnatural captivity he carried with him, but in that wood he felt something unfathomably German – the fairy tale. He knew with half his mind that he was drawing near to the castle of an ogre – he had forgotten that he was the ogre. He remembered asking his mother if bears lived in the old park at home. He stooped to pick a flower, as if it were a charm against enchantment. The stalk was stronger than he expected, and broke with a slight snap. Carefully trying to place it in his scarf, he heard the halloo, "Who goes there?" Then he remembered the scarf was not in its usual place.

'He tried to scream, and was silent. The second challenge came; and then a shot that shrieked as it came and then was stilled suddenly by impact. Otto of Grossenmark lay very peacefully among the fairy trees, and would do no more harm either with gold or steel; only the silver pencil of the moon would pick out and trace here and there the intricate ornament of his uniform, or the old wrinkles on his brow. May God have mercy on his soul.

'The sentry who had fired, according to the strict orders of the garrison, naturally ran forward to find some trace of his quarry. He was a private named Schwartz, since not unknown in his profession, and what he found was a bald man in uniform, but with his face so bandaged by a kind of mask made of his own military scarf that nothing but open, dead eyes could be seen, glittering stonily in the moonlight. The bullet had gone through the gag into the jaw; that is why there was a shot-hole in the scarf, but only one shot. Naturally, if not correctly, young Schwartz tore off the mysterious silken mask and cast it on the grass; and then he saw whom he had slain.

'We cannot be certain of the next phase. But I incline to believe that there was a fairy tale, after all, in that little wood, horrible as was its occasion. Whether the young lady named Hedwig had any previous knowledge of the soldier she saved and eventually married, or whether she came accidentally upon the accident and their intimacy began that night, we shall probably never know. But we can know, I fancy, that this Hedwig was a heroine, and deserved to marry a man who became something of a hero. She did the bold and the wise thing. She persuaded the sentry to go back to his post, in which place there was nothing to connect him with the disaster; he was but one of the most loyal and orderly of fifty such sentries within call. She remained by the body and gave the alarm; and there was nothing to connect her with the disaster either, since she had not got, and could not have, any firearms.

'Well,' said Father Brown rising cheerfully, 'I hope they're happy.'

'Where are you going?' asked his friend.

'I'm going to have another look at that portrait of the Chamberlain, the Arnhold who betrayed his brethren,' answered the priest. 'I wonder what part – I wonder if a man is less a traitor when he is twice a traitor?'

And he ruminated long before the portrait of a white-haired man with black eyebrows and a pink, painted sort of smile that seemed to contradict the black warning in his eyes.

PENGUIN CLASSICS

THE INNOCENCE OF FATHER BROWN
G. K. CHESTERTON

'How in blazes do you know all these horrors?' cried Flambeau.
The shadow of a smile crossed the round, simple face of his clerical opponent.
'Oh, by being a celibate simpleton, I suppose,' Father Brown said. 'Has it never struck you that a man who does next to nothing but hear men's real sins is not likely to be wholly unaware of human evil?'

With his round face, pipe and umbrella, the shambling, bespectacled priest Father Brown is an unlikely detective – yet his innocent air hides a razor-sharp understanding of the criminal mind. As this first volume of his adventures shows, the clerical sleuth has an uncanny ability to bring even the most elusive wrongdoer to justice.

PENGUIN CLASSICS

THE INCREDULITY OF FATHER BROWN
G. K. CHESTERTON

'That sort of thing may be very well for crypts and cloisters and all sorts of moonshiny places. But ghosts can't get through a closed door in an American hotel.'

Father Brown, the shrewd and modest clerical detective, encounters miracles, ghosts and prophets in this third volume of ingeniously plotted tales. From South America to New York, his keen observation is a match for any mystery - even when he finds himself missing, presumed dead, in his own coffin . . .

Penguin Classics

THE SECRET OF FATHER BROWN
G. K. CHESTERTON

'You see, I had murdered them all myself . . . I had thought out exactly how a thing like that could be done, and in what style or state of mind a man could really do it. And when I was quite sure that I felt exactly like the murderer myself, of course I knew who he was.'

Unassuming super-sleuth Father Brown has such brilliant powers of deduction that he knows more about crime than the criminals themselves. In this fourth volume of stories, the shabby priest unravels baffling conundrums involving, among others, a flying fish, a man with two beards and the Worst Crime in the World.

read more

PENGUIN CLASSICS

THE SCANDAL OF FATHER BROWN
G. K. CHESTERTON

'It would not be fair to record the adventures of Father Brown, without admitting that he was once involved in a grave scandal. There still are persons, perhaps even of his own community, who would say that there was a sort of blot upon his name. It happened in a picturesque Mexican road-house of rather loose repute . . .'

After many years in the priesthood, Father Brown knows human nature and is not afraid of its dark side. In this fifth and final series of mysteries, the clerical mastermind confronts slander, passion, superstition, high crimes and misdemeanours, outwitting some quite extraordinary and villainous adversaries on the way.

PENGUIN CLASSICS

THE MAN WHO WOULD BE KING: SELECTED STORIES
RUDYARD KIPLING

'They tell me that one never sees a dead person's face in a dream. Is that true?'

Rudyard Kipling is one of the most magical storytellers in the English language. This new selection brings together the best of his short writings, following the development of his work over fifty years. They take us from the harsh, cruel, vividly realized world of the 'Indian' stories that made his name, through the experimental modernism of his middle period to the highly-wrought subtleties of his later pieces. Including the tale of insanity and empire, 'The Man Who Would Be King', the high-spirited 'The Village that Voted the Earth Was Flat', the fable of childhood cruelty and revenge 'Baa Baa, Black Sheep', the menacing psychological study 'Mary Postgate' and the ambiguous portrayal of grief and mourning in 'The Gardener', here are stories of criminals, ghosts, femmes fatales, madness and murder.

Part of a series of new editions of Kipling's works in Penguin Classics, this volume contains a General Preface by Jan Montefiore and an introduction discussing Kipling's reputation and influence, the ambivalence of his writing and the fascination with 'otherness' expressed in his short works.

Edited with an introduction by Jan Montefiore
Series Editor Jan Montefiore

PENGUIN CLASSICS

THE THIRTY-NINE STEPS
JOHN BUCHAN

'My guest was lying sprawled on his back. There was a long knife through his heart which skewered him to the floor'

Adventurer Richard Hannay has just returned from South Africa and is thoroughly bored with his London life – until a murder is committed in his flat, just days after the victim had warned him of an assassination plot that could bring Britain to the brink of war. An obvious suspect for the police and an easy target for the killers, Hannay goes on the run in his native Scotland, where he must use all his wits to stay one step ahead of the game – and warn the government before it is too late. One of the most popular adventure stories ever written, *The Thirty-Nine Steps* established John Buchan as the original thriller writer and inspired many other novelists and filmmakers including Alfred Hitchcock.

In his introduction to this new edition, John Keegan compares Buchan's life – his experiences in South Africa, his love of Scotland and his moral integrity – with his fictional hero. This edition also includes notes, a chronology and further reading.

Edited with an introduction by John Keegan

PENGUIN CLASSICS

LOVE AND MR LEWISHAM
H. G. WELLS

'He was no common Student, he was a man with a Secret Life'

Young, impoverished and ambitious, science student Mr Lewisham is locked in a struggle to further himself through academic achievement. But when his former sweetheart, Ethel Henderson, re-enters his life his strictly regimented existence is thrown into chaos by the resurgence of old passion. Driven by overwhelming desire, he pursues Ethel passionately, only to find that while she returns his love she also hides a dark secret. For she is involved in a plot of trickery that goes against his firmest beliefs, working as an assistant to her stepfather – a cynical charlatan 'mystic' who earns his living by deluding the weak-willed with sly trickery.

A biting critique on the spiritualist craze sweeping the nation, and a considered exploration of one man's conflict between love and ambition, *Love and Mr Lewisham* is the first of Wells's satires on social pretension in Edwardian England. Part of a brand new Penguin series of H. G. Wells's works, this edition includes a newly established text, a full biographical essay on Wells, a further reading list and detailed notes.

Introduction by Gillian Beer

Textual Editing by Simon J. James

Notes by Simon J. James

PENGUIN CLASSICS

MAURICE
E. M. FORSTER

'People were all around them, but with eyes that were intensely blue he whispered, "I love you"'

Maurice Hall is a young man who grows up confident in his privileged status and well aware of his role in society. Modest and generally conformist, he nevertheless finds himself increasingly attracted to his own sex. Through Clive, whom he encounters at Cambridge, and through Alec, the gamekeeper on Clive's country estate, Maurice gradually experiences a profound emotional and sexual awakening. A tale of passion, bravery and defiance, this intensely personal novel was completed in 1914 but remained unpublished until after Forster's death in 1970. Compellingly honest and beautifully written, it offers a powerful condemnation of the repressive attitudes of British society, and is at once a moving love story and an intimate tale of one man's erotic and political self-discovery.

The introduction, by David Leavitt, explores the significance of the novel in relation to Forster's own life and as a founding work of modern gay literature. This edition reproduces the Abinger text of the novel, and includes new notes, a chronology and further reading.

Edited with an introduction and notes by David Leavitt

THE STORY OF PENGUIN CLASSICS

Before 1946 ... 'Classics' are mainly the domain of academics and students; readable editions for everyone else are almost unheard of. This all changes when a little-known classicist, E. V. Rieu, presents Penguin founder Allen Lane with the translation of Homer's *Odyssey* that he has been working on in his spare time.

1946 Penguin Classics debuts with *The Odyssey*, which promptly sells three million copies. Suddenly, classics are no longer for the privileged few.

1950s Rieu, now series editor, turns to professional writers for the best modern, readable translations, including Dorothy L. Sayers's *Inferno* and Robert Graves's unexpurgated *Twelve Caesars*.

1960s The Classics are given the distinctive black covers that have remained a constant throughout the life of the series. Rieu retires in 1964, hailing the Penguin Classics list as 'the greatest educative force of the twentieth century.'

1970s A new generation of translators swells the Penguin Classics ranks, introducing readers of English to classics of world literature from more than twenty languages. The list grows to encompass more history, philosophy, science, religion and politics.

1980s The Penguin American Library launches with titles such as *Uncle Tom's Cabin*, and joins forces with Penguin Classics to provide the most comprehensive library of world literature available from any paperback publisher.

1990s The launch of Penguin Audiobooks brings the classics to a listening audience for the first time, and in 1999 the worldwide launch of the Penguin Classics website extends their reach to the global online community.

The 21st Century Penguin Classics are completely redesigned for the first time in nearly twenty years. This world-famous series now consists of more than 1300 titles, making the widest range of the best books ever written available to millions – and constantly redefining what makes a 'classic'.

The Odyssey continues ...

The best books ever written

PENGUIN 🐧 CLASSICS

SINCE 1946

Find out more at www.penguinclassics.com